C903048677

Dead Flowers

D1333469

Praise for Nicola Monaghan

'Monaghan's convincing characters swing unpredictably between terrifying and tender, and the often violent encounters usually have a bleakly funny edge'- *Independent*

'A gripping, mile-a-minute British debut. Enthralling'
- *Kirkus Reviews*

'Monaghan's novel is direct and deceptively simple. In spite of suffering there are surprising touches of humour and tenderness that bloom like flowers on asphalt' - *Times*

'Monaghan's is a powerful, loving, and honest new voice'
- **AL Kennedy, author of** *Paradise* **and** *So I Am Glad*

'The pace and claustrophobic atmosphere also serve to make this an almost unbearably tense read at times'
– *Daily Mail*

Also by Nicola Monaghan
The Killing Jar
Starfishing
The Okinawa Dragon
The Night Lingers and other stories
The Troll trilogy

Dead Flowers

A DR SIAN LOVE MYSTERY

NICOLA MONAGHAN

VERVE BOOKS

First published in 2019
VERVE BOOKS
an imprint of
The Crime & Mystery Club Ltd,
Harpenden, UK

vervebooks.co.uk

All rights reserved
© Nicola Monaghan, 2019

The right of Nicola Monaghan to be identified as the author of this work has been asserted in accordance with Section 77 of the Copyright, Designs and Patents Act 1988.

This is copyright material and must not be copied, reproduced, transferred, distributed, leased, licensed or publicly performed or used in any way except as specifically permitted in writing by the publishers, as allowed under the terms and conditions under which it was purchased or as strictly permitted by applicable copyright law.

Any unauthorised distribution or use of this text may be a direct infringement of the author's and publisher's rights, and those responsible may be liable in law accordingly.

ISBNs
978-0-85730-803-0 (epub)
978-0-85730-802-3 (print)

Printed in the UK by Clays Ltd, Elcograf S.p.A.

For my parents

October 1967
A Whiter Shade of Pale

The Loggerheads pub, Nottingham

It was Saturday night glad times in the Loggerheads pub and Harry was propping up the bar with his skinny red streak of a pal Bobby O'Quaid. An old man a couple of tables away tipped his hat at the pair of them. Harry lifted a hand to wave then slicked back his dark hair, pomade leaving a sticky film on his fingers.

The three old crows who sat together in the corner most nights and drank gin until they fell over were cackling away. The oldest one shouted out. 'Oi, Harry, come and chat with us, duck.'

Bobby turned to him with one raised eyebrow. 'They're after your body again, Harry. Watch 'em, that's all I'm saying.'

'Well, I havenay had sisters afore, so could well be tempted,' Harry said, laughing and slapping Bobby on the back. The carpet sucked at the soles of his shoes as he walked towards their table.

The three women grinned at Harry as he approached. Not a one of them had a full head of hair and their mouths were missing several teeth, except the smallest who had perfect chops that could only be false. 'Hello, my lovelies,' he said. 'What're ye lassies up to tonight?' He fixed them with his lively blue eyes and gave them the big smile that he knew made ladies' hearts beat a flutter.

'Gladys'us brought her tarots,' one of them said. The one with the false gnashers was holding a pack of cards.

'I'll do a reading for you, if you want, me duck,' Gladys told him. 'You don't have to cross me palm with silver or owt like that. I just like the cut of your jib.'

'I'm no sure, lassie,' Harry said. 'I'll no have a thing to do with that carry-on.' His voice was playful, though, at odds with the words. 'Ah, gwaan then. What harm's in it?'

Gladys glanced up at him through her lashes, looking weirdly coquettish. She handed him the deck to shuffle. Then she took the cards back and dealt them on to the table in a cross formation. Harry had seen this before; his Granny Mac used to do the tarot. She swore by them and would deal the cards whenever she had a decision to make.

The old woman turned the cards face-up, one then another, announcing them as she went. Bobby strolled across and watched over Harry's shoulder. 'The King of Swords,' Gladys said, 'oh my, good-night.' She turned more cards. 'Now don't be startled, young man. This un's death but don't take it all literal.' She looked up, and her eyes met Harry's. 'The Trent'll run red with the blood of trees before you see your end,' she told him.

Harry and Bobby exchanged a doubtful look. Then Harry lifted a hand to his forehead, play-acting a dramatic shiver and making the old ladies laugh. Gladys continued to slowly turn cards over and announce their names.

'The Three of Swords.' Turn. 'The Wheel of Fortune.' Turn. 'The Lovers.' This card had a picture of a half-naked couple on it, wrapped up in each other and tangled with ivy.

'Ooh err,' said Bobby, elbowing Harry with a smirk on his face.

'There's a big future for you here,' Gladys said, looking at Harry with a very level gaze. She glanced down at the table with a frown. 'You'll have fame, be in all the papers. They'll talk about you long after you've passed on from this world.'

Harry let out a comic gasp, then clasped his hand over his mouth.

'More than that,' she said. 'You'll be king of your world.'

Gladys smiled in a far-off way.

The tallest woman spoke, her voice rich and deep. 'King of it all,' she said, her words like an echo. She pointed at a card. 'Wheel of fortune,' she said, 'and the King of Swords.' She smiled and tapped the side of her nose, as if there were an in-joke that Harry should know about.

Gladys turned her head to take in the whole cross again. She pushed at one or two of the cards, adjusting their positions ever so slightly against the scratches in the wood.

Bobby pointed at the Lovers' card. 'What's this 'un about?' he said, winking at Harry.

'I see a beautiful young woman. Oh, yeah, one heck of a looker, she is, this gell,' the third old bird piped up. 'I see you, nearly half a century after the day you both get wed, wrapped in each other's arms.'

'What about me?' Bobby nudged Harry again. He was enjoying this a bit too much.

'You'll do alright,' Gladys said. 'You'll be happy, in the end.'

'Fame and fortune sounds better, being honest.'

Gladys smiled like she knew all his secrets, rocking gently in her chair. Dancing to her own tune. 'I see something good here for your children,' she said, and left it at that.

'What about my weans?' Harry said. 'How many? Will they be happy and rich?' He was grinning and catching Bobby's high mood.

Gladys grabbed the cards and cleared them quickly. 'The Tarot don't tell you everything,' she said.

The women turned towards each other then, and back to their glasses of gin and orange. Whatever they had wanted from Harry, it was over now.

'What the hell were that about?' Bobby said, as they walked back to the bar. 'Blood of trees!'

Harry shrugged. He wasn't smiling anymore. The way she'd suddenly packed up the cards when he'd asked that question about children had put the willies up him.

They stood at the bar and he ordered two more pints of mild. He thought about the cards. The pints were handed over and he took a big gulp. Bobby stood beside him, staring into space as he took his first sup.

'Penny for 'em,' Bobby said.

Harry took another gulp of his drink and shrugged. 'Naw, I cannay believe in any of that shite, anyways,' he said. But he closed his eyes and all he could see was a picture from the cards; three swords piercing a heart, and blood. Blood, gurgling and bubbling and thickening like it was boiling in a pot, leaking all over the sticky floor of the pub and pooling at his feet.

October 2017

HOME

The former Loggerheads pub (permanently closed), Nottingham

Sian dropped the box on the bedroom floor and a cloud of dust flew up, making her cough. She looked around and was hit by nostalgia so heavy that it felt like a presence in the room. She hadn't been in the top rooms of the Loggerheads public house for years and it was dragging her back in time.

Kris appeared at the door carrying two boxes with such ease that he made them look empty.

'I see we have the usual Sian Love approach going on here,' he said. He walked over and placed the boxes carefully against the wall. 'You'll break your stuff.'

'I barely own anything breakable,' she said.

Kris turned towards her and raised one eyebrow. 'Previous house moves?'

'Oi!' Sian aimed a playful slap at his shoulder and he ducked away from her. She couldn't help smiling as she saw the laughter in his warm brown eyes.

'How you manage to run a methodical lab and not just break all the test tubes is beyond me.' His voice was teasing.

'Work's different,' she said, taking him seriously, although her forensics research role didn't involve handling test tubes or equipment very often these days. 'I'm handling people's DNA, all their innermost secrets. It's more important than a few books and knick-knacks.'

Kris grinned. 'It suits me if you break things. Gives you an excuse to call someone tall, dark and handsome to help you fix it all up, Love,' he said. He had this affectation of calling her by her surname like this, a habit formed when she'd been his boss, back when they'd first met working together on the local murder squad. Sian liked it, though.

'Excuse me, but I can fix my own things, thanks,' she told him, her grin carrying in the tone of her voice.

'I'm just trying to help you here, giving you some good excuses for getting me over. Your loss if you can't see that this is for your benefit.' The words got quieter as he headed towards the stairs.

Sian looked around the room. It was going to take forever to unpack all of this stuff. She pushed a box aside and picked up a suitcase. She could at least put a few things in the closet. She reached up, opening the door, and was hit by a long-forgotten scent of old cloth and mothballs. It filled up her mouth and nose and, for a moment, she couldn't breathe. She was back with her Uncle Rob, years ago. She could hear his voice, as clear as if he were here in the room. *Ran off with a Scotsman, Sianey.* And she could see the clothes she'd found that day, smell them again. Classic, figure-hugging dresses with floaty skirts, high, glamorous heels, and silk stockings.

Sian held on to the cupboard door handle, dizzy and confused. *A Scotsman, a black man, the milkman*, Uncle Rob had changed it every time he told the story. She knew now that those clothes could never have been his wife's, even if she had existed. They'd been from a different era altogether, like something the femme fatale in a film noir might have worn. Sian's fingers tingled again with the feeling of silk and she was filled with longing, and with fear that she hadn't known her uncle at all.

All at once, Sian needed to be out of that room. She needed to not be alone. She rushed on to the landing and galloped down the stairs, taking them two at a time, her heart racing. She swung off the bottom step, holding on to the banister. She had to stop herself short to avoid colliding with Kris, who was waiting in the hallway.

'What next?' he said.

She shrugged. Kris grabbed her and pulled her into a kiss. She pulled away and noticed Elvis sitting neatly and calmly by the back door.

'You need to bark, boy!' she said, opening it wide for him. 'I'm not psychic.'

'Maybe he is and he doesn't understand why you're not getting him,' Kris said. He put on a silly, dreadful American accent. 'What's that, Elvis? There's a boy stuck down the well?'

Elvis strolled outside and dug at a patch of concrete. Sian watched him, the urgency of his claws and sniffing. It reminded her of earlier that day, when he'd lost his precious teddy toy underneath the sofa.

'Tea?' Kris asked her, cutting across her thoughts with a warm smile.

'That'd be nice,' she said. It would be. Nice. And Kris was nice, too, wasn't he? He'd looked after her, been there and pretty much saved her life, more than once, since they'd first met on the force over a decade ago. She really needed to get over whatever was holding her back with him.

Sian sat down on one of the fold-out chairs in the kitchen as the kettle boiled. She'd scrubbed and scrubbed the cupboards and surfaces in here but the colours still looked muted by grime. Kris got up and dug in the boxes on the worktop, pulling out some teabags and a couple of mugs. He turned towards Sian. 'OK, DCI Love. I've known you for long enough now. What's wrong?'

'Nothing.' Sian was shaking her head. 'And I haven't been a DCI for a very long time, matey.' She wasn't sure she wanted reminding of how senior she'd been by the time she'd left the force, how complicit that made her feel about everything that she'd seen, even if she had walked out in protest. She'd hated the blurred lines of policing, the corruption and sexism she'd seen, and the racism too, directed at Kris.

'Well, I ain't going to call you Doctor Love.' Kris clicked his tongue against his teeth. 'Not gonna happen.' He rolled his eyes. 'Come on, it's never nothing. I'm not that young and naive.'

'Two years!' Sian was talking through a broad grin. 'You are literally two years younger!'

Kris shrugged. 'Gotta take my advantages where I can find them, babe. Wouldn't even beat you in a fight.' He took milk out of the fridge and turned to look straight at her. 'So, c'mon. What's up?'

Sian let out a long sigh. 'Oh, I dunno. Can't put my finger on it. Just being back here after all these years.'

Kris glanced across at her and for a horrible moment Sian thought he was about to come over and hug her. But perhaps he really had known her long enough. He carried on making the tea and then brought the mugs over, plonking one down in front of her on the pasting table that she was using as her temporary dining furniture. 'Weird circumstances. You're still grieving for him and now, moving into your uncle's place. Everything here must remind you of him.'

'Yeah,' she said. She half-smiled. 'Although I haven't got a clue why he left it all to me.'

'Families are weird,' Kris said.

'Especially mine.'

Kris cocked an eyebrow. 'Not stupid enough to get drawn in by that,' he said.

They let the silence rest for a moment and both sipped at tea. Sian cupped her hands around the mug and felt it warm her.

A loud scratching sound came from the other side of the kitchen door along with a gentle whimper. Sian got up and walked into the hallway; Kris followed. They both watched Elvis, who was scratching at the cellar door. 'Leave it, boy,' she said. Then louder, 'Leave it!' Elvis came away, a good boy. Her dog was also ex-police; retired now but very well trained. 'There must be something there,' she said. 'He only does that when there's something there.' She swung the door open and clicked on the light, spotting something furry and matted on the top step and recoiling for a moment, thinking it was a rat. She realised it was just his teddy toy. The door didn't quite catch properly, and the bear must have slipped the other side and got shut there.

'Ah ha!' Kris said. 'The big softy.'

Sian laughed lightly, handing Elvis his toy. Her dog bounded off and sat down with it, chewing at one of the cloth ears. Her toolbox was on the hallway floor, waiting to be taken down into the cellar, and she placed it in front of the door to keep it shut.

'Can we go out or something? Get a drink.' A tight fist of anxiety squeezed her stomach.

'Sure,' Kris said, making the word sound uncertain.

Sian grabbed her coat from where she'd slung it over the top of the living room door. Elvis padded after her. 'Not this time, boy,' she said. She checked her pocket for her keys. Glancing up, she saw Kris locking the back door. As if he lived here, too.

Kris walked down the hallway, squeezing past her and out into the street. Sian turned, taking a last look at Elvis. 'You be a good boy,' she said. 'No digging or scratching at things. OK?'

He tipped his head to the side, as if trying to understand what she was saying. She smiled at him, which made him tip his head to the other side.

'You coming?' Kris called back, yards up the street already.

NICOLA MONAGHAN

Sian turned from her dog and shut the door, locking it. She could feel the broken coin on her uncle's old keyring, cold against her hand. Uncle Rob had left her a pub but he'd also left her this weird mystery; half of a Mizpah love pendant. Somewhere in the world there was a second half coin that would fit with this one perfectly, completing the words of its broken promise. She had no idea where it had come from but its existence put a very different light on his jokes about a wife who had run away.

ALES

The Pitcher and Piano, High Pavement, Nottingham

'My uncle used to call this place Twat Church,' Sian said, gesturing around at the drinkers in what used to be the Unitarian Church before it was bought and renovated by an upmarket pub chain.

Kris laughed loudly and brought a hand to his mouth to stop himself spitting beer. 'You shouldn't swear like that, young lady. In the house of God!'

'Yeah, well, God moved out a while ago, and all the twats moved in.' The old building was packed with drunk, noisy groups; more than one of them looked like stag parties. A few tables away, someone shouted 'who are ya' and his friends joined in so loudly it swallowed all the air.

Sian tipped her head back as she took a swallow from her beer, taking in the high ceiling and the stone arches along the side that had been turned into balconies. There were several large stained-glass windows and even the framed mirrors on the walls were arched to fit with this style. It was very in keeping with where the building had come from.

'Better to turn churches into pubs than to turn pubs into luxury flats,' Kris said.

Sian gave him a level stare. 'The Loggerheads hasn't made any money for about a million years.'

'Yeah, but maybe your uncle wasn't a businessman. With you at the helm, it could be a different story.' He slid a hand around her waist.

'Oh, my uncle was very definitely a businessman.'

'Oh, really?' There was a sudden light in his eyes. 'A "business-man?"' He made air quotes with one hand.

Sian nodded. This had been code on their squad for someone who did a certain type of business, not much of it legal. She let out a small nostalgic laugh. 'He joked when I joined the force that he wouldn't be able to talk to me anymore.' She looked up at Kris. 'Cos, y'know, you don't talk to police.' She imitated a strong Nottingham accent.

'Your family gets more interesting by the second.'

'Believe me, they really don't,' Sian said, looking over his shoulder at one of those arched mirrors behind them, sensing trouble somewhere. She saw the reflection of two men the other end of the bar doing the drunken wankers' dance, edging themselves closer, then further away from one another, on the brink of a fight. Sian felt her chest tighten. She checked where the exits were. She looked at the men, assessing their weights and heights and anything around that might help immobilise them if necessary.

'So, c'mon, Love, what's the problem with the Loggerheads?' Kris stepped back so that he could look into her eyes. 'It's a bit creepy, I'll give you that.'

Sian took Kris's hand, manoeuvring him away from the potential fight and towards an empty table. 'You're sounding like my mum, now,' she said. 'Don't move into that pub, it's a dark, bad place.' She was putting on a fortune teller voice, each word heavy with meaning. Her eyes were still on the two men, though, and she was relieved to see a bouncer intervene and tell them to leave.

'Whoo-oo-ooo!' Kris said, making a token effort of waving a hand and wiggling his fingers. 'But you're better than that. You don't believe in that shit.' It was left unsaid between them, the crime scenes they'd witnessed together. Sian had always been struck by the absence around a dead body; that was what unnerved you, not the sense of any kind of spirit or presence in the room.

DEAD FLOWERS

With a deep breath, as if she were about to dive underwater, Sian took another swallow of her beer then came back up for air. 'I dunno. I've always had a weird time at that pub. I ran away to Uncle Rob when I was fifteen,' she said. 'I'd just found out that David wasn't my real dad and I was furious. Uncle Rob took me in but he told my mother I was there and she turned up screaming like a banshee.' She stared down at the table, remembering it so clearly, the twist to her mum's face. She'd thought it was rage at the time, pure, blind anger, but now, as she tried to picture it again, she saw fear there instead. 'She threatened to drag me out the place by my hair.' She was shaking her head and felt the prickle of tears in her eyes. She pulled against the feeling, her throat tightening. 'I think I was more upset with Rob, in the end. He was supposed to be my cool uncle who played the drums and owned a pub. But he went straight off tittle-tattling to my mum.'

Kris looked thoughtful and was quiet for a moment. 'Quite a big deal, something like that. What it does to a family,' he said.

A sip of drink, marking time whilst she gave herself space to think.

'How'd you find out? Birth certificate?' he asked her.

Sian let out a bitter little laugh. 'No, nothing as simple as that. It's David's name on my birth certificate. But he has the wrong colour eyes.'

'You what?'

Sian waved her beer about as if to illustrate what she was saying. 'You can blame good old-fashioned O-level biology,' she said. 'Two blue-eyed parents can't have a brown-eyed child, etcetera. I read that, and kept staring in the mirror to see if my eyes were really some kind of odd shade of green that gave the impression of brown, or had some blue in there somewhere, right in the middle near my iris. I tried to persuade myself that what I'd read had to be wrong. But it nagged at me until I blurted something out in the middle of a row like a total cliché. You know the drill, the "you're not my dad!" obligatory teenage strop.'

'Did they deny it?' Kris's eyes were shining.

'Well, I was bloody expecting them to, but no. Mum just crumbled. She sat down, fell back, actually, as if I'd punched her. And she said, *no, he's not*. And then started giving me the third degree about who'd told me. When I explained about the eye colour she seemed relieved.' Sian shook her head. 'I couldn't believe they'd lied to me all those years. Lied to the bloody registrar too, the pair of them. Mind you, poor old dad. I mean, David dad. He probably didn't know that long before I did. I dunno. He just seemed gobsmacked by the whole thing.'

Kris had gone very quiet and was staring at her. She hadn't meant to say as much as this.

'What about Tom?" he asked, finally, and Sian realised he'd been trying to work out how to phrase the question about her younger brother.

She laughed; a sharp, bitter sound. 'Lovely Tom? No, David's his dad, because he's lovely Tom and life is always lovely for him. That's the rule.'

'You make it sound like you don't think he's very lovely at all!'

'Sorry.' Sian sat up straighter. 'It's not his fault. Him and his lovely blue eyes.'

'Okaaaay,' Kris said.

'Anyway,' she said, running a hand through her blonde, cropped hair. 'It was all wrong, my premise. I know that now. There are a bunch of ways that blue-eyed parents can have brown-eyed kids. My genetic father might very well have blue eyes for all I know. It's all much more complicated than that biology class.' She paused and looked at Kris. 'I just happened to have been right at the same time as being wrong,' she said.

'That's fucking mental.'

'Yup.'

'And you said your family wasn't that interesting,' he said.

'Fucked-up is not the same as interesting.'

They both sipped beer at the same time and their eyes caught. Kris put his glass down and reached across the table for Sian's hand. 'And you're not even as fucked-up as you should be,' he said. He cleared his throat. 'Sorry, that was supposed to be funny but came out wrong.'

There it was; that tight, pinching squeeze of anxiety again. She leaned back in her chair and looked around the crowded bar. She considered getting another drink but staying out didn't appeal. 'Listen, I'm knackered. I'm going to go home. Get an early night.'

'On your own,' Kris said. It was a statement not a question. Sian pulled at the corners of the label on her beer bottle and didn't say anything. She knew that she needed to be better than this with Kris, that the way she pushed him away had broken them up before. But she couldn't help it.

Kris downed the last of his beer then shook his head. 'What's wrong, Sian? We getting a bit too close?' She noticed the use of her first name and knew that she'd upset him.

'I'm just tired.'

Kris stood up and put on his jacket. 'Fine,' he said. He waited for a moment, like he was expecting her to change her mind. Then he zipped up his coat and walked away.

Sian watched him go through another mirror. She felt like everyone in the bar was watching him leave, watching the two of them. But, actually, he was walking slowly, with his usual lazy swagger and she wouldn't even have realised he was pissed off if she hadn't known him so well. She wished she could stop upsetting him and just be normal. One day, he'd decide he'd had enough of her nonsense, the way her ex had promised her when he first heard they were together. *He'll realise you're a psycho bitch soon enough.* She could hear the words, her ex-boyfriend's voice, so loud and clear that she almost expected him to appear in the arched glass of the mirror as she stared into it.

She turned on instinct, the ghost of an itch in the middle of her shoulders like there really was someone behind her. But there was nobody there.

CELLAR

Narrow Marsh, Nottingham

Sian came down the steep steps past the Contemporary Art Gallery, her eyes tracing the Nottingham lace patterns in its concrete walls. She could feel the history around her; Narrow Marsh, as it used to be, full of crime and squalor. She felt separated from the slums and violence by the finest of membranes, like if she pushed hard enough she could burst through and find herself years back in time.

The sign from the old Loggerheads pub was rattling in the wind, making a crashing sound against its frame. Sian checked up and down the street for any signs of trouble but could see nothing except leaves being blown and buffeted against the pavement. She could hear Elvis, barking and howling the other side of the door. He wasn't usually that bothered when she went out for a couple of hours but the combination of the high winds and being somewhere new were probably to blame. She dug into her bag to get her keys and his barking got more urgent. 'It's just me, you silly sod,' she said. She opened the door and he came bounding over, doing the dance of love he did whenever she came home, nuzzling her, then rocking from back to front paws. She leaned down to give the German Shepherd a proper scratch behind his ears and let him lick her nose, then locked and bolted the front door, shutting out Narrow Marsh and the dark.

Elvis ran through the hallway to the back door. Sian grabbed the key from a hook on the wall; he was trying to force the door open before she could unlock it. Finally, he burst outside and jumped into the air, barking at the night sky. The house felt damp and chilly so Sian went into the kitchen and turned the heating on. She wasn't sleepy enough for bed. She rooted through the boxes searching for something to drink, and glasses. She could only find an old bottle of amaretto and the plastic beakers from the bathroom. She poured herself a drink and slipped through to the living room, collapsing on the sofa and kicking off her shoes.

Sitting back, Sian tried to relax. She took a sip from her drink. It had a thickness and a rich, high taste. She couldn't shake the idea that part of the slick flavour was old toothpaste. She heard Elvis, scratching at the cellar door again. She ignored him for as long as she could. Then he popped his head into the room and stared at her. 'Fine,' she said, putting down her drink and walking back through to the hall. She closed and locked the back door. 'I can see I'm not going to get any peace here. Let's go and find out what's down there.'

Sian moved her toolbox and opened the cellar door, flicking on the light switch. There was a bright flash below and then darkness as the bulb blew. 'How's that for a sign,' she muttered, with a nervous laugh. She tilted the door back and reached into her toolbox, finding a torch. Then she picked up the box in case she needed tools when she got down there. Elvis scratched at the door again then looked up at her expectantly. 'You know, boy, the rule is never go down into the cellar.' She smiled at her own joke. And then she pushed open the door and he barged past her and rushed down the stairs, barking.

Sian followed him, shining the torch ahead of her. She tripped slightly as she misjudged the last step then righted herself. At the bottom of the stairs there was a high, sweet smell, reminiscent of old bins. She put the toolbox down on the floor. Elvis was scratching at the far wall and turned towards her, barking. He started to whimper and then pace the floor in a way she'd never seen him do before.

Sian felt the temperature of the room drop. She knew this was the effect of adrenaline on her body but the feeling struck home, nonetheless. Because Elvis wasn't any old retired police dog. He was a cadaver dog. Elvis had been trained to find the dead.

July 1970
Band Of Gold

The Loggerheads pub

It was a hot and humid midsummer evening and the sky had only bothered to darken to a vague kind of indigo. Angela Donnelly had left her husband seven days previously, and looked full of the same kind of doubt as the sky. Her sister Marilyn was skipping down Cliff Road ahead of her, drunk on the wonder of the night, as well as the cherry brandies that were dancing in her belly. Angela had been drinking too, but she wasn't skipping anywhere.

Marilyn tipped open the door to the Loggerheads pub and the sound of people having fun came roaring out. Angela followed to the door but turned at the last minute, looking carefully down the street behind her, checking. Trying to see into the shadows down alleys and twitchells. There wasn't a soul lurking in any of the dark places.

The lounge was packed to the rafters with a Saturday night crowd, their bellies full of beer and freedom. A Beatles song was coming out the jukebox and there were shouts and jeers from men playing skittles in the alley out back. Marilyn was at the bar, holding out a ten bob note like it was a ticket for something. Angela stood behind her, pulling at her borrowed minidress as if to stretch it longer. She turned and looked around for a table. A man nearby waved over at her. He was very good-looking, with lots of dark hair and intense blue eyes. Self-consciously, she smiled back. She fluffed her hair, which was cut into a short fashionable bob. The right kind of haircut for an independent modern woman who wanted to make a new start.

Angela grabbed the half pint of lager and lime Marilyn had handed her and they both headed over to the fellow, who was sitting with a pal and gesturing at a pair of spare seats at the table.

The man looked up at her and smiled, his eyes soft 'Glad to meet ye, hen,' he said, with a very strong Scottish accent. 'It's no every day I meet such a beautiful wee lassie as yoursel.' Angela blushed bright red. She pulled at her dress again before sitting down.

'My name's Angela,' she said, holding out her hand stiffly. The man took her fingers in his and kissed them. The blush bit deeper into her cheeks.

'Angela, Angela, Angel girl,' he said. He made it sound like a song. 'I'm Harry, and this here's my pal Bobby Q.' He indicated his friend, a tall youth with red hair, who was grinning and chatting with Marilyn like everything was already decided. Harry held out a packet of Park Drive to Angela and she took one. He lit her cigarette and then his own.

Angela smiled at Harry. 'Why Bobby Q?' she said.

'On account of the darts,' Harry said. 'He puts Q up on the score-board, from his surname, because there isnay any other Qs.'

Angela tried to think of something else to ask him. She loved his accent. She wanted to listen to him speak.

'Bobby's driving to Skeg next Sunday and says there's space for us in his motor car,' Marilyn said. She winked at Angela, who stared back and tipped her glass a little bit too quickly. She coughed and spluttered.

Harry patted her softly on her back. 'That one got a bone in it?' he said, making her laugh and cough some more.

'Bobby's from Ireland,' Marilyn said.

'Originally,' he said. 'Well, I were born there.' He had a Notting-ham accent now.

'Like my da and, well, like, erm, lots of other people I know,' Angela said. She sounded like she'd swallowed as many words as she'd spoken. She took a drink, like she was washing something down. Marilyn and Bobby had started up their own conversation again, giggling with heads close together, and Angela watched as her sister slipped from her chair and on to Bobby's knee.

'Your da and other people?' Harry said, amused.

'Yes,' Angela said. She looked past Harry, over his shoulder, scanning the room.

Harry turned his head to follow Angela's gaze. Quickly, whilst he was looking away, she pushed her hand into the pocket of her minidress and slipped off her wedding ring. She took a deep swallow as he turned back towards her.

'Someone ye looking for?' Harry said, turning back.

Angela shook her head and forced a smile. 'You're from Scotland,' she said.

Harry laughed, showing all his teeth. 'No getting anything past ye, is there, eh?' He took a big swig of his drink, still smiling broadly. 'Glasgow,' he told her, although it sounded like a struggle for him to pronounce the w. 'You been?'

Angela shook her head. 'We went caravanning up to the Lake District once. That's as far as I've been. But my da told me Scotland was very beautiful. Not as nice as Ireland, though, he'd always say.'

'I'll raise a glass to that,' Harry said. 'To Ireland and its many beauties.' He winked at Angela, and softly placed his hand on the space between her shoulders, lightly touching her back. She could feel the heat of his fingers against her bare skin.

'Oh, you charmer, you,' she said, but she raised her glass.

'So, are you courting?' he said. 'Nice wee lassie like yoursel. I'd have thought the boys were queuing up.'

Angela shook her head. Her eyes were wide and panicked.

'Naybody important, eh?' Harry said, as if he were deciding it.

Angela didn't correct him. A flush rose from the pale skin at the base of her neck and into her cheeks. And then Bobby kissed Marilyn, and Harry turned towards Angela, grinning. Angela took a last drag from the cigarette and stood up, stubbing it out into the ashtray. Her legs were shaky as she walked towards the back of the pub.

The toilets at the Loggerheads were the other side of a backyard. Angela went into the ladies', pushing the door hard so that it rattled on its hinges. The sounds of people having fun were muffled and far away. She locked herself in a cubicle. She put the toilet seat down and sat on it, her head in her hands. They were just having a drink and a chat with Harry and Bobby. Marilyn could do what she wanted but Angela didn't have to join in with any shenanigans.

Opening the door, she went over to the sink. She splashed cold water on to her face, rubbed it into her cheeks. She'd had too much to drink. It was all right for Marilyn; she was more used to this kind of thing.

Angela glanced up into the mirror and caught her own eyes. Then Jack's behind her. He was standing so close she could feel his breath against her neck and smell the alcohol. She turned towards him.

'You've been following me,' she said.

'So?' he said. 'You're my wife, supposed to be. I have a right to know what you're on with.' His voice was low.

'Leave me alone, Jack.'

Angela tried to duck past Jack but he grabbed hold of her dress. A seam ripped as he yanked her hard towards him. She struggled away from him and managed to get out through the door and into the yard. She was breathing hard and fast. Then she pulled away from him again and her wedding ring flew out of her pocket. They both stared as it bounced across the yard, making musical sounds as it hit one stone, then the next.

'Bitch!' Jack shouted. He flung himself at Angela and wrapped both of his arms around her middle, jerking her back towards him. She screamed; loudly. Then he shoved her, throwing her with some force into the back wall of the pub. She was winded and struggling for breath. She managed to stand up and he pushed her to the floor again. Then he picked her up, grabbing her by the collar of her dress and pressing her into the wall.

Jack pulled Angela towards him and then thrust her hard into the wall again. Her eyes watered.

'What the bleddy hell do you think you're playing at?' he said, spitting the words into her face.

Angela turned her head away from Jack. She was crying, letting out pathetic little moans begging him to *stop, please*. 'Nowt's going off I don't even know them blokes.' She could smell his breath, sour from the drink.

'Exactly,' Jack said. 'My mam always said you was a wrong 'un.' He brought his face close. His eyes were narrow and menacing and his teeth were gritted. His mouth made a sharp line, the same as the time he'd bitten her, right on the cheek. 'Sitting in the pub with fellers you don't know. Sitting there, carrying on, in clothes like them.' He nodded down at the minidress.

'Hey you!' The voice had an authority about it as it carried across the yard. That Scottish accent again. Harry. 'See you with the broken nose.'

Jack let go. Angela fell to her knees. She pushed herself up from the cobbles and pulled in deep draughts of air. She stood up, holding on to the wall and wobbling on her heels. Harry was squaring up to Jack. He wasn't as tall or broad as Angela's husband, but there was something about him that looked serious.

Jack puffed out his chest. 'I an't got no broken nose.'

'Oh aye?' Harry said. Then he headbutted him – hard and full in the face.

Jack staggered backwards then stood up straight and lurched back towards Harry. He wiped blood from his nose. 'You think yer a hard man, eh?' he said, snarling.

'Harder than you, son, I'll tell ye that for free,' Harry said.

'Right, so it's this 'un, then, what you're knocking off?'

Jack looked from Angela to Harry and back again. He spat on the floor. There was a flash of movement and a loud crack. Harry had punched Jack hard and fast. Jack reacted after the punch had landed, his hands windmilling halfway to his face. He fell backwards on to the ground and tried to jump straight back up, then fell a second time and lay still, making Angela think of the skittles from the alley behind the public bar.

'C'mon,' Harry said, gesturing to Angela to take his hand. She stared at Harry like she was trying to work out what he was offering. She was shivering and Harry took his jacket off, placing it over her shoulders and making comforting noises.

Harry ushered Angela towards the pub. Jack came to and sat up, looking dizzy and annoyed. 'Oi! That's my missus!' he called after them. His voice was loud but broke up at the edges.

'Go inside,' Harry said, waving Angela towards the door. But she stood there, looking at Jack.

'She's no yer wife, pal. No nay more.' Harry's angry voice sounded like a growl. 'Ye think ye the big man, eh? Knocking her about like that? Eh?'

'You don't understand what she's been on with, all the cheek and lies,' Jack said, getting to his feet but swaying.

'I couldnay care less if she shagged the pope,' Harry told him, walking back over. He grabbed the front of Jack's smart shirt, popping some of the buttons, and then pushed him backwards. 'You no got the message yet?' He punched him again, knocking him to the floor. He gave him a couple of kicks while he was down there and

Jack groaned in pain. 'Ye hear me now, pal? Eh?' He kicked him again, harder, and right in the mouth. 'Eh?'

Harry pulled Jack up by the collar and examined his face; it was smeared with blood and his nose was definitely broken. 'That enough for ye yet, laddie? Ye want a bit more, eh?'

Jack's head was weaving around so that it almost looked like nodding.

'Well, then? Ye want a bit more, aye or naw? Answer the fucking question, big man.'

With some effort, Jack shook his head from side to side.

Harry pulled him closer. 'Ye sure? Can easily be arranged, sonny Jim.'

Jack shook his head again and Harry let him go. Jack landed on his arse, and then pulled himself to seated against the wall. He was crying. 'I love you, Ange,' he said, through sobs.

'Ye mibbe should have thought about that afore you went around walloping her,' Harry muttered. Angela didn't say anything. She stood next to Harry, shaking under his smart suit jacket. Harry turned towards her. 'You his missus, hen?'

Angela shook her head. 'No,' she said. She sounded very sure about it.

'Right, then,' Harry said. 'We're gony go back in. We're gony sit down and have a drink and you, laddie, you're gony get tay fuck out this pub and you willnay be coming back. I swear to God that if I see ye here again, ye'll be leaving in a box. Ye get me, pal?'

Jack nodded through sobs.

Harry turned to Angela. She took one last look at her husband. 'Goodbye, Jack,' she said. And she took Harry's hand and walked into the pub.

The Wonder Of You

The Left Lion, Nottingham Market Square, a few days later

Harry leaned against the large stone lion in front of the council house, smoking, and keeping an eye out for Angela. The fight with her husband in the Loggerheads a few days ago felt like an age longer, but he liked her, despite the complications. He glanced up Long Row, looking for women getting off the buses. The big clock on the tower behind him ticked towards the hour. Then he spotted a girl in a neat white dress, pulling at its hems as if to make it longer, and he recognised the gesture before he could be sure of her face. A few moments later, she was standing in front of him.

'Aren't ye a sight for sore eyes?' he said.

Angela smiled up at him, blinking into the sunshine and pulling at the dress again. She threw away what was left of her cigarette then stubbed it out with a platform heel.

'That means ye look lovely,' he said. 'Beauti—' Harry was interrupted by the chimes of Little John behind them, striking seven. He tried to raise his voice to be heard above it and then gave up and waited until the bongs finished. 'Bang on time, too,' he said. 'A feat no often heard of in the female of the species.'

'Oi!' Angela said.

Harry held out a hand and she took it, blushing a little. 'Ye're no one a them women's libbers, are ye?' he said.

Angela shook her head, vigorously. 'Course not.'
'I was thinking we'd get a wee drink or two on the way and then go for a meal at the Savoy hotel. What do ye think?' he said.

'It sounds nice,' Angela said.

Harry lifted her hand and kissed it; she shivered at his touch and he loosened his grip, but she didn't let go. They walked together hand in hand, not talking.

'Here?' Harry said, outside the Dog and Bear. Angela nodded and smiled, and he held the door open for her. She walked through.

There was a gentle buzz of chatter and laughter around the pub. Harry gestured for Angela to sit down and asked her what she wanted to drink. Then he went up to the bar and ordered a pint for himself and a cherry brandy for the lady.

He sat back down with the drinks. Angela took a sip and smiled at him, looking hesitant. Harry took a sip from his drink too and tried to think of something to say. Then he spotted the jukebox across the room.

'Will we put some music on, hen?' he said. As he waited for the answer, he realised the question was more important than he'd planned it to be.

Angela's smile broadened and she stood up and headed over with a spring about her. Harry slipped his hand around her waist as they stood by the machine. She flipped through the songs, turning to Harry, who nodded encouragement and put some coins in.

'Are ye Beatles or Stones?' he asked her.

'Stones!' she said, as if it were a rude question. 'And the Kinks. They used to gig up here a lot. Marilyn—' she seemed to stop herself. 'Marilyn got on well with that Ray Davies one,' she said.

Harry laughed. 'Was she knocking him off?' He tried to imitate a Nottingham accent.

Angela looked away and blushed. She was sweet-looking, with her cheeks all rosy like that.

'The Kinks,' he said, 'aye, that isnay too bad. I can live with that.'

Angela pressed the buttons and a 45 single dropped on to the turntable. Then there was that sound of the needle hitting the vinyl, finding its groove with the tiniest of crackles. Harry loved that noise. She'd picked 'Waterloo Sunset' and the opening chords filled the air like magic. He took her by the arm and they walked back over towards the table.

Then Angela smiled up at him and started to sing the opening lines to the song. Harry couldn't believe what he was hearing. Because Angela could sing. Not like him and Bobby Q, just about able to hold a tune and get away with it if the guitars were loud enough. Angela had a voice that held on to the notes and carried, louder and more impressive than the record. He knew the real thing when he heard it, and he was hearing it now.

They sat down and the chorus started, and then Angela seemed to notice him watching and stopped, looking embarrassed. 'What?' she said.

'You havnay half got a voice on ye,' he said. 'Beautiful.'

She looked down at the table. 'I didn't mean to show off,' she said.

Harry took hold of her chin and turned her head up so that she was looking at him. 'What ye talking about? With a voice like that it'd be a crime to no show it off!' He was beaming all over his face. This was it. The missing piece that his band, the Midnight Roses, had been looking for all along. A singer with class like she had. 'Ye could be famous, ye know that?' She was easy on the eye, too, which wouldn't be any harm.

Angela shook away from his grip. She looked around the room; anywhere and everywhere except back into his eyes. 'I'm not sure about that,' she said, 'not that I'd want to.' She smiled. 'I do love singing. We used to go down to my da's local, when he was still around, and everyone had an instrument or they'd sing. I wasn't even the best.' She let out that kind of happy laugh mixed with a sigh that people do when they remember something good that they'll never experience again.

'Your da's no with us nay more?' Harry said.

'No,' Angela said.

'What about your maw?'

Angela rolled her eyes. 'My mam? She's not going nowhere in a hurry.'

Harry laughed, lightly, at that. 'You two no the best of pals, hen?' he asked.

Angela looked into her drink. 'She says I should go back. That marriage is for life.'

He snorted. 'Aye, and life isnay long for naybody married tay a bastard like that yin.'

She looked up, shocked.

'Sorry,' he said. 'What's that word you like round here?' He screwed up his face as if concentrating. 'Bugger, naw, hang on. Bogger! To someone married to a bogger like that one.' He did his impression of her accent again.

Angela's hand shot up to her mouth as she laughed and tried to keep her drink in. 'Sorry,' she said. She struggled to get any words out through the giggling. She pulled a handkerchief from her pocket to wipe at her face and the top of her dress.

'Ye got a big family?' Harry asked her. 'Well, obviously, I've met wee Marilyn. There more of ye bonny lassies? Any laddies?'

Angela nodded, and examined the contents of her glass with a sudden focused air. 'Seven of us all told, the ones what are still alive,' she said. She smiled but it was the kind of smile that comes through something else, fighting its way up from under less happy feelings. 'Keeps the old witch busy at least.' She looked Harry right in the eye, a light dancing in hers, as if shocked at herself for the mildly bad language about her mother. 'The rest are all younger, so keep her very busy,' she said.

Harry swilled his drink around. The glass was getting close to empty. He wondered if he wanted to stay with her here or move to another pub.

'You going to read my tea leaves in that?' Angela asked him, that light dancing in her eyes again.

Harry got the sense he was bringing the devil out in her and he liked it. He grinned back. 'Ye ken much about that, eh?' he said. 'Tea leaves and fortune telling? Believe in it?'

Angela nodded with enthusiasm. Her eyes widened and she looked suddenly very earnest. 'My old mammar read the tea leaves, my mam's mam,' she said. 'And she reckoned I'd inherited the second sight too.' The words came out fast, garbled, as if she were unsure of herself. 'I don't know. I wouldn't know where to start with it,' she added.

'A fortune teller once tellt me I'd be famous,' Harry told her. He'd never told anyone this. He'd only ever talked about it with Bobby, who'd been there, and then only a handful of times, making a joke of it.

'Well, then you will,' Angela said, with absolute certainty.

Harry stared at Angela. He remembered the cards that old Gladys had dealt and what she'd told him, her false teeth slipping in her mouth as she spoke. Fame and fortune and that card with the naked couple and the vines. A love that would last. Was this it?

He leaned over and took her hand, kissed it, all chivalrous. 'I think ye will too, hen. Named for Angels and the voice o' one too,' he said, with his most charming smile. And he saw Angela melt a little into the compliments and pictured the day when he'd be able to come in here and pick his own record, on the jukebox, and hear her voice any time he chose. He could see the both of them, in fifty years' time, wrapped up in each other's arms, exactly the way old Gladys had described.

October 2017

DOOR

Beneath Loggerheads

Sian shone the torch around the cellar. It was a small space and she estimated that it stretched about halfway along underneath the kitchen and a metre or so into the backyard. She waved the beam around the walls. She had no idea what she was looking for. She glanced up the stairs behind her. Maybe she should call Kris and get some help. But it was probably nothing. She'd feel ridiculous if she dragged Kris all the way over here and they found a few old socks in a box in the corner of the room.

There was a crack in the wall at the back. Sian followed its path up, around and then down with the torch. It was the outline of a door, hardly there, as if it had been plastered over a very long time ago. Sian walked over and pulled at its edges with her fingers. The plaster was old and dry, and it flaked away easily. Elvis was sniffing at the wall; he started scratching at the plaster too. She tried to tell herself it was nothing. But she remembered what she'd told Kris earlier, when Elvis was looking for Teddy. He didn't behave like this for no reason; there was something the other side of this wall and it wasn't his teddy toy this time.

Remembering the toolbox she'd brought down, Sian took a few steps back to find it. She dragged it towards the far wall and hunted inside with the light. She found the lump hammer she'd bought in case she needed to carry out more drastic renovations. She picked it up then placed the torch on its side near the left-hand wall, plunging the room into twilight. This job required two hands. She lifted the hammer and slammed it into the wall.

Plaster fell in lumps to the floor. The dust made her cough and she sneezed three times. Elvis took a huge step back from her and whined. She cleared her nose with one big sniff then lifted the hammer again, swinging it hard. She swung it over and over again, stopping a couple of times for breath and to cough. Her running and martial arts kept her fit, but this was a different type of effort. Finally, there was a massive crack as the plaster gave way. Sian picked up the torch and walked closer. She shone the light around and inspected her handiwork.

There was an old door, white speckled and emerging from underneath the plaster. The unpainted wood looked damp and rotten. She could feel her heart beating, see her chest moving faster and not just from the effort. There was a cave back here, one of the many that hid in the side of the cliff. Doors didn't spring up by themselves, growing in random places like plants, except in the kind of daft stories her uncle used to tell. Doors led somewhere; that was the point of doors.

Sian found a chisel in the toolbox and used this and the hammer to clear the last of the plaster away from the edges of the opening. She chipped away until the door was fully exposed. She looked for a handle or a lock but there was nothing obvious. She pushed against the door. There was no give, as if it were locked or barred. She pushed harder. Still nothing. She went back to the toolbox and found a crowbar. Bracing herself, she jammed it in to the edge of the door and levered. There was a crack and Elvis howled. She hammered the crowbar in deeper, then levered hard again. There was more loud cracking, more dust. She tried again. And again. Despite the state of the wood, she couldn't break it open. Sian threw the crowbar to the floor. Then she took a short run up and rammed her shoulder into the door.

DEAD FLOWERS

The wood gave way and Sian slammed right through to the other side. She landed with her foot twisted and felt something crack. She fell hard, slamming into the floor. The torch was flung from her hand. It clattered into the far wall and the room was thrown into darkness. She choked and spat out dust. There was a searing pain in her ankle and heel, and the shoulder that she'd barged the door with was burning. She sat up, her hand brushing against something weird and cold. There was a sound like the clink of fine china.

It felt different here from the cellar. It was a touch colder and there was a weird kind of silence, like being underwater. The sweet smell was stronger. Like flowers that had been left in water for weeks after they'd died. Sian had seen exactly this at one of the crime scenes she'd attended and the rotting flowers had added a high, sweet undertone to the stench of death that made it even more disturbing.

Sian lay on her belly and reached out around her, searching for the torch. She could hear Elvis sniffing and moaning somewhere nearby. Her hand found something slender and cool. It felt like leather or plastic that had been chilled. There was a lump of nausea in her chest as she held on to it and she let go, reached further. There; the feeling of the plastic torch, slightly warm from use. Sian pushed herself up to seated and switched the torch on. She focused on the object she'd been holding and let out a choked gasp. It was a hand.

Dried-up flesh like beef jerky lined the bones; nails like filthy daggers thrust out of the ends of what was left of the fingers.

Sian shone the torch around and flashes lit up more bones. A tibia and fibula, definitely human. She jerked the light away, illuminating a pelvis, almost bare but for scraps of what might have been flesh or clothing. There were shoes too, lying on the floor nearby, the kind of glamorous stiletto heels that Sian would never wear. Even in the half light, she could tell that they were red. She shone the torch upwards and found one rictus grin, then a second.

She yelped. Then she bit her lip and breathed. She shone the torch around again and started to hyperventilate. 'Oh God oh God oh God.'

Sian held a hand to her mouth and tried to control her breathing. The corpses were not quite decayed down to the bone and appeared to have been partially mummified, probably because of the cold, dry air in the cave. The glamorous shoes were the style they wore in the 40s or 50s, she thought, although she was no expert in fashion. They looked as if they'd been kicked off in a moment of carefree abandon and Sian didn't like to think about the mechanisms that had actually arranged them so jauntily. The shoes made her think of Dorothy in the *Wizard of Oz*, clicking her heels together and chanting *there's no place like home*.

Sian reached into her back pocket for her phone, but it wasn't there. It was highly unlikely there was a signal down here, anyway. She turned and shone the torch behind her. Elvis was lying flat on the floor. He growled when the light hit him then cried, a sound that was almost human. She was shaking through all of her limbs so completely that it felt like every cell in her body was vibrating. She was terrified but tried to rationalise it. Whoever these people were, they were many years past the stage where they'd be any harm to her. Elvis started whining, loudly. She heard him scramble back out from the cave and lie the other side of the door, whimpering.

Sian pressed against the side then the bottom of her injured foot. It felt like a sharp blade was ripping through her heel and calf. She pushed herself up to seated then standing. Her damaged left foot looked out of shape and flatter than normal, but she could put a little bit of weight on it; enough to limp about. She had to use the torch-light to find the door again, and had a moment's panic that it might have slammed shut behind the dog, trapping her with these other poor souls. She forced herself to stop panicking then she saw that the door was open. She stumbled back through. She emerged the other side to a light whine from Elvis. He tried to lick her hand clean, the one that had been holding the beef jerky limbs, but she pulled it away and firmly shut the door to the cave.

Sian climbed up the stairs, leaning against the wall and keeping the weight on her right foot as much as possible. She limped into the kitchen and leaned against the sink, scrubbing her hands with soap and very hot water. She couldn't get the smell out of her nose or from under her nails and she kept scrubbing. Then she went back through to the hall to look for her phone in her coat pocket. She knew she should really call the police but there was just no way. She knew too much about how they operated to want to trust any of this to the murder squad, to Dominic fucking Wilkinson, one of the major reasons she'd left the force.

Instead, she rang Kris. She listened to her handset; one, two, three, four rings. She hoped he wasn't asleep already, or mad enough with her to ignore her call. But just as she was expecting to hear his voicemail kick in, he picked up. 'Hello,' he said.

Sian wanted to tell him she needed his help but the words stuck in her throat. She swallowed. 'Can you come over?'

'Ha!' he said. 'I knew you'd miss me.' He sounded sleepy but pleased to hear from her.

'Please. Just come,' she said. She hated how desperate she sounded. 'I've hurt myself.'

'Oh my God,' Kris said. His voice had changed completely, as if he'd suddenly woken up. 'What's wrong?'

'I fell. I'm OK but I think I've broken something.'

'I'll be ten minutes,' he said.

'Thanks,' Sian said, and she put down the phone.

TIME

Loggerheads

It felt like Kris was taking forever but when Sian looked at her phone, she saw that it had only been eight minutes. She was lying on the sofa and staring at the ceiling, imagining faces emerging from the stains and pock marks in the paintwork. Elvis climbed on to the far cushion, curling himself up and placing his chin on her legs. 'Next time, I'm adopting a dog that sniffs for drugs,' she told him. But she was stroking his head and enjoying his warmth beside her.

Just as Sian decided she should ring Kris again, Elvis sat up taller and let out a deep bark. She tried to stand up, forgetting about her injury. It was more painful than before and she struggled to put her weight on it. She hopped and limped to the door, opening it as Kris went to ring the bell.

'Oh,' he said, stepping back in surprise.

'Very advanced and sophisticated visitor sensor system,' she told him, gesturing at her dog. 'Wait.' She reached towards him. 'I think I need your help.' The words came out squeaky.

Kris put an arm around her and walked her back through to the living room like they were doing the three-legged race at primary school. He looked down at her as he helped her sit down gently on the sofa. 'What happened, Love?'

'Not quite sure where to start,' she said. 'Except that I need a drink.'

'You need to go to the hospital.'

'Alcohol is a painkiller. And an anaesthetic,' she told him. 'It's treatment.'

'I see, Doctor Sian.' His voice dropped with resignation. 'Fine. But you're coming to the hospital, after.'

Sian half-nodded. She was walking on her foot, albeit with increasing difficulty, and tried to persuade herself that she hadn't broken it. Except she had felt a snap so perhaps a broken bone was the better outcome; ligaments took even longer to heal.

She picked up the toothpaste glass and handed it to him. 'Go through to the kitchen and refill this. And get yourself one if you want. The amaretto is on the side.'

Kris nodded.

He returned moments later with the drinks and passed a glass to Sian. 'So,' he said, 'how'd you do it?'

Sian took a sip first, stalling, rolling the thick liquid around her mouth and savouring it. 'Elvis was keen to explore, so we both went down to the cellar.'

'OK...'

Sian reached out a hand and rubbed her foot and ankle. 'Yeah, there's more.'

'Oh?' She had all of his attention now.

'Maybe sit down.'

Kris did as he was told. He looked at her from the armchair. 'What happened, Sian?' His face was turned up towards her and he held his head to the side, the same way Elvis did.

'I found *something creepy in the cellar.*' Her voice sounded sing song like a playground chant.

'You what?'

Sian took a breath. 'I've found remains down there.' She gestured with her glass towards the floor. 'Human remains. Old.'

'Definitely human?' he said. 'Bones?'

Sian shrugged. 'Yes, definitely human. And mostly skeletal, I think. I mean, it's dry and cold down there and I think there might be a bit of mummification. But they can't be that old because there are some scraps of clothes. And a pair of shoes. Based on those, I'm thinking 1950s but I'm no expert.'

'Oh my God,' he said.

'Yeah.'

'How long did you say this place had been in your family?' he said.

Sian poked at the ice in her drink with a finger. 'I said forever but I was exaggerating a bit.' She made eye contact with Kris. 'You going to come take a look?'

'We should be careful. Don't want to contaminate the scene, Sian.'

She finished her drink with a flourish and banged her glass down. 'You coming or what?'

'Can you manage it? How bad's your foot?'

Sian frowned. 'I can manage,' she said. But when she put her foot down the pain was deep and sharp and she reached for Kris.

'You're not fit for this. We need to go to A and E.'

Sian shot him a filthy look and picked up the torch from the coffee table.

'Fine,' he said. He grabbed her around the waist and helped her hop to the door, shutting Elvis in the living room. The dog's whining followed them down the hallway.

'Sit me down here,' Sian said, at the cellar doorway, passing Kris the torch. She sat on the top step and then bumped down from stair to stair. At the bottom, Sian clung to Kris as she hopped across the cellar. She showed him the hole she'd made in the back wall. She pushed the door and he shone the torch ahead of them.

'There's a cave,' he said.

'Yeah. Go have a look.' Sian shoved the door open wider for him and held tight on to the frame, her bad leg wrapped around her good one.

Even though he knew what was coming, Kris took a step back, his breath coming in sharply as he saw it for himself. 'Fuuuck, Sian,' he said, 'yeah, that's the real thing.'

'OK, now imagine this is the house you inherited from your uncle and have just moved into,' Sian said. They stood in silence for a few moments, staring at the human remains. The shock wearing off slightly, Sian was starting to look at what she'd found as a crime scene, instead of something from a horror movie. One of the corpses was, indeed, partially mummified. That meant there would be some DNA. The other was skeletal. Both skulls had cavities in them and, although Sian was no pathologist, she'd bet on gunshots because one was a keyhole shape, the way she'd seen in photographs at college. As well as tiny scraps of clothing, there was jewellery; a single pendant with a fine chain on the mummified body and several heavier chains on the other.

'Who are these people?' Kris asked her.

'I don't know,' Sian said. She moved closer, tried to get a better look at the pendant. Then she realised what it was and took a step back, her hand shooting to her mouth.

Kris examined the scene, getting in close then moving away and turning to Sian. 'These people were murdered. We need to get out of here and seal it up, as soon as possible. Get you patched up then call this in.'

'I'll be fine,' Sian said. Her heart was pounding and she didn't feel fine at all, but it had nothing to do with what had happened to her foot.

Kris shook his head. 'Sian, I can see just looking that there's something wrong with that foot. It's not the right shape.'

'It's just a sprain,' Sian said. She put her foot down as if to prove it but let out a yelp and pulled it straight back up.

'Yeah, so I see.' Kris's voice was loaded with sarcasm. He looked up from her foot and into her eyes. 'Look, you've had a shock and I don't want to labour this and make a big deal, but I don't think this kind of stress is going to help your other issues.'

'We can't just leave this to *them*,' she said. She made the last word sound dirty.

'Come on, Sian, these are my colleagues you're talking about. Your colleagues, once upon a time.'

'Yeah, well, I left for a reason.'

He took a deep breath then blew out air, slowly, before speaking again. 'I get you, you know I do. But what are you suggesting we do? Seal it up and leave it?'

Sian stood facing him, her arms folded.

'Come on,' he said. 'We have to call them, you know we do.' He sounded completely reasonable.

There was a standoff between the two of them for a moment, the room silent and tense. Sian thought about telling him about the clothes she'd found upstairs when she was little, and her uncle's stories of disappearing wives. About what the pendant might mean. But it was all so incriminating that she couldn't do it; even telling Kris was too disloyal.

'Kris, I need to know the truth not just whatever convenient answer the local murder squad come up with to get this off their books. You know what they're like.'

Kris stood there for a few moments staring at Sian. When he spoke again, his voice was quiet and level, the words slow. 'I'm going to make this really simple for you, Sian,' he said. 'I care about you too much to see you throw everything away and I'm sorry; I won't help you do anything stupid.' Kris turned, holding his hands out to her; reluctantly, she let him help her towards the cellar steps. They stopped talking for a moment and focused on getting back up, Sian sitting down and propelling herself backwards with one foot until they got to the top.

Kris pulled her back to her feet. 'We're going to go to the hospital then we'll come back and call this in. And, when the police come, we will trust them to do their jobs, OK?' he said.

Sian's grip tightened on his arms but she didn't reply. They stood in the cellar doorway for a few moments getting their breath back.

'Mum knew about this,' Sian said.

'Eh?' Kris's face screwed up in confusion. 'Course she didn't.'

'Don't you remember, though? All she kept saying when the will was read was how I'd be sorry I ever got this place, that there was nothing but badness here.'

'She was mad that he'd not left anything to Tom, though, wasn't she?' Kris reminded her.

'Yeah, but it was more than that. She knew.'

'This won't be anything to do with your mum. Come on.' Kris's voice was gentle now. He paused, as if carefully assessing the weight of what he needed to say next. 'Your uncle, I dunno. You said he was into all sorts and I don't know if you were messing with me. But, like you said, those red shoes are from before his time. Rob and your mum would've been babies when they were in style.'

'She tried everything she could to stop me moving in here short of chaining herself to the front doors.' Sian felt her eyes fill up. She cried when she was angry; it was one of her design faults. But she had learned that the best thing to do was not to make a point of it, not to make a sound.

'Sian,' Kris said. He made her name sound like a tragedy.

Nothing upset Sian more than sympathy. She pushed Kris away and turned heel, trying to storm off. The pain as she stamped down her bad foot was like someone had pitched a dagger right through her heel. 'Fuuuck!' she yelled, frustrated, grabbing on to the wall to stop herself falling.

Kris took hold of her with firm hands. 'Come on,' he said. 'Let's get ice on your foot, and pain relief, and let's get you to the hospital.'

Sian's eyes met his, her face a picture of defiance.

'Let me help you, Sian,' he said. The statement sounded deeper and more serious than she wanted to think about.

The silence stretched between them, Sian's eyes watering with the pain from her foot. 'Fine,' she said, at last, her teeth gritted. And she let Kris walk her to the living room, one step, then the next.

BREAK

The Queen's Medical Centre, Nottingham

Every movement the nurse made was soft and slow. Sian wanted to brush her off and jump down from the bed. She wasn't a patient person at the best of times but all she could think about was the pendant and how she should have stayed down in the cellar long enough to grab it, rather than letting Kris drag her back upstairs. The nurse placed Sian's foot down on the bottom end of the bed. The bruises were really coming out now, in vivid purples and blues. 'It's your fifth metatarsal. We call this fracture "the Beckham", after its most famous victim,' the nurse said. She stroked Sian's foot then pulled on an elastic support without touching the skin. She wrapped the leg tightly in bandages and began painting on the plaster. The sensation was cool and pleasant.

'Do you really need to plaster all the way up to my knee?' Sian said. 'It's a little bone in my foot I've broken.'

The nurse glanced up as she painted. 'The proper cast will be just up to your ankle,' she said. 'But this one's a bit crap, really, and needs to go all the way to the knee, yes.'

Kris was sitting nearby, absorbed by his phone. Sian glanced over and could see he was googling the Loggerheads pub. She couldn't make out the full text of his search, or what the results looked like.

The nurse wrapped more bandages around Sian's leg. 'How long you two been together?' she said. The tone of her voice was casual but Sian caught something in her eyes. This happened a lot with Kris, women fishing for the status of their relationship. It served her right for going out with someone this good-looking. More than one of her friends had compared him, breathlessly, to Idris Elba, and she had rolled her eyes and said she didn't see the resemblance at all, other than them both being black.

'About eighteen months,' Sian told the nurse. 'In total, anyway.'

'In total?' The woman raised her eyebrows.

'We had a shaky start.' Kris said this casually, still focused on his phone, although Sian knew she'd hurt him badly at the time.

'Oh, I see.' The nurse sounded playful. ' Well, mister on and off, time to earn your keep so that maybe you get to keep her this time. Go down to the shop and stock up on paracetamol. I'm going to give your good lady some strong painkillers but she'll want something else in between. Oh, and bring coffee, because coffee's always good. Maybe add a couple of sugars for the shock.'

'No sugar,' Sian said.

Kris patted his pockets for his wallet. He found it and stood up, half waving as he walked away on his errand. Sian smiled as she watched him, thinking how much he liked to be useful and wondering if the nurse had spotted that in him.

'Sorry,' the nurse said. 'I don't mean to interfere.'

'It's alright,' Sian said. 'He needs instruction.'

'Yes, don't they all?' The nurse cut the bandage and put everything down on the table beside her with a whisper of a sigh. 'Actually, I wanted to get rid of him for a minute. I just want to check that everything's OK.'

Sian let out a shock of laughter. 'It's very far from OK.' She indicated down at her leg.

'That's not what I mean.'

Sian's throat spiked with sickness as she realised where the conversation was going. The nurse had been fishing about Kris, but not the way Sian had assumed.

The nurse placed a hand on her arm and Sian glared at it like it was a foreign object.

'For God's sake.' Sian swung her legs so they were hanging off the bed, as if she were planning to jump down and walk away.

'Ms Love, I'm sorry, but this is a safeguarding issue. Your medical records have a note. I don't mean to upset you.'

Sian was looking at her half-plastered leg. 'All of that was years ago. And it wasn't him. Kris isn't like that.'

The nurse picked up another roll of bandages and undid the wrapping. 'The note's from five years ago, which isn't that long in the scheme of things. I was just concerned. Can I call you Sian?'

A nod.

'Sian, I was concerned with you saying it's on and off.'

'I didn't really say that,' Sian said. She managed a bitter, little laugh. 'Kris's mad ex-girlfriend is far more likely to try to beat me up than he is. He would *never*.'

'OK,' the nurse said. 'But I had to check. Professional duty. Now, are you going to let me finish off plastering your leg up?'

Sian nodded and lifted both legs back on to the bed. 'Please don't say anything to him,' she said.

The nurse began rolling a second layer of bandages around her foot. 'And, bingo, now I'm worried about you again.'

'You don't need to be. I just don't want it all dragging up again. He gets really overprotective and it drives me mad.'

'OK.' The nurse didn't sound convinced but she didn't say anything else. She carried on wrapping bandages around Sian's leg, then painting them with the plaster. It seemed they needed layer after layer and even the smell reminded Sian of papier maché in primary school.

Sian tried to forget about what the nurse had said, closing her eyes and trying to pretend none of it had happened. But her eyes snapped open. She had to make this woman understand that it really wasn't Kris. It felt important. 'I'm telling you the truth. You really don't need to worry about me, not with Kris.'

'You sure?' the nurse said, meeting Sian's eyes with her own.

'Yes, honestly,' Sian assured her.

'People who say honestly are usually lying.' Kris's voice carried ahead of him. He walked back in, a carrier bag dangling over one of his wrists and two Styrofoam cups steaming with hot coffee in his hands. He held out one of the cups towards Sian like an offering. 'I brought sugar in case you changed your mind. Also, this is from a machine and will probably taste nasty.' Kris took a sachet from his pocket and handed it to her.

'Ta,' Sian said.

'I was just telling Sian she mustn't put any weight on her foot. Not in this cast. She promised me but I'm not sure I believe her.'

Kris sat down, stirring sugar into his own coffee then handing the plastic spoon to Sian. 'You got that right and you've only known her five minutes,' he said, looking up. 'I'm going to ring a taxi, Sian, and I'll carry you if I have to.'

'Ha! Good luck with that,' she said, taking a drink. Kris was strong, but she was tall and a good eleven stone, almost all muscle. He wouldn't be carrying her anywhere she didn't want to go. 'And I'll have those painkillers now, please,' she told the nurse.

'These are proper, so they might knock you out a bit,' the nurse said. 'No driving or operating heavy machinery, OK?' She made the instruction sound like a joke. She took the coffee and handed Sian a plastic cup with pills in, and another one of water.

Sian tipped the pills into her mouth and washed them down. 'Thanks,' she said, holding out the empty cups.

'Right, you need to rest here for twenty minutes. Give the plaster time to dry.' The nurse handed Sian her coffee back, then looked at Kris. She seemed satisfied that things between them were all right. She patted Sian's leg with an air of finality. 'I'll leave you to it,' she said, and left the treatment booth, closing the curtain with a whoosh as she walked away.

'I was putting weight on it fine before,' Sian said. She tried to slip herself off the bed.

Kris frowned, placing a hand on her shoulder. 'Stay there.' He made several jabs at his phone screen. 'I'm calling the squad direct. It'll take them a while to get people out, anyway.' Sian could hear the ring tone on the other end of the line and wanted to grab the phone, stop him. She heard the tone cut short.

'Hey, Guv. DS Kris Payne,' he said. He made eye contact with Sian as he spoke and she knew without needing to ask that, of all the people who could have picked up, the 'guv' in question was Dominic Wilkinson. 'Yeah, I need to call something in. It's a cold one.'

Sian shivered as if responding to those words. Her foot throbbed and she had a weird sensation of wanting to run away, and feeling trapped.

July 1970

In The Summertime

Cliff Road

Marilyn held hard on to Bobby as the car skidded on to Cliff Road. Harry was driving very fast and air tore from one open window to the other, making both of the women shiver. Harry laughed and manoeuvred the car up on to the pavement with a bump. 'Gettout and I'll park up,' he said, slurring the words.

Marilyn took a final drag from her cigarette, then opened the door and stumbled out of the car. She stubbed her fag out under the sole of one of her stilettos, lifting the heel and feeling elegant. She turned to Bobby, who was holding out a hand. She grinned. She couldn't believe that she'd only known him a week or so.

Bobby took hold of her and spun her around, underneath his arm, like they were dancing at the Palais. Then he swept her into his arms for a kiss.

'Have I caught the sun?' Marilyn said, pulling away from him and swinging his hand as they walked through the doors to the pub. She felt like she had. She felt like she'd brought some of the seaside back with her, the heat on her skin and salt in her hair.

'You look beautiful a bit sun kissed,' he said.

'Not just the sun, either,' she said with a shameless grin.

He laughed, a sharp, hard sound. 'Have I got a tan?'

Marilyn brushed a hand across his cheek. His face was red and she was sure that there were more freckles than this morning. The only thing about him that was brown was his lovely, warm, laughing eyes. 'You have,' she said. 'You'll have to watch it or they'll be saying I ran off with a black man!'

'Ha! Can you imagine your ma's face?' Bobby said.

'She'd be OK, just so long as he's a Catholic!' Marilyn announced. Mrs Callaghan would have a big problem with Bobby because he wasn't but Marilyn didn't care. She was a grown woman and would not be told what to do, not anymore. She'd seen where that had got her sister.

They both giggled, and then Bobby kissed her again. Marilyn spotted her sister, standing on the pavement looking a bit lost and left out. 'Ah, c'mon Ange,' she said, and walked over to hug her.

Angela gave a reluctant smile but shrunk away from being hugged. Marilyn had noticed how hard she'd held on to the car seat on the drive home. Her sister had always struggled with car journeys; they'd had to stop on trips to Skegness when they were children, five little ones having to pile on to the pavement to let Angela out to throw up.

'You OK?' Marilyn asked, waving Bobby on ahead of them.

'I think I'm in one piece,' Angela said. She was rubbing at the sunburn on the tops of her arms.

'Stop doing that,' Marilyn said, taking hold of both of her sister's hands. 'You'll make it peel.'

Angela stared at her and looked like she might cry. Sometimes Marilyn felt like she was the big sister. She squeezed Angela's hands and swung them slightly.

'We had fun, didn't we? At the seaside? On the pleasure beach, and ice creams and fish and chips. It was a lovely day.' Marilyn glowed with pleasure at the memories.

'We did. I had a nice time. But I didn't enjoy Harry the one-eyed driver. I didn't like that at all.'

Marilyn grinned. That had been Harry's own joke, and he had closed one eye and then the car had weaved about less.

'He scared me,' Angela said. 'I thought he was going to kill us all.'

Marilyn pulled her sister towards her, forcing her into a hug. 'But he didn't, though, Ange. We're all fine.' She patted her sister's back. 'Come on,' she said.

Angela rolled her eyes but she followed Marilyn into the pub. Bobby was sitting at a table waiting for them. He'd already got the drinks in.

'I asked for umbrellas and cherries,' he told them. There was even one of each sitting atop his pint and he made both the women laugh as he took the umbrella and opened it over his head, like he really planned to go out in the rain under its protection.

Angela got up to go to the loo. Marilyn watched her go, wondering whether to follow. Worrying about history repeating itself with the ex-husband. But Jack hadn't been seen anywhere near the pub since he got beaten up by Harry. He'd be mad to come back. And stupid. In Marilyn's opinion he was at least one of the two and it was always best to keep your eyes open.

She smiled at Bobby, and stretched like a cat. 'What a great day. We're fun together,' she said. She leaned back and took a drink, then grinned. 'And Harry and Angela, that is so romantic. He's so nice to her.' She was shaking her head. 'A real gent, just what she needs after that bogger.'

'Yeah, a gent,' Bobby said. There was something flat about his voice, though, as if he were not convinced.

Marilyn leaned forward, her eyes wide. 'What you trying to say?'

Bobby sat up straighter, seeming to recover himself. 'Nowt,' he said. 'Nothing at all. He really likes her, I can tell. And I've known him a long time.'

'Yeah.' Marilyn was sitting back in her chair, her voice floaty with her mood. She was all romance today and refused to believe in any of the shadows she saw dancing across her boyfriend's face. 'He does. He really likes her.'

DEAD FLOWERS

'And I really like you.' Bobby leaned towards her, grinning. 'Really like you.'

Marilyn smiled back and took the cherry from his drink, dipping it into the foam on top of his beer then popping it into Bobby's mouth. He chewed through a grin and then kissed her. The kiss tasted sugary sweet.

You Can Get It If You Really Want

The Loggerheads pub

Angela walked back towards the public bar. She was shaking, still holding herself tense from the car. Now she rubbed her arms, where they were smarting pink from the sun. Marilyn and Bobby were feeding each other cherries from their drinks and playing with the umbrellas, staring into each other's eyes.

Then Harry arrived, sweeping into the Loggerheads like he owned the place. He gave her a broad, warm smile and she couldn't help but return it, walking towards him.

'Let me get my wee lassie a drink,' he said, taking her hand and kissing it with a theatrical bow.

'I already have a drink,' she said.

'Then ye shall have another,' he told her, putting on a posh voice and pulling her towards him. He deposited her back at the table like it was a dance move, and walked to the bar.

Angela sat down with the lovebirds and then Harry came over with more drinks for everyone. Like they hadn't already had their fair share. But Angela sipped her cherry brandy and Harry was sitting opposite her, looking into her eyes as he started his next pint. She felt better.

'A Whiter Shade of Pale' came on to the jukebox and Angela sang. Harry watched her, and joined in on the chorus, taking her by the hand. 'The face o' an angel and a voice e'en sweeter,' he proclaimed. Then he pulled her to her feet and he kissed her.

Bobby and Marilyn had been snogging all day but Harry had been quite restrained; the odd peck on her hand or to her cheek. This kiss was lingering and deep, like a movie kiss. Angela pulled away feeling dizzy.

Harry held her gaze, his bright blue eyes like ice melting into water. Angela knew he wanted more than just kissing and it scared her. 'I can't,' she said. 'Not yet.'

They both sat back down and Harry took hold of her hand across the table. 'Nay body's asking ye tay do a thing,' he said.

Angela's lashes fluttered over her eyes. She glanced away, then back at Harry. 'I know,' she said. 'But I know you want to.'

Harry rubbed her hand with both of his and smiled. He reached for her face and tilted her chin up so she was looking at him properly. 'Everything's fine. There's nay rush.' He kissed her forehead. 'I'm a gentleman, ye'll see. I'm no gony rush ye.'

Angela felt her insides melt. She suddenly felt more inclined to go home with Harry and this made her breathing quicken. She lit up a Park Drive. Then someone called Harry from across the bar and he got up to talk to them. 'Jonno!' Bobby shouted, loudly. And he got up and went over too.

'You OK?' Marilyn asked, leaning towards her sister across the table. Her voice was gentle.

'I think so.' Angela could feel herself blushing. 'He wants me to go home with him.' She said this as if it were a fact although, actually, he hadn't said this. Not out loud.

'Of course he does!' Marilyn's glow was lighting up the world around her. 'And you can, if you want to.' She winked then laughed. 'It's 1970! Not the Dark Ages.'

'I don't know,' Angela said. 'I'm still married.'

'Yeah, to that horrible sod.'

'Oh Marilyn, don't say that.'

'But he is. I don't care.' Marilyn's eyes glinted as she lit up another cigarette.

Angela nodded. 'Mam'd have my guts,' she said, leaning forward in conspiracy and feeling daring.

'Mam'd have both our guts for just being here drinking. But it's not up to her no more.'

Angela nodded. She had to concede. 'It feels quick,' she said.

Marilyn leaned across the table. She grabbed her sister by the hand, vehement and smelling of vodka. 'Life's short, Ange. You're only twenty and you've had a bleddy hard time. You do what you want. Don't let anyone or anything tell you what's OK, alright? Least of all Mam.'

Angela nodded. She squeezed her sister's hand back in return. Th men were on their way back to the table. Harry's face was full of joy to see her again, and he sat down with a soft gentle hand against her back. She liked him. She trusted him. It was a new decade and things were different.

A record slipped on to the jukebox and in the moment of fuzzy static as the needle went down, Angela decided she was going home with Harry that night. She was an independent modern woman, and she could do what she wanted.

October 2017

CRIME

Loggerheads

The taxi driver stopped and turned the radio right down, cutting off a cheesy eighties song mid-chorus. Sian opened the door and placed her crutches on the ground. Kris jumped from the front seat and appeared next to her.

'Wait. Come here.' He was raising his voice.

'Can't even let me try with the crutches.'

'When you're out of the car, maybe,' Kris said. He pulled her from the vehicle with a jerk and steadied her on the pavement. 'Bloody independent, modern woman!' He said this like it was swearing and Sian gave him a warning glare.

She placed the crutches down properly and stood, steady and balanced. 'See? I'm fine. If you want to be useful then go pay the driver.'

Kris reluctantly turned away and Sian headed towards the door. She caught her good foot on a paving stone and almost tripped over but Kris was too busy to notice. Then he was beside her again. 'You OK?' he said. 'Here, let me help.'

'Stop fussing,' she said. 'I need to learn to get about by myself.' Elvis had started to bark from the other side of the door.

'Fine,' Kris said. He pulled her keys from his pocket and slipped them into the lock. 'Just call out if you need help.'

'OK,' she said, noticing the coin dangling from her keyring as he unlocked the door.

'Yeah, right.' Sian couldn't see Kris's face but she could almost hear him rolling his eyes.

Elvis was standing the other side of the door as it opened. He licked Sian's left hand, then stepped aside. Sian hopped on the crutches through the hallway and then leaned against the banister. Kris hovered behind her but did not interfere. She was lucky she kept herself fit, although her arms weren't nearly as strong as she'd have liked and her left shoulder was still sore from the accident. She swung herself down the hall and then into the living room, launching herself on to the nearest chair and throwing down the crutches. Elvis followed her in, settling down on his bed in the corner of the room and closing his eyes. He opened one eye, as if to check that everything was OK, then stood up, turned and settled right down again. 'I think we both need a drink,' Kris said. 'Yeah?'

Sian nodded. 'Can I have my keys?' she said.

'Sure.' He was frowning as he dug in his pocket then threw the keys to her. 'Although I'm not sure where you think you'll be going in a hurry.'

Kris walked off towards the kitchen. As soon as he was out of sight she took hold of the keyring and detached Uncle Rob's special coin. She slipped it into her pocket just as her boyfriend returned. He was holding two glasses clinking with ice and amaretto and handed one to Sian. He sat down in the other armchair and put his feet up on the sofa.

'How long do you think they'll be?' Sian said.

'Dunno,' Kris said, with a little shrug. He let out the smallest of laughs. 'Hardly the golden hour.'

Sian laughed lightly, too. The golden hour was that first hour after you found a murder victim, when all the evidence and forensics were fresh and the killer might still be nearby. The golden hour for the poor chaps downstairs probably happened before she was born.

Sian took a sip of amaretto. It felt too thick against her tongue and throat and its sweetness and burn reminded her of childhood medicine. 'Do you think they were murdered?' she said.

'Well, the holes in their heads would appear to be strong indicators. We need to wait and see what forensics say, though. Keep an open mind.' He sat up straighter and gestured towards a leather bag propped up against the sofa. 'Can I borrow your laptop? I can remote access a couple of the databases and find out a bit more about this place.' He was already pulling the bag towards him.

'Yeah,' Sian said. 'Help yourself.'

The computer lit up Kris's face. He chewed on a hang nail on his left little finger and then typed with two fingers and a thumb on each side, his hands held stiff like lobster claws. His eyes widened and narrowed as he carried out tasks and opened more windows, thoroughly absorbed in the screen. She put both crutches together in front of her with their handles inward, to make a stand, the way she'd been shown in the hospital, and pushed down. It was easier to get to standing this way than she'd expected.

Kris glanced up. 'You OK?' he said. But his attention was back on the computer straightaway. That suited Sian.

Swinging herself into the hallway, Sian closed the door behind her. She felt lightheaded and wasn't sure if this was the amaretto-codeine combination, or just having been awake for so many hours. She needed to get the pendant from downstairs, and check if what she suspected was true. She thought about the detectives she knew on the force, and the forensics team that often sent the very hardest work to her lab at the university. With the exception of Kris, she didn't trust a single one of them to find the truth so she'd need to do that herself, even if it meant taking a risk or two. Sian headed through to the kitchen, placing her crutches very carefully balanced against a worktop.

Boxes were piled on the floor. The one marked 'bathroom' was near the top. Thank God for Kris's help packing or it wouldn't have been half this organised. She sat down and pulled the box towards her, carefully peeling the tape from the cardboard. Digging into the box, she found a packet of hair dye and quickly extracted a sealed pair of plastic gloves, putting them into her pocket. She searched through the box for something sharp and suitable, something that would be more or less sterile. Her tweezers were no good; they'd retain traces of her own DNA no matter how much she washed them and she was going to need to amplify anything she found, so traces would matter.

There was a manicure kit near the bottom of the box, still wrapped in plastic. Sian got on to her knees and shuffled over to the sink looking for the poop scoop bags. She nudged the open packet aside with an elbow and found a sealed one, ripping it open and taking out several bags, placing the packet of gloves and the manicure kit inside one of them, tying it up. Not bad at all for an improvised sample kit. She took another bag and stretched it across the bridge of her nose, tying it at the back of her head to make a protective mask. She picked up another unopened packet of bags and shoved it in her pocket. Before she could think about it enough to change her mind, she grabbed the torch from the worktop and tucked it under her armpit, heading back towards the hallway on her crutches.

The living room door was still closed tight. Suddenly aware of the noise she might be making, Sian placed one knee then the other slowly on to the carpet then took her time putting her crutches down as gently as possible. She opened the cellar door carefully. It made the tiniest of creaks and she glanced at the living room door again. She slipped down the steps on her bottom, lighting up the way in front of her with the torch. Every stair seemed to take an hour as she moved carefully, to avoid making a sound. She balanced the torch on its end against the bottom step, so that it lit up the whole cellar. Then she dragged herself along the floor on her hands and knees.

DEAD FLOWERS

Through the door and in the cave, the light was duller and muddy. That suited Sian; she didn't really want to see everything in high contrast for this particular little 'assignment'. Now she was faced with the human remains, even in this dull light, she wasn't sure she could do it. But she had to. She crawled over until she was right next to the bodies. Sian reached for the pendant and jerked it towards her sharply. The chain snapped easily and the pendant fell gently into the palm of her hand.

The silver half-coin glinted in the dim light. She took the other coin from her pocket, the one from her uncle's keyring. Placing them side by side, along the fake cracks, she saw that they fitted perfectly. She let out her breath, not realising she'd been holding it. She couldn't read the words in this light, but she knew what they said. The same as every Mizpah pendant in the world. *The Lord watch between me and thee, when we are absent one from another.* Sian was pretty sure she had found her uncle's runaway wife. With another man, just like he'd told her, although they hadn't got very far. But who the fuck was the man? Well, he'd left a few clues about that, in the remnants of flesh that still lined his bones. In fact, that could tell Sian everything about him, if she was lucky. She pulled out the packet of gloves and opened it, putting them on carefully. Then she ripped open the manicure kit and took out the scissors.

Sian reached for the man's leg, gagging slightly as she felt the cold, leathery texture through the thin plastic gloves. Gently and slowly, she pushed the scissors into the mummified flesh on his right calf. She had to dig deep into the tissue to guarantee that she'd find a place that was protected from contamination from her own DNA, since she'd fallen over down here earlier. She didn't need much of a sample and the less the better, so she snipped off the tiniest of slivers. She held the scissors away from her own body and everything else in the room then pulled several of the small plastic bags from the sealed packet, placing one bag inside a second, then a third, and carefully dropping the scissors right into the inner bag. She tied up the bags and pushed the muscle back together at the top. The pathologists would probably notice, anyway, but the alternative was having no way into this investigation herself, and she couldn't cope with that. She hadn't left her own DNA or fingerprints here and, although there were limited options for who else might have done this, she was confident she could style it out.

She shoved everything deep into her pocket. Then she reached for the second corpse, just to make sure. Searching its surface with her gloved fingers, she confirmed what she'd thought before; this one was just bone. The bones were no longer fully connected and she could have stolen the tibia or fibula from its leg, or even a metatarsal like the one she'd broken in her own foot. That would definitely be noticed, though, and it was fraught with danger, stealing a human bone and trying to hide it. Besides, the kind of DNA she'd get from the bone wasn't nearly as useful. Sian leaned back and pulled off her gloves and the bag from her face, putting them into her other pocket.

Crawling back towards the stairs, Sian wrestled for a moment with how to get herself back up. But it wasn't that difficult a climb. She dragged herself up by the handrail and used her knees to push from one stone step to the next, resisting the urge to rush in case she made too much noise. It was agony; wanting desperately to be upstairs, but remaining careful and slow so that Kris didn't hear her. She knew that once he'd got his head into an investigation, he often lost himself in the details on the computer. She hoped his searches about the Loggerheads would keep him busy for long enough. As she came up the last few steps she got a little careless and knocked the wall and door lightly. But she was soon closing the cellar door and using the wall to get herself upright, then reaching for her crutches. Not a moment too soon as the sound of Elvis barking erupted. She could hear him scratching the living room door, trying to get into the hallway to protect them all.

DEAD FLOWERS

Kris walked out from the living room. 'This'll be them,' he said, staring at her as if trying to work something out.

Sian looked down at her legs, dust covered and grimy from the cellar. The once white plaster that the nurse had so carefully applied to her left leg was a filthy brown-grey colour.

Kris turned towards the front door, then back to Sian. She heard the cellar door creak behind her and realised it was still slightly open. Kris stared towards her pocket and his eyes widened. She glanced down. One of the plastic gloves was sticking out. Without thinking, she shoved it back in properly.

'What the fuck, Sian?' Kris said.

'Kris!' she called after him. But he had already turned towards the door. He stepped in a confident, urgent way. It reminded her of what he had always been like at a crime scene. Sian leaned on her crutches and her head dropped. Kris opened the door and she heard the deep voices of the police officers as they walked over her threshold.

SCENE

Loggerheads

Sian sat on the sofa with her plastered leg stretched over the arm. Kris was standing up, bouncing on his toes. Elvis whined, scratching at the bottom of the door. He barked, but backed off as a youngish officer in uniform walked in, followed by a man of about Sian's age. The woman smiled at Sian, then held her head to the side. Sian disliked the pretend empathy; it was only Elvis she'd ever seen do this and mean it. She knew immediately that these were the family liaison officers.

'Cuppa tea?' the woman asked, with the kind of almost smile people use when bad things have happened.

'No, thanks,' Sian said. Kris sat down on the sofa next to her.

'I'm Sergeant Lizzie Meadows,' the woman told them. 'And this is my colleague, DI Jon Breen.'

Sian nodded, and wondered what a DI was doing on a family liaison team. Breen was staring at her, as if he were trying to work out where he knew her from. His eyes were a weird, almost see-through blue and Sian found them vaguely unsettling.

'DI Breen?' Kris said. 'You guys the FLOs?'

'Y'can call me Jonny,' Breen said. 'I know you're both police.' He had a weird hybrid accent that was part Nottingham and part County Wicklow, like he'd moved here from Ireland when he was a teenager.

'I'm *ex*-police,' Sian said, with emphasis on the ex.

'We're not going to condescend to you,' Meadows told her. 'We know you know the drill.'

Sian nodded and lay back against the sofa.

Meadows sat down on one of the armchairs. 'How's the foot?' she asked, sounding awkward.

Sian shrugged. 'Still broken.' A little laugh. Kris placed his hand gently on her knee but Sian wasn't sure if he was comforting her, or warning her to behave.

Meadows turned her head again, the ghost of a smile on her lips. 'You must be wondering who on earth it is down there.'

Sian stared back at her over the top of her water glass. Was she actually kidding? Part of a FLO's role is to get under the skin of family members, act as a spy for the investigation, but did Meadows imagine that Sian had forgotten that? Sian didn't say anything.

'You any idea, then?' she asked. 'Who it is?' She might not be very subtle but at least she was getting to the point, now.

Sian shook her head. 'None at all.' She placed the glass down and swung her leg on to the floor a bit too fast. 'Ouch,' she said. Elvis came over and started licking at the big toe that was sticking out of the end of the plaster; she pushed him away. 'Far as I know, my uncle, Robert O'Quaid, lived here for years. Before that, I have no idea. None at all.'

'And your man Robert was Bobby Q, right?' It was the guy this time, friendly Jonny.

Sian met the DI's eyes. 'What?' She cleared her throat, trying to work out if she'd heard that name before. 'I never knew him by any other name, just O'Quaid.'

Jonny's smile twitched at the corners, like he was holding something more genuine back. 'OK.' He made a note. 'Did you ever meet his wife? Did he ever talk about her?'

Sian didn't say anything for a moment. She could see from Breen's face that this wasn't a guess, that he'd already done some digging into her uncle. The runaway wife; she wasn't made up. Which meant that it could be her down there wearing the other half of that pendant. Although she'd suspected it, hearing it out loud was a shock.

'What?' Breen said, looking puzzled. 'You didn't know he was married?'

'No,' Sian said. 'He was single, all my life, as far as I knew.' This wasn't the whole truth but she didn't want to tell these people about her uncle's jokes. She glanced at Kris, whose attention was on the male officer, as if he were trying to work something out about him. 'Let's not mess about here. I know what you're getting at. But there are two people down there. That doesn't fit the man who killed his wife narrative.'

Jonny's smile stayed the same, with that tickle at the edges. 'That's true all right. Then again, maybe he caught them together up to no good?'

'In the cellar?' Sian said.

'Come on, now, we're both trained detectives. This might not be the original crime scene, yeah?' There was an amused air to the guy's voice; he sounded almost flirtatious.

'Okaaaay,' Sian said, stretching the word. 'I see what you're saying. Like I said, if he was married then I didn't know that.' She took a breath and felt everyone waiting for her to say more. 'Look, my uncle loved me. Was very protective. And he left me this place in his will. Do you think he'd have done that if he'd known there were dead bodies in the cellar?'

'Anything else we should know about him?' It was the woman this time. Meadows.

'Nothing. My uncle lived alone. I'd never heard about this Bobby Q name or that he was married. He never mentioned anything about a wife.' She closed her eyes against the lie then opened them again. 'Bobby Q? Where do you get that name from?'

Meadows ignored her question. 'And the rest of your family? How can we get hold of them? We'll need to talk to them all.'

'I have one brother, Tom, who lives out in East Leake. My dad died in '92 of a heart attack. My mum moved to Spain with her new partner ten years ago. That's all of us. I can give you phone numbers.' Sian watched Jonny as she spoke. His eyes danced, as if he knew a different story.

Meadows tucked away her notebook and pen and looked up with a more measured smile. 'We need to find you somewhere else to wait. You, and your friend.' She nodded at Kris.

'You know, I would like that cup of tea,' Sian said. She just wanted-ed Meadows and Breen out of the room at this point, long enough that she could sort out her head.

Meadows nodded and got up. Both of the officers left the room and the door swung shut behind them. Sian rubbed at her toes. They were feeling a little numb but that was better than itching.

'What do you know that you're not telling anyone?' Kris was whispering but he sounded cross. 'What's going on, Sian?'

Sian felt her lips go tight. She wasn't about to tell Kris any more than any of the others. This was family, and there were limits, even with people who seemed to be on her side.

'They're going to notice that you messed with the scene,' Kris whispered. He was frowning, but he took her hand and held it tightly.

Sian shook her head as if shaking away the idea, even though she knew it was a problem. 'I doubt they'd notice if I'd dressed the poor sods up for Halloween.'

The door opened again and the younger FLO was back. She held out a mug to Sian and then sat down on the arm of the sofa. 'Your neighbour across the way, Mr Parker, says you can go and sit with him for a while. Although he's not happy to have the dog in the house. Says he's allergic.'

Sian took the tea and blew on its surface. 'I don't know any of my neighbours, thanks. And I won't go without my dog.'

'I can take Elvis to his day care. He can't stay here anyway,' Kris said, his voice very quiet.

Sian shot him a look; such betrayal.

'That's decided then,' Meadows said.

'No, it's not,' Sian said. 'I don't see why I should have to go anywhere, or my dog. I've done nothing and, as you said, I know the drill.'

'Well, you can't stay here.' The FLO glanced from one to the other of them. Her mouth hardened. 'I can organise a room at the station if you'd prefer.'

Sian glared at the young woman, who flinched away. She had a moment's temptation to be stubborn, and force her to follow through and take her to the police station. Or to refuse to move and force Meadows to arrest her, see how well she handled that. But she held her breath and placed her mug gently on the coffee table.

'Fine,' she said. 'I'll go over to the neighbour's for a few hours.' Her voice was full of false cheer and came through a tight smile. She'd let the little FLO win this one, like that thing her mum used to say about picking your battles. She had a feeling, with Dominic Wilkinson on this case, she might have a lot more fighting to do.

VIEW

A house on Cliff Road

Sian ran a finger down the rich, silky material of the curtains, opening them just a twitch as she leaned against the window ledge. Some of her neighbours were being far less subtle, standing as close as they could to the yellow tape in front of the pub and staring as forensics officers dressed in white suits rushed back and forth with evidence bags and Tupperware containers. There was a bit of a buzz on the road now and a few reporters and a small TV crew had turned up, making Sian glad that she'd agreed to leave the Loggerheads. She watched everyone going about their business. The police and CSIs looked orderly, organised and professional, although experience told Sian not to be convinced.

A large black car pulled up outside the pub. An unmarked police car, Sian knew straightaway. The door opened and she slunk backwards from the window as she saw Detective Superintendent Dominic Wilkinson climb out of the driver's seat. Tall and pale in a very serious black suit, with salt and pepper cropped hair and stern blue eyes, he exuded a special kind of gravitas that had helped him rise through the ranks very quickly. Helped him hide what he was underneath that image, too. Sian could feel her heart racing and she took a couple of deeper breaths to try to ground herself. The young FLO walked out into the street and he spoke to her, his hand territorially on her arm in a way that made Sian wonder if there was something more between them. She hoped not, for the young woman's sake.

'Excuse me, ducky.'

The high, tight voice came from behind her. Sian turned. Mr Parker was standing there, holding out a cup of tea.

'I know you said no sugar but I put a couple in. For the shock.'

Sian took the cup and tried to smile, taking a sip and holding back a wince at the sweetness. 'Thanks, Mr Parker,' she said.

'Call me Les,' he told her.

Sian nodded.

Les perched himself on the arm of his settee. 'Who d'ya think they've found there?'

He was digging, she knew, but Sian just shrugged. 'No idea,' she said. She wished Kris would hurry back from dropping Elvis at day care.

'I wouldn't put owt past that place,' he said, talking as if the pub itself were the guilty party.

Sian turned from the window. She realised that he had no idea of her connection with the pub and its history, with her Uncle Rob. She put down her tea and hobbled over to the armchair on her crutches. 'Oh yeah?' she said, as if this were a question.

'Oh, yeah,' Les said. 'That place's seen all sorts over the years. Some better'n others. He were a good 'un, Bobby Q, you know, what had it before you.' He got up and brought her tea over to her, a beneficent smile on his face.

'What is this Bobby Q thing?' she asked. She didn't like this new name of her uncle's, didn't like the way it made her feel like she'd never known him at all.

'Oh, he were famous.' He nodded and shrugged at the same time, an odd gesture that older men in Nottingham seemed to be the masters of, especially when they had an opinion. 'Him and them other boggers. Not famous famous, you know, but well known round here. They had a band.'

Sian took a sharp breath in. 'He was in a band?' That couldn't be right. Her Uncle Rob? She knew he played the drums and that he'd recorded with the studios on some session work but he'd never said anything about being in a band, not even as a joke. How could he not have told her?

'That's right. What were it they called themsen? It'll come to me. And before him, that other pair from the band had the pub.'

'Who was that?' Sian had gone into her gentlest interrogation mode, her voice sweet and soothing.

'Them two,' he said, as if Sian knew them. 'They were on the telly, you know. Airs and graces, they had. *Ideas*.' He made the last word sound immoral and disgusting. 'Not sure as I remember *his* name but I went to school with Angela Callaghan. *Opportunity Knocks* it were they went on. You probably won't remember that programme.'

'I do,' Sian said. 'It was on when I was little.'

'Well,' he said, 'the Scots feller she were with. Mac summat his name were. Maybe Tommy?' He stared into his cup of tea. 'No. Harry,' he said, 'that were it. Harry Mac. He went off the rails after losing out on the telly. Drinking. Shouting his mouth off. More than once she chucked him out and someone off the road called the coppers.' He took a prim-looking sip from his mug. 'Not me, I hasten to add.'

'No,' Sian said, understanding straightaway. She might not have been born and bred on Cliff Road but she was from the same stock. She wondered what Les would think if he knew she'd once *been* a 'copper', and quite a senior one at that. 'Do you think his wife called them?' she asked. She tried to sound casual and unpractised; no clues.

Les laughed; a light, musical sound. 'Ange? No way. Not on your nelly, gell. Ange wasn't like that.' He was shaking his head. 'You don't think it's her, do you, what they've found?' He sounded upset.

'I don't know,' Sian said. She stopped herself short, realising she was about to tell him there were two bodies down there. He didn't need to know any of that.

Les went quiet and stared into his cup of tea. Sian stared at her neighbour. She realised that he'd been thinking about this for years but told no one, except perhaps other people on the street whom he might have had the chance to gossip with. All of them, everyone living on this street had had some idea that bad things had gone on at the Loggerheads pub. And that included her uncle, who, it turned out, had a whole life she'd never known a thing about.

The doorbell rang. Les smiled and put down his tea. 'That'll be that nice police officer,' he said.

'Yes,' Sian said, 'I'll bet it is.' She tried to tone down the note of sarcasm but failed.

Les was staring at her as if deciding something. 'You don't half look like your mam,' he said, smiling. 'She were a beauty, too. And you got her attitude.'

Sian was taking a sip of tea and choked, coughing.

Les patted her on the back. 'Got a bone in that?' he said, with a laugh.

Sian watched him go to answer the door with a smirk on his face and wondered what kind of game he'd been playing with her. He'd known who she was all along. She put down her tea. People never told her she looked like Ruth and Sian had always assumed she must look like her biological father.

Moments later, Les walked back into the room with Meadows. The FLO's mood had changed completely; her face was aglow. Sian stared at her, trying to work out what was going on.

The young woman turned towards Les. 'Can you give us a moment?' she said.

He nodded and left the room.

Meadows waited until he'd closed the door behind him. Sian imagined that he was probably waiting just behind it, anyway, one ear pressed against the wood.

'They want to do some excavations,' Meadows said. She smiled, weirdly, as if she knew she shouldn't but couldn't hold it back.

'Where?' Sian asked.

'There's another room that's been boxed in, on the ground floor. There used to be a skittle alley there.' Her voice was breathless and Sian realised that the young officer was excited.

Sian remembered that space, had been inside it a bunch of times. It didn't seem likely that there was anything to find in there. Besides anything else, Elvis had shown absolutely no interest in this part of the old pub.

'Apparently, there's a stud wall blocking the entrance that's pretty recent,' Meadows told her.

Sian sighed. 'Look, I don't imagine I have a choice, anyway, do I?'

'Well, no, not really.' Meadows couldn't meet her eyes. 'I'm telling you as a courtesy.'

'I don't understand. What are you expecting to find there?'

Meadows didn't say anything. And Sian realised that they thought there would be more bodies. For fuck's sake, they thought they'd found a new Fred West or something and, for all she knew about this 'Bobby Q' bloke, maybe they had. Meadows was excited, imagining the case of her life here at the pub, convinced that they'd found something very big indeed.

July 1970

Spirit In The Sky

A house on Cliff Road

Angela was woken by Harry, snoring beside her. It felt like the middle of the night but there was a gap in the curtains and sunshine spread out from it like the light from a projector. She felt drunk and her head was spinning. She sat up slowly and slipped the covers to the side. She scratched at her upper arm then felt itchy all over, as if there were something wrong with the sheets. Angela was overwhelmed with the feeling she shouldn't be there, in this bed, with this man, that she needed to leave. She stood up too fast, and had to steady herself against the wall to stop from falling.

Harry turned over in bed, letting out a snuffle. He lay on his side and the snoring stopped. The whisky bottle he'd brought up to bed sat on his bedside cabinet, almost empty. Angela looked at the man on the label, standing on a hillside with his kilt blowing in the wind and staring at her, judging her for what she'd just done. She smiled as she remembered Harry, drunk the night before, telling the man on the whisky bottle just how big the band was going to be now he'd found an angel. She needed to go before she changed her mind.

Angela rooted around on the floor for her clothes. She pulled on her knickers over aching legs. It hadn't felt wrong last night but now, with a bright square of light on the wall and the man standing judgement on the whisky, it did. She wasn't sure she believed in God and she wanted to believe in Twiggy and free love, but she felt ashamed. She could hear her mother's voice, talking about loose women and declining morals, and Angela knew what she'd say about women who did what she'd done last night when they were still married to someone else.

It was the early hours of Sunday morning and the air felt still, the street outside was dead quiet. Angela padded down the stairs and to the back of the house, locking herself in the bathroom. She splashed water on her face and pushed her hair behind her ears. She might be a fallen woman, but there was no way she was about to look a right mess out and about on the streets of Nottingham where someone might see her. She took deep breaths and managed not to be sick.

Back in the hallway, she looked for keys to let herself out. There was no hook, and no mat to hide them under. She tried not to make a sound as she searched frantically; she was starting to panic. There was nothing to be seen, so Angela examined the door. She undid the bolts and tried the handle. It had one of those Yale catches that lock themselves when you close it behind you. She glanced nervously up the stairs. She liked Harry but she wasn't that modern and she couldn't do this. She sighed, and checked that she had her handbag, coat and keys, and that the silver watch her mammar had given her was safely on her wrist. Then she let the door shut behind her and heard the lock click.

It was a bright, fresh morning, the sun high in the sky. She could hear birdsong and the chimes of Little John in the distance. She breathed in the cool sharp air and it shocked her lungs, making her feel sick again. She walked past the Loggerheads pub, where they'd been drinking last night, and up Cliff Road towards town. The old caves of Narrow Marsh were open to the world like a mouth full of fillings. She was soon at the steps that ran up into the main part of the city centre. She climbed them, stopping once to catch her breath.

A church rose above her like an iceberg from the sea and she wasn't sure if it was the lightness of breath or the drink still on her but it was the most beautiful building she'd ever seen. She was sure she'd be struck down as soon as she entered its walls but she felt compelled to go in. The sign outside said 'Unitarian Church', which definitely wasn't Catholic. But it was a church, and it was Sunday, so she pushed open the door.

Angela stood for a moment in the entrance, breathing fast and wondering if she was allowed to go in. The church smelled posh; of furniture wax and flowers dissolving into water. Coloured shafts of light flew from the stained glass and blessed the pews beneath. It felt grand, the kind of place that belonged to those who wore brand new clothes every Sunday. Her mam had always said, though, that God was for everyone, and it was hours before any service was likely to take place. Angela took a deep breath and went inside.

There was a severe-looking pulpit at the front of the church, so foreign and different from what Angela was used to that she almost wanted to go and stand in it, see the view. She chose a pew towards the middle and genuflected, making the sign of the cross before entering the row. There were soft red cushions on the benches. She put one on the floor in front of her and knelt. The scent of furniture polish seemed to fill her up as if it were God's spirit she was breathing in. She pressed her hands together and closed her eyes and prayed. *Please let it all be OK.*

A hand on her shoulder made her jump straight up to standing and swivel on to a back foot, ready to – what? – she had no idea but both her hands were in the air, like a boxer's.

'Hey, Angel girl.' He made this sound like the beginning of a song.

'Harry!' Her voice had a screech to it.

He placed his hand gently on her arm as if to calm her and his words were as soft as cotton on newly bathed skin. 'What're ye doing?'

Angela sat down on the wooden bench. She looked up at Harry. Then she laughed. 'I was praying for my mortal soul.'

DEAD FLOWERS

'Budge up,' Harry said. Angela shuffled along as requested. Harry took a second red cushion and put it behind his back, wriggling around to get comfy. She turned towards him and he touched her cheek. 'So ye feeling a wee bit guilty about last night?'

'No,' Angela said. 'Yes. Oh, I don't know.'

'A good Catholic lassie, eh?'

Angela nodded. She realised she was crying as Harry brushed her tears away with his thumb.

'Ye really think God's that auld fashioned, hen?' He smiled, broad and warm. 'Baby, Jesus is alive and well, wearing flared jeans and winklepickers, on his way to Woodstock with flowers in his hair.' He put on an American accent.

She choked on her tears as she laughed at that image.

Harry took her hand and held it in his, gently pressing against one finger and then the next. 'Our preacher always used to say that God is love. And me and you, we're all about love. Honestly, that cannay be wrong in my book.'

'My mam would say that a lot were wrong with it.' She was shaking her head. 'God might not be old-fashioned, but she is.'

Harry reached forward and took a hymnal from the bench in front of him. 'Trust me, it'll be alright in the end. And if it isnay all right, then it cannay be the end.' He placed his hand on the leather book. 'I swear it on the Holy Bible.'

'That's not a Bible,' Angela said, but the words came through a smile.

'It's close enough,' Harry told her. 'C'mon,' he said, with a nod towards the door, 'I was gony make us a wee bit o' breakfast.'

Angela hesitated. She looked at the pew in front of her, the red cushion on the floor. Then up to the grand pulpit, to the stained glass. As she looked up, the colours brightened, the sun coming out from clouds above them. It felt like a sign.

Harry stood up, holding out a hand. Angela felt a kind of surrender come over her. She wanted to believe in him. *All you need is love,* the gospel according to John, Paul, George and Ringo. Angela wanted to walk off into the future with Harry and put her faith in love and music, so she took his hand and held on tight.

Ain't No Mountain High Enough

Mill Caff

There was no mistaking Big Pat Walsh; six-foot-four and half as wide, with a broken nose from the boxing. No irony in this nickname. He was sitting at a table eating breakfast. He took a massive swig of tea and wiped at his tomatoes with a slice of fried bread. Harry walked over, taking him in. There were two things people said about Big Pat Walsh and the first was that he wasn't a man you talked about.

Walsh looked up and made eye contact as he chewed; he nodded up and to the side, a silent hello. Harry could see why he scared people. There was something brutal and dead in those nut-brown eyes. But Harry was still high on the back of his first proper night with his new love, and he wasn't afraid of anything. He sat down and leaned back in the chair opposite Pat.

The woman from behind the counter came over with a cuppa for Harry, and he added lots of sugar and waited for Pat to speak, stirring the tea vigorously.

'So, I hear you fancy yourself for a go at running the Loggerheads,' Pat said.

'Not one for small talk, eh?' Harry said. He was smiling, though.

'Nah, fuck that.' Walsh had a strong southern accent. London or nearby. Harry wondered if he'd come to Nottingham in similar circumstances to himself, on the run from someone bigger who would have killed him if he'd stayed. Of course, those psycho twins had run everything down there, and he couldn't imagine Walsh putting up and shutting up to anyone, not based on the rep he had up here.

'Aye.' Harry sat up straight, puffing his chest out slightly. 'Been a regular down that pub for a few years now, pal. Everyone kens who I am and they ken that they cannay mess with me, too.'

'Yeah?' Walsh leaned forward, narrowing his eyes. 'Look, I don't doubt that you can run a pub, mate. But I got business interests that need looking after in that place and I need to find the right man for that job, too.' He grabbed a toothpick from a packet in the middle of the table and went to work on his front incisors. 'You get my drift?'

Harry smiled, and tilted his head to the side. 'Does Ronnie Kray suck cock?' he said.

Walsh grinned and chewed on his toothpick. 'Funny,' he said. He waved the toothpick in Harry's general direction. 'You're definitely funny, though I'd be very careful who you said that to.'

Harry stared him out and took a big sip from the strong tea. It was stewed tasting, and he grimaced as he put down the mug.

'It needs someone strong,' Walsh told him. He slammed down the toothpick then flicked it across the table, pointing a finger at Harry. 'Someone who can stand his ground, you know what I mean?'

'Aye,' Harry said. 'I've worked with auld George Kinnock. And the O'Reillys over in Cov. I'm naybody's fool, I can promise ye that.' He dropped the names that he was sure Walsh would have heard of from his previous life without mentioning anyone who would pay money for his current address.

Walsh picked up a fresh toothpick and started chewing it, examining Harry's face as if he were trying to work something out. His eyes narrowed. 'You married?' he said.

Harry shook his head. He held on to his tea tightly. 'No yet. Though I met a lovely wee lassie, just now, and I have high hopes.' He thought about what Pat might like to hear about Angela, what might pull him on to Harry's side. 'A lovely Irish *cailin*,' he said, pronouncing the Gaelic properly. He knew that Angela was only really half Irish, and that she was English enough to use *colleen*, the anglicised version of the same word, but why let facts get in the way?

Pat waved a second slice of fried bread around before dipping it. 'It's the brewery, see. You gotta be married. I can fix a lot but I can't do nothing about that one.'

The two men stared at each other for a few moments. 'I'll sort it,' Harry said, breaking the silence.

Pat nodded through a mouthful of food. It was a small gesture but it was all it took.

October 2017

VISTA

A house on Cliff Road

Sian was still reading everything she could find online about the pub and about her uncle, Bobby Q, and his band, when she was startled by the sound of the door behind her. She lost her grip on the phone and had to lunge to catch it, putting too much pressure on the bottom of her cast.

'Sorry to make you jump.' Les Parker was back in the room. 'You've got a visitor.'

Behind Les, in the doorway, was her mother. Sian sat up straighter. 'How did you get here?' she said.

'Trains, planes and automobiles. All the usual ways,' her mum said.

'I'll leave you to it,' Les said, looking from one to the other of them and seeming awkward. He retreated out of the door and closed it quietly behind him.

Ruth walked over to inspect Sian more closely. 'What happened?' She leaned over, a deep frown cutting into her brow. 'Please tell me this isn't boyfriend related.'

'No!' She pulled her leg away from her mother. 'Course not. I'm still with Kris.'

'Ah, the decent young man,' her mother said, sitting on the sofa. 'That's good, so.' She was putting on that phony half-Irish accent, one of her more annoying affectations.

'How did you hear?' Sian said.

'Les messaged.'

'Oh, Les did, did he? You two friends then?' Sian could feel her own face screwing up, her throat tightening. And then a weird thought, remembering what Les had said about her mother being beautiful. Was he her biological father? She tried to remember if he had blue or brown eyes.

'He got in touch through Facebook,' her mother said. 'I've known him since I was six,' she added, as if this made some kind of difference.

Sian longed for simpler times when one's parents couldn't connect to the dial-up modem never mind add each other on Facebook. She did the add-ups, though. There was no way that her mother could have got here this quickly, not all the way from the Costa del Ex Pat Wankers. 'Where were you when you got Les's message?' she said.

Her mother's face clouded. Her head dropped and her eyes focused on the floor. 'Look, I was going to get in touch. Tom was going to ring you and get you over for dinner. Help us sort everything out.'

Sian let out a snort. 'Everything?' she said, thinking that this would be some kind of miracle.

'You know what I mean.' Her mother's voice was quiet, gentle. Soothing. She was good at that kind of thing and Sian had moments of wondering at the manipulativeness. It was usually psychopaths who were this good at this stuff, wasn't it?

Sian was hit by the impulse to cry so strongly that it caused a pain in her throat and jaw; that design fault again. But she was not going to give her mother the pleasure of that. She gritted her teeth.

'I told you not to move in there.' Her mum's voice was quiet, without a hint of satisfaction.

'Did you know?' Sian almost growled the words. 'Did you fucking know?'

'Please don't swear.'

'Answer the question,' Sian said, wondering where her mother got off telling her not to swear. She was a stone's throw away from fifty, not a sulking teenager, and she had good reason to feel disturbed by what was happening.

'Of course, I didn't know, Sianey.'

'I don't believe you.'

Her mum let out a big sigh. 'I've never liked that place. Never. That's all I knew.' She looked like she was making an effort not to roll her eyes. 'Honestly, honey, this is as big a shock to me as it must have been to you.'

'Oh, come on. You didn't find them down there, so you are not as shocked as me, I promise you. And you knew that Uncle Rob was in that band, that he called himself Bobby Q. You both lied to me about that.'

'We didn't lie to you, we just didn't tell you about it. It all happened before you were born, ancient history. It messed up Rob's head and he wanted to leave it all behind.' Her mum held her gaze like a practised liar. Sian had learned a lot through police interviews; it'd all be loads easier if people were worse at lying, their body language giving away their dishonesty with glances up and to the right, or an inability to make eye contact. Proper liars, who made a habit of it, they knew that the first person they needed to convince was themselves and, after that, the rest was easy.

'I can't believe you were in the country and hadn't told me.' Sian's voice was low. Dangerous. 'Staying with Tom, and neither of you bother to ring or text.'

Her mother swallowed hard. 'I thought we both needed a bit of space,' she said. 'After all that was said about the will. It got very nasty for a while.'

'Yeah, well that was months ago. You could have at least let me know you were here.' Sian crossed her arms and felt her body tighten. 'So, tell me about my uncle's friends from the band. And his wife. Everything.'

A frown twisted her mother's face. 'You probably know more about them than I do,' she said.

'I only know what Les told me.' Sian watched her mother swallow again, the curve of her throat moving in and out.

'What else did Les say?' her mum asked.

Sian sat and considered this, watching her mother twist and fidget in her seat. What might Les know that her mum didn't want her to find out? Sian would have liked to have let her suffer but she couldn't; it wasn't her nature. 'He just said that two of them lived at the Loggerheads before my Uncle Rob, and that they were a bit up themselves. That they went on the telly and then the bloke went off the rails.'

Ruth breathed in sharply; she'd been holding her breath. 'That's about the strength of it,' she said. 'Although Harry was always a bit of a nutter.'

'And Uncle Rob was on the telly?'

'Aye.'

Sian wondered why her mother couldn't just say yes, like a normal person. *Aye* wasn't even properly Irish.

'What else did he tell you?' Ruth asked, again.

'Nothing,' Sian said. 'Oh, actually, no, that's not true. He said something about me looking like you and you being a beauty. Which proves he's blind.' She caught her breath and then realised what she'd said. 'About me looking like you, not the beauty thing.'

There was a strained smile on her mother's face; it looked like a lot of effort.

'What else is there to tell?' Sian said. She stared right into her mother's blue eyes, hoping for the truth at last.

'Nothing,' Ruth said, glancing away.

'You're lying!' Sian's voice was rising with her emotions. She reached for her crutches. 'You can't even tell the truth now. Well, it's all going to come out!' She pushed the crutches into the floor, the way she'd been taught, but with her rush and her temper it was hard to get her balance.

Her mother came over to help. Sian tried to resist but Ruth was insistent and helped her to her feet.

Sian held on to her mother and looked her right in the eye. 'You know I used to think he was joking, Uncle Rob. I used to think he was *so* funny.' She was only just holding off the tears and her mouth was hurting with the effort. 'His wife'd run off with a Scotsman. I thought it was all one big joke.'

'Oh, Sian. Please tell me you didn't tell the police that.'

Sian pushed her mother away and nearly fell over. 'Of course not!' Her voice was a screech. 'Sometimes I wonder if you know me at all.' She was shaking as she started to make her away across the room. She struggled with the door knob. All she wanted was to storm out and it was impossible.

'Sian.' Her mother's voice snuck up on her, soft and gentle.

'Do not touch me,' Sian said. She lifted one hand. 'Don't you dare.' She finally managed to wrestle the door open and got to the other side of it, shutting it behind her sharply.

Les Parker was standing in the hallway, close enough to the door that he had to jump out of the way.

'Everything all right?' he said.

'Oh, everything's just wonderful,' Sian told him. She hopped past him on her crutches towards the front door and he rushed past to open it for her.

Sian stood out on the street and reached into her back pocket for her mobile phone. There were still loads of police and CSIs coming and going from the Loggerheads, and Dominic was doing an interview with the TV crew, looking serious and professional. She sat down on the wall in front of her neighbour's garden and let herself cry; a sweet, silent relief. She made no noise and no drama and you would have had to look closely at her face to see the hot, bitter tears that streaked it.

Sian's mother was a liar, it was as simple as that. There were so many lies. She would never trust her again.

TUNDRA

Cliff Road

The sound of a car door closing made Sian look up. She saw Kris coming down the street towards her.

'Hey,' he said, as he got closer.

Sian rubbed her neck and stretched. She reached for her crutches but they were slightly too far away.

'You OK?' Kris said, walking to her and handing her the crutches.

Sian shrugged. 'Not really.'

'What happened?'

Sian shook her head. She looked up at him, squinting against the morning sunshine, which was hitting the tops of her eyes. 'Can we go somewhere?'

'Sure,' Kris said. 'I thought I could take you out for breakfast or something. Then back to the fracture clinic to get the proper cast on that foot. What do you reckon?'

'Am I going to get a lecture?'

Kris frowned. 'I think we need to talk.'

'Fine.' She indicated towards the house behind her. 'Les hung my coat up and I left in a hurry. It's still there.'

Kris raised one eyebrow, a talent that had always made Sian jealous. 'Les, is it now?'

'Yep, my pal, Les.' She rolled her eyes. 'Shit, I know a neighbour now, too, and I'll have to say *hello* and all that rubbish. This is just a *disaster*.'

'I'll fetch it,' Kris said, 'to protect you from, you know, any untoward friendliness.' He walked down the path and knocked on the door.

Sian hugged herself, cold without her coat. She glanced up again and saw Dominic Wilkinson, standing outside the Loggerheads and staring over at her. His gravity seemed to suck in the air around him, making him a deep dark space, and she stared at him thinking this must be what it would be like to see a vampire, if such things existed. He looked as if he were deciding whether to cross and talk to her. She felt colder still, all over, and shivered, wanting to get up and rush away but feeling trapped and stuck to the spot.

Then Kris was back with her coat, holding it out in front of himself like a prize. He turned, following Sian's gaze across the road behind him. Then he saw who she was staring at and understood. 'Come on,' he said. 'We should go.'

'Yes.' A cough. She grabbed the crutches and got herself to her feet. Kris was standing by, slightly stooped and with his hands out as if to catch her. She gave him a look and he backed off. Even though she couldn't put her left foot down, she felt pretty steady. You didn't get to fourth Dan in anything without having strong core muscles. She swung herself along the pavement next to Kris, keeping pace with him.

Kris smiled as he pressed on the keys to open the car. 'Warsaw diner?' he said, suggesting a place that was one of their regular favourites.

Sian considered it. They sold proper hash browns and it was usually busy and loud in the diner. 'OK,' she said.

'Hold on. Lean against the car here.' Kris helped her balance against the back passenger door, opening the front. He took hold of her again, almost lifting her up to load her into the car. He went to put the crutches on the back seat.

'No!' Sian called to him. 'I need them with me. In case.'

'In case of what?' Kris was leaning against the car and holding the door open.

'I dunno.' She looked at the road ahead. 'In case of emergency.' Kris flicked his tongue against his teeth and shook his head. 'Fine,' he said. He placed the crutches beside her in the front seat and when everything was out of the way of the door, he closed it firmly but carefully.

Kris was very quiet, and Sian kept glancing over at his face as he drove. The radio was on Smooth FM. She re-tuned to Radio 1 and then ramped up the volume. Kris pressed the 'silence' setting and caught her eyes in the rear view mirror.

'You wanna tell me what you took away from that crime scene?' he said.

'Didn't take long to get to the lecture part,' she said.
Kris ignored the snipe and kept his eyes on the road. 'You took some kind of sample, right?'

Sian let out a deep sigh. 'I just want to know who that is, in my house. I think I have a right.'

'Oh yeah? Finders keepers, like in primary school?'

'That's not what I said, Kris.' She swallowed. 'Anyway, I only got a sample from one.'

'Oh,' Kris said. 'That's all right then.'

There was the beat of the road, the growl of the engine.

'Where did you put it?' he asked.

'In the freezer.' She stifled a giggle and shook her head. She wanted to tell him it was in the amaretto bottle, too, but she couldn't get the words out. She'd tried to approximate the way she would have usually preserved a sample, in high percentage ethanol and a very deep freeze.

'It's not funny, Sian!'

She was properly laughing, though, could hardly breathe with it.

'Sian, for fuck's sake. You gotta take this seriously!'

She couldn't speak, though. It wasn't that she didn't take it seriously. Part of the laughter was the shock playing out. She tried to breathe.

Kris pulled the car over, sharply, to the side of the road, so fast it felt like a skid. He turned to Sian, his face tight with anger. She flinched away. The smell of burning rubber filled her nose and throat and she knew she was going under. There was nothing she could do to stop the past as she felt it barrelling towards her like a car crash.

Another car, a dark Mercedes just like this one. The scream and the screech of brakes and that exact same smell. *FOR FUCK'S SAKE SIAN YOU FUCKING BITCH*. The loud thumps against the dashboard set to smash it up and Sian shaking and shrinking back into her seat. Reaching for the car door, for the little metal latch that opens it but, as she hears the click of the door opening there's another screech of tyres. Accelerating back into the road and Sian thrown straight into the dash and grabbing hold of the handbrake to stop herself falling out. The car weaving all over the road and the g-force pulling and pushing her as she holds on with all the strength she can, then pulling too hard and the handbrake coming up. The car spinning, the tyres burning as it screeches to a stop. Trying to scramble out of the door but strong, strong hands grabbing her and...

'Sian!' Kris had hold of her, his hands on both of her shoulders, and was looking into her eyes. 'Look at me.' She was half aware of being in the right car, with the right man, but it felt like watching from above. She was shaking, her teeth chattering. She looked into Kris's eyes. 'Sian,' he said. His voice quivered. He pulled her closer, kissed her forehead. 'Sian, please.'

Sian stared at the thick wires of dark hair on Kris's head, then at the leather seats and the interior of the car, pale blue and not black like that other car. She saw her foot, in a cast in the passenger footwell. Moment by moment, piece by piece, she grounded herself, brought herself back to the present. She sucked in a sharp breath and blew it out slowly. Then she burst into tears.

'Sorry,' he said. His voice was quiet now and he sounded contrite. 'I'm so, so sorry.' He kissed her forehead and pushed back her hair.

Sian flung herself back in the seat and wiped away her tears. At least he'd seen her like this before and she wasn't going to have to explain it all over again. It took her a few moments to compose herself and Kris sat back in his seat and left her alone. She managed to make the shaking ease off with deep, focused breaths.

She turned towards him. 'Sorry,' she said.

'No need for you to be sorry, this is my fault,' he said. 'Are you feeling OK?'

She nodded. 'It's not your fault. I think it was that look Dominic gave me from across the road that's set me off That on top of my mum turning up,' she told him. 'At Les Parker's.'

'Your mum?' Kris stared out through the windscreen. 'How did she find out what was going on? Wait a minute, how did she even get here, from Spain?'

'She didn't come from Spain. She's been staying with my brother.'

'Wow!' Kris's voice sounded almost admiring.

'I know, right?' She let out a very short, bitter laugh. 'Apparently Les added her on Facebook,' she said.

'Parents, eh? And their actual own lives.' He was shaking his head. 'I can't believe she was at Tom's and didn't get in touch with you. And as for Tom.'

'I know,' she said. 'There'll be more bodies in that cellar if they're not careful!'

Kris laughed, lightly, but his eyes were far away. 'I'm really worried about you, Sian.'

'I get it,' she said. 'Look, I know I shouldn't have done it, but I have now. I panicked. I dunno.' She examined her fingernails. 'I just needed to do something.'

'And what next? I mean, what you going to do? Take your sample into your office at the university? Really?'

She chewed at a nail. 'Maybe.'

'And then what? How much info you going to get from old DNA like that? And what you going to do even if you get a full profile? Check it against the police database?' He leaned his head down on the steering wheel. 'You haven't thought this through, Sian.'

'Next time you find a pair of fucking skeletons in your cellar let's see how well you think things through,' she said. She had to bite her lip to stop herself from laughing again. *Hysterical.* She could hear her ex's booming voice again, as clearly as if he was sitting in the car with them. *Completely lost your shit.*

Kris smiled at her and reached a hand towards her hair. She let him brush it out of her eyes. 'OK, point taken. But you're a professional, Sian. You're putting everything on the line here, your job and maybe even your freedom. Does that not worry you?'

Sian sighed. 'Not nearly as much as the idea that Dominic Wilkinson is trying to make out my uncle was Fred West,' she said.

'Nobody thinks that, Sian.' Kris started up the car again, checked his mirrors. 'And just because Dominic's an arsehole, that doesn't mean he's being an arsehole about this.' He indicated and pulled out.

'My mum was shitting herself. Worried about what Les might have told me. Which is fair enough because that bloke likes to gossip,' she said.

'So, did he tell you anything you didn't already know?'

'A few things.' She cleared her throat. 'Like my uncle was in a band that was almost famous and had a whole other name and life I didn't know about before I was born.'

'Honestly,' Kris said, 'the cheek of that generation with their own lives.'

They were quiet for a minute or two. Sian knew they'd soon be at the diner, which was just as well as she hadn't eaten for hours. She was so hungry she felt a bit sick. They turned on to Derby Road, St Barnabas Cathedral looming over the hill towards them. She shielded her eyes from the harsh morning sun that was peeking into the top of the car window. She flicked the sun visor down, hesitating for a moment. A flash of a large hand, slamming the sun visor back up, the plastic making a sharp slap against the inside of the car and the voice growling *leave it there*.

She had to remind herself that she was here with Kris, and that he didn't do things like that. She held on to the sun visor, to her seat, kept herself in the right moment, with the right man.

He pulled over and parked the car. 'Wait there,' he said. 'Don't you dare try to get out by yourself. This is not an emergency.'

Sian rolled her eyes, but she waited. Kris helped her out from the car and handed her the crutches. She pushed them into the ground and hopped towards the diner.

'That looks like hard work,' Kris said.

'It is.' She was getting used to it, though. Already, it felt a lot easier than it had the night before.

They were at the door of the diner and Kris stopped still. 'I'm not going to mention what I saw in your pocket again. Not ever. You will need to deal with it now. And you'll have to take any consequences. Just do me a favour, OK?'

Sian gave him a nod to carry on.

'Stop doing stupid things.'

FREEZING

Loggerheads: crime scene

There'd been a long wait at the fracture clinic and it was mid-afternoon when Kris brought Sian back to Cliff Road. He pulled up outside the Loggerheads, which was still buzzing with police although Sian saw, with relief, that the TV crew were no longer camping outside. Her stomach flipped. She didn't want to be here. She didn't want to know what else they might have found.

Kris turned towards her. 'You ready?' he said.

'Yes,' she said, thinking she needed to stop lying to Kris. She glanced over at the pub and then looked him in the eye. 'No,' she admitted. 'But let's do this.' She let him help her from the car and into the street. It was easier to walk now she had the proper cast on and was allowed to put her foot down and use the crutches to minimise the weight on it.

Kris knocked on the front door and Sian stood balanced on her crutches. A uniformed officer opened the door.

'Yeah?' he asked.

'Here with the homeowner.' Kris said. 'Can we talk to someone senior about what's going on?'

The guy nodded and went back inside. Moments later, the door opened and Dominic Wilkinson appeared. He seemed incredibly tall so close by and at the top of the doorstep. The sight of him took Sian's breath away and she stepped back, stumbling and having to grab hold of Kris.

'Sian,' he said. Then he glanced down his nose at Kris, as if he could smell something bad. 'DI Payne.' A female plain-clothes officer appeared behind him; a slim, attractive woman with long blonde hair.

'I just wanted to pick up some stuff I doubt it needs authority at the superintendent level.' Sian was trying to make a joke, to get past the chill of fear she felt so close to him, but it didn't help.

Dominic half-smiled. 'In that case, I'll leave you in the capable hands of my good woman here.' He gestured behind him with a leer, and Sian knew that he'd meant to give her the impression that the woman was more than just his second in command. 'Now, if you'll excuse me, I'm a busy man.' They stepped aside and he strode past them towards his unmarked car.

The woman moved into the doorway and held out a hand. 'DCI Julia Swann. Can I help you?'

Kris shook her hand, then Sian, who had to juggle with her crutches first.

'Just wondering what's going on,' Sian said. 'When I can get my house back.'

Swann looked her up and down. 'Dunno,' she said. 'Not today. We have a lot more to do in terms of forensics and so forth.'

'You found something else?' Sian tried to sound casual.

The officer looked up into the sky then levelled her gaze at Sian. 'I can't really discuss that with you.'

Kris flashed his ID. 'Come on,' he said. 'I'm Missing Persons now but I used to work with you guys.' He jabbed a thumb in Sian's direction. 'She did too.'

The woman looked from one to the other of them, considering that. She sighed. 'Look, I didn't tell you this, OK? We haven't really found much else. Just a load of old stuff someone had sealed in a room. Women's clothing. A few old photos and some records and newspaper clippings. We don't even know if any of it is relevant at the moment. But we will need to keep looking.'

Sian frowned. 'Fine,' she said, knowing that there wasn't really any other choice but to resign herself to this.

'Listen, I'd find somewhere else to stay for a bit. God knows how long we'll need to be here and when we're done, it'll be a right mess,' the DCI told her.

'Not so easy when you've got a dog,' Sian said.

Swann looked genuinely concerned and Sian suspected it was the mention of the dog that had drawn out the empathy. She got that; she liked dogs more than people, too.

'Don't you have a friend or someone who might help?' Swann said. She sounded so sympathetic that Sian was half expecting her to offer her a place to stay in her own home.

'She totally has somewhere to go,' Kris said. 'Come on, you, stop playing for sympathy.'

'Fine,' Sian said. She put on a sickly sweet, breathless voice and fluttered her eyelashes madly. 'I'm so excited! We're moving in together already! Can we get married, too?'

Kris rolled his eyes. Now, it was him who was getting the compassionate looks from DCI Swann. Sian didn't like that so much.

She smiled at the detective. 'Can I get a few things, you know, an overnight bag? Happy to be accompanied by one of your uniforms.'

The woman nodded.

'I'll wait in the car,' Kris said. Then, a very quiet mutter under his breath so that only Sian would hear it. 'Don't let her out of your sight.'

'What?' Swann called after him.

'Nothing!' he said, all cheerful and sing-song. 'Just talking to myself.'

Sian smiled and followed the officer into the pub. Swann called over to a young man. He looked fresh-faced but was hardly the uniform Sian had suggested. Probably a DC but Sian would need to watch herself. She smiled at him.

'Follow me,' he said, his accent smooth and private schooled. He was wearing a pair of tailored trousers that hung from his hips to show the Ralph Lauren label on his underwear.

They headed upstairs with the occasional awkward smile passing between them, but no words. The young man looked like he wanted to pick her up and carry her to speed things up. The image of the skinny youth buckling under her weight made Sian smile.

Outside the bedroom, Sian used one of her crutches to point at the suitcase she wanted. 'Can you carry it for me?' she said. Kris had insisted she pack one bag as if she were going away, with enough things that it would be the only one she'd need to dig into for a few days. She was suddenly very grateful for his relentless need to organise everything properly. 'OK,' she said. 'There's just a couple of things I need from downstairs, now.'

'Downstairs?' The young detective sounded hesitant.

'Yes,' Sian said, with conviction. Before he could argue or think about it much more, she swung away from the room and towards the stairs, moving as fast as she could with her crutches. At the top of the stairs, she handed one to the young man and used the banister instead. He stood close as they walked down. In the hallway at the bottom, she took her crutch back off him and was off towards the back of the pub ahead of him.

DCI Swann was standing outside the back room and whatever was going on in the excavation was hidden by a privacy screen. 'Hello?' Swann said. 'Can I help you with something?'

Sian threw the DCI a massive smile. 'From the freezer,' she said. She kept moving and tried not to think too hard about what she was doing. She swung her body across the kitchen, trying to find out exactly how fast she could go. She flung the freezer door open, digging inside for the bottle.

'My amaretto!' she said, handing it to the dazed and confused young detective with a flourish. 'Can you tuck it into the bag for me? Not going anywhere without that.'

'Do you keep that stuff in the freezer then?' the lad asked. 'I thought that was just gin.'

'Oh, the freezer's good for all sorts of things,' Sian told him, with a wink. He blushed, and suddenly seemed as young and inexperienced as he doubtless was. Sian headed for the door and the nice young man carried out the sample she had stolen from the body in her cellar. If it hadn't been so weird and so very, very wrong, it could almost have been funny.

August 1970

I'll Say Forever My Love

Nottingham Castle grounds

The ice cream man plunged his shoulder deep into the freezer and pulled out the strawberry split Angela had asked for, handing it to her with a flourish. Harry juggled between his pockets and the 99 he was eating, pulling out notes to pay.

The sun beat down. The icy chill of the lolly made Angela's head hurt, so she stopped eating and walked. The grass was pristine and the castle walls and bandstand made Angela feel posh just being near them. The flowers were arranged to make pictures and patterns.

'It's been a lovely day, Harry,' she said.

'It has that, darlin'. It has that.'

They walked up the steep path towards the castle. They stopped for a breather halfway and Angela glanced down to see something red all over her hand and leg. For a moment, she thought she was bleeding, and she dropped her lolly with a shocked 'oh!' Then she laughed, realising it was just the ice lolly she'd half-forgotten, melting on to her skin. She pulled out a handkerchief to try to wipe the stain away.

'Let me help ye, there, hen,' Harry said, pulling out his hanky too. He dabbed at the sticky red liquid on her hand then, with a wink, on her leg. 'Out damned spot!' he said, and Angela laughed with him, but wasn't sure why it was funny. Then his hand wandered further up her skirt and she looked around to check no one could see, and let him lick her leg in a pretence at cleaning it. He stood up, pulling her close, then they kissed. She could taste strawberries on his breath. Angela closed her eyes, enjoying the moment. When she opened her eyes again, Harry was on one knee.

'What you doing?' she said. 'Get up!' She had no idea what he was messing about at. 'You'll have the knees of your trousers out!' she said.

'Angela Callaghan, will ye marry me?'

'Stop messing, Harry. Get up! This isn't funny.'

But he pulled her towards him and stayed exactly where he was. Then he reached inside his pocket and pulled out a small, dark box.

'Oh Harry, what are you going on about?' Angela didn't even know where to look. But then she let her gaze settle on the box. It was velvety, and a very dark blue colour. 'What are you doing, Harry?'

'I think it's called proposing,' he said, grinning up at her.

'Harry. We've known each other five minutes.' She pulled hard on his arm, tried to get him to stand up.

Harry stood and pulled Angela towards him for a kiss. He leaned back again. 'So what? I havenay felt like this about naybody in my life. What about you?'

Angela considered his question. She'd certainly been happier in the last few weeks than she had been for a very long time. Harry was a gentleman but she barely knew him. It was easy to be charming for a while; she'd seen that with Jack.

'Ye havenay to answer in a rush,' Harry said. He took her hand and they carried on up the path towards the castle.

'I really like you, Harry. I'm just not ready yet.'

He swung her around to face him. The sun was shining up above them, over the castle, illuminating the scene like stage lights. It felt very romantic.

'When I met ye, I couldnay believe I'd met someone so pretty and sweet that actually liked me too,' he told her. 'Then I heard your voice; the voice of an angel. And I thought, I'm no gony let this one go.' He paused and looked up to the sky and then back down at her. 'We're meant to be together, of that I am certain, lassie. And I'm gony keep asking this question until I hear the right answer!'

'My mam'll never wear it,' she said.

Harry laughed, looking over her head and sounding slightly hysterical. Maybe that was it. Maybe the sun had sent him loopy. But he turned back to Angela with that light in his eyes. 'I'm no asking her,' he said.

Angela reached for his shirt, her fingers bothering a button. 'She has to give her permission, though, Harry. I'm only twenty.'

'Naw,' he said, firmly. He was shaking his head. 'That changed, remember. In January. It isnay like that nay more if ye're past eighteen.'

Angela stopped, staring at Harry. He was right, of course. She had forgotten about that new law. There were other laws, though, important ones. 'I'm still married to Jack.'

Harry waved a dismissive hand at this. 'I couldnay care less, darlin. We'll get married anyway. As far as I'm concerned that auld man o' yours is dead. That's what we'll say. Naybody's gony notice little auld ye and me.'

'Harry, it's *illegal*.' She made the last word sound incredibly serious and important.

He let out a choked laugh and shook his head. 'We'll get ye divorced if you insist,' he said, 'but truthfully, my love, I couldnay care less for them and their rules. Fuck 'em.'

Angela looked at the castle wall. His vehemence was catching and she wanted to say yes, a nagging voice somewhere telling her that she shouldn't let a chance like this go with a man like Harry. 'I'll say yes when I've known you a bit longer, I'm sure I will. If you can only wait,' she told him.

'Aye. I'll wait as long as I need to,' Harry said, looking wise and patient. Angela remembered that he'd been patient about getting her into bed, and that he hadn't, in the end, needed to be. His patience had rushed her. Was that his game?

'Can I tell ye a wee secret that'll mibbe change yer mind?' he said.

Angela nodded, intrigued.

'Yer wee sis and my best pal have got plans, just next weekend, to run off up tay Gretna Green and get theirsel hitched. How's about that? Why no make it a four? And at Gretna, there definitely isnay need to worry oursel about yer maw.'

Angela's hand shot to her mouth and she let out a small squeal. 'Really? Marilyn? And she hasn't told me?'

Harry smiled in a knowing way. 'O'course she hasnay. Worried ye'll go tell yer ma and she'll put a stop to it.'

Their mother would stop her. She was livid with both of them. With Marilyn for *running around with a detty heathen*. With Angela because *I never left when yer father hit me. I covered up the bruises, and I din't tell no one, because marriage is holy between two people and no-un else*. But Angela didn't want that same marriage her ma thought was holy, didn't want to be part of that same world that decided two people who loved each other couldn't be together because a slightly different kind of priest splashed water on their heads.

'I would never tell Mam,' Angela said.

'Naw, course ye wouldnay. Yer wee sister kens that. She wasnay gony put ye in that position, that's all,' he told her.

Placated, Angela took a deep breath and looked into Harry's big blue eyes. They welled up with love towards her and a lump formed in her throat. She had to swallow to stop from crying.

'You really love me?' she asked him, staring into his eyes and looking for the least bit of deception in them. They were clear and blue as the sky.

'Aye, hen. Ye cannay doubt it, surely?' Harry's voice made everything sound so obvious.

'You think we should do this?'

Harry nodded, vehemently.

Angela looked at Harry and all she saw was a man who loved her, and who wanted them to be together for the rest of their lives. And she couldn't help but want that in return. 'Yes,' she said, her voice a whisper.

'Say it louder, else I cannay be sure ye mean it,' Harry said.

'Yes,' Angela said, more clearly and firmly now. 'Yes!'

Harry smiled in that way that lit up his entire face. And he took her arm and spun her, like ballroom dancing, then waltzed her up the hill and towards the castle.

Bridge Over Troubled Water

The Loggerheads pub, a couple of days later

Harry noticed that the Loggerheads was packed with youngsters; girls in miniskirts who almost made him wonder if he was doing the right thing, courting Angie so seriously. Their fellas, looking Saturday night smart, not mods exactly but on their way to being. Harry had a vision for the pub, of the cave at the back and bands playing, the music bouncing off its unusual acoustics. Now he just needed to get everything signed and official with Angela so he could get the pub.

Bobby was at the bar, being chatted up by a woman who looked underage. He was grinning down at her and patted her bottom before picking up two pints and heading back to Harry. He put down the glasses and sat down, giving Harry a grin and a big thumbs-up.

'Cheers, pal,' Harry said, taking a big sip. He turned towards Bobby looking thoughtful. 'I hear auld Gladys has popped off, the one who read my fortune?'

Bobby was nodding.

'Bet she didnay see that coming, eh?'

Bobby burst out laughing and missed his mouth with his beer, grabbing a hanky out of his pocket to wipe himself down. 'You're a right bogger, you are,' he told Harry, and they laughed together.

Both men went quiet and sipped at their drinks. 'How's yer wee lassie, then?' Harry asked, after a few minutes.

'Marilyn?' Bobby licked away a foam moustache that the beer had left on him. 'Not sure about that one. She's a bit flighty.' He shook his head. 'Not sure she's the right gell for me, if I'm being honest.'

Harry nodded, gulping down beer. 'She's a doll, though,' he said. 'And mad about ye. She tellt me as much!'

Bobby's face folded into a doubtful expression, his eyes squinting at the idea. 'She gets mad with me easy,' he said, 'I don't know about owt else.'

Harry laughed. 'Well that's lassies for ye,' he said. He tapped the side of his nose. 'If ye don't wantay murder her, and she isnay gony murder you, then you're ontay a winner, take it from me.'

Bobby looked doubtful but his face relaxed and Harry seized the moment.

'I'll let you intay a secret,' he said. He put his pint down dramatically and sat back in his chair. 'We're getting hitched. Me and Ange. We're running off tay Gretna, all romantic and that. You two should come with.'

Bobby choked on his beer. 'And get married?' he spluttered, grabbing his hanky again and patting at his shirt. 'Me and Marilyn?' He made the idea sound ridiculous.

'Aye.' Harry didn't miss a beat. He knew if he made it sound obvious then he'd more chance of getting what he wanted.

Bobby was laughing, and wiping down his shirt. 'Jesus, Harry, you nutter.' He shook his head.

Harry kept his gaze level, until Bobby's eyes caught his. 'Ye got yersel a good yin there, pal. You dinnay want to lose a lassie as fine as her. She sees her sister getting hitched when we all met the same day, she's gony be asking questions!'

Bobby stared back. His whole attitude had changed. 'It's too soon,' he said. 'I like her, but not this quick.' He was shaking his head. 'That's a big promise to make someone you don't know that well.'

Harry waved a hand in the air and pulled a doubtful face. 'Listen, pal. Promises are like noses.' He paused for effect then grinned. 'Made to get broken!'

Bobby laughed again, lightly this time.

Harry winked. 'Ah c'mon,' he said. 'She's a cracker. And keeping ye more than happy in the bedroom department, eh?'

Bobby blushed, his pale skin glowing red with it, but he was grinning, those warm brown eyes full of fun. 'No complaints from me on that score,' he said, nudging Harry as he drank.

'My old granda used to say it right on that,' Harry told him. 'If there isnay a problem in the bedroom, then there isnay a problem.' He let out a short, sharp laugh. 'Or ye can get off tay bed and forget all yer problems!'

Bobby laughed loudly. 'Got that one right,' he said.

The two pals drank in companionable silence for a while. The buzz around them in the pub was pleasant and soothing. A girl came over to Harry for a light, glancing at him through big, dark lashes as he lit a match for her.

'Listen, pal,' Harry said, watching the woman retreat to the group she'd come in with. She was wearing green flares that pulled tight at the top, and they showed off her arse very nicely. 'Between ye, me and the table here, Pat Walsh is gony give me this pub. There's space here for a barman to live in, with a wife, if ye hear me.'

Bobby nodded. He drank more beer.

'Job. Free place to stay so you can get out from under yer maw's hair. All the beer you can drink. And the chance to make a bit o' dough helping me out with Pat Walsh and his crew.' Harry counted off the perks on his fingers. 'But the brewery willnay wear it if you're no married.'

'OK,' Bobby said. He looked thoughtful.

'Aye, well best if ye don't take yer time over it too much, pal. Me and Ange, we're off next weekend, you ken?'

'OK,' Bobby said. 'I'll think on it and let you know by Thursday.'

'Ye do that,' Harry said. But he could see he was halfway there, or more, by the look on Bobby's face. Sex could make a man do pretty much anything, Harry knew that. He glanced at the woman in flares again, then back at Bobby.

Aye, sex was powerful. It had persuaded better men than Bobby O'Quaid to make the biggest mistakes of their lives.

Can't Help Falling In Love

Gretna Green, the following weekend

It was a grey day and the clouds loomed over them like a warning. Harry looked up at the sky and grimaced. The register office looked like a scout hut; not exactly romantic, but it would do the job. The girls had climbed from the car and were straightening out their matching white dresses and smoothing down hair. They fussed around each other, picking off invisible bits of fluff from one another's clothes and looking nervous.

'You going to put on the shoes now?' Marilyn asked her sister.

Angela looked doubtful but Marilyn took them from the bag and put them on the pavement. 'They're our something new,' she said. 'You have to wear them.'

Reluctantly, Angela slipped off her flats and put on the red stiletto heels. Now the girls' outfits matched perfectly. The dresses were simple, but cinched at the waist to show off their figures. Harry smiled at the look of the shoes on Angela, liking the way they brought out the curve of her legs.

Marilyn opened up the back of the car and took out the flowers. She placed the two white bouquets on the top of the Austin Princess, and brought buttonholes over for the men. She smiled as she pressed Harry's to his lapel. She smelled amazing, the scent of the buttonhole combining with the Lily of the Valley perfume that he'd helped Bobby pick out for her when they first started courting.

'They're midnight roses,' she told Harry, pinning his on with a kiss and then a smile. 'Like your band!'

Harry grinned back at her. He couldn't help thinking that he wished that it had been Angela thinking about the band like that, buying flowers to match his heart. His wife to be was standing by the hedge looking like she might throw up. He looked at her and, for the first time in ages, he saw someone else's wife.

He walked over, placing an arm around her gently. 'Ye OK, hen?' he asked.

She nodded, looking up from where she was bent over. 'Car sick,' she said.

'Ye sure that's all?' he said.

Angela was bent right over herself, as if she couldn't stand up, so he crouched down next to her.

'What's wrong?'

'Harry, we're breaking the law,' she whispered. Her body lurched forward and she heaved.

'We're in Scotland. You're no married in Scotland, are ye?'

Angela stared back at him as if she hadn't considered this idea.

'You been worrying yoursel about this all this time and didnay tell me?' Harry said.

Angela leaned over further, grabbing hold of her knees.

Harry pulled her to standing then kissed her. There were tears running down her cheeks, so he kissed those away, too.

'I am married in Scotland, Harry. Aren't I? It doesn't work like that.'

He grinned. 'Ye shouldnay worry about these things. Not now I'm looking after ye. Anyone come along asking after ye will be getting short shrift from me. You get me?'

Angela smiled through her tears, and nodded.

'I'm looking after ye now. Ye just remember that, hen.'

He took her hand and led her towards the register office; the other two were waiting at the gate. They all walked in together, finding the little wedding room at the back. It was small, but there was just the four of them and the registrar, so it felt empty and echoed.

'You all ready?' The registrar asked them. He had a Borders accent, that weird middle ground between Scottish and English that Harry hated. He'd far rather people sound plummy and English than like they were trying to.

'Aye, we're set,' Harry told him. He looked around at everyone else and they nodded. He noticed that Bobby's little nod wasn't so certain, his pal looking almost as worried as Angela. Marilyn, though, was glowing. She never had doubts about the things she did. She was the kind of person who lived, and danced, and drank and did nothing without meaning it. And, as he thought about her this way, he half-wished she was the sister he was marrying.

The registrar glanced from one to the other of them and waited until he'd seen a nod from each of them. Then he started the service, those words so familiar about gathering to join in matrimony. Now things were moving, Angela looked more relaxed.

'If anyone here knows of any lawful impediment why these persons here present should not be married, then he should declare it now, or forever hold his peace.'

The four young people looked at each other, eyes popping from one to another, everyone wondering if one of them would say it. But the chapel stayed silent. Then the registrar nodded and Harry mopped his brow and mouthed 'phew', his standard joke at this point of a wedding service. The serious man officiating rolled his eyes, but a smile crept on to his lips.

The smile was still catching as he got each of them to declare that they 'knew not' of an impediment. Bobby was slouching and looked like he might faint. Harry hoped his pal would hold it together until the end of the ceremony. Was that too much to ask, really? He was only giving his life away to help Harry get the things he wanted, after all, not that much of a big deal.

Fifteen minutes later, the four of them emerged into the sunlight. Marilyn reached into her pocket and pulled out a box. Confetti. She burst it open with a cry of joy and threw it over the rest of them. They all ducked and Angela squealed loudly as the white petals flew into the air.

Harry drove them all to the blacksmith's shop, which was where people used to get married, back when you could do so where you wanted just by holding hands and saying a few words. They went inside and stood next to the anvil for a blessing. Marilyn took photos of them all with a polaroid camera. There was a hiss as it spat the pictures out, which smelled of melting plastic. Then she handed the camera to the shop girl, who took a picture of all of them, shaking it to cool before handing it back, so that it wouldn't smudge.

Outside, they sat on a bench and talked about which pub to visit first, having acquainted themselves with the entirety of Gretna's nightlife the previous evening. Harry handed out presents to the ladies in smart boxes from H Samuel. It'd taken him ages browsing the shop to decide what to buy everyone but, in the end, he'd settled on Mizpah pendants, golden coins with a promise of love. You split the coins along a crack stamped in at the factory and wore half each, as if the coins would always join you.

Marilyn opened hers and pulled the coin out, waving it in the air and looking overjoyed. 'I've always wanted one of these!' she said, hugging Harry hard and then showing Bobby how they needed to split it.

'I ain't wearing no necklace,' Bobby said.

'Don't be so daft' Marilyn told him. 'Course you are. It's romantic!'

'No way. I ain't a puff'

'For crying out loud, it isnay queer to wear jewellery. Mark o' a real man,' Harry said, patting the sovereigns and chains around his own neck. 'Where I come from, ye go out wearing enough gold tay bury ye, if needs be. And we're no puffs!'

'No way am I wearing it.' Bobby's face was set.

Marilyn looked livid. 'You always have to spoil everything,' she said.

'Just put it on your keyring or summat.' Angela's voice was soft conciliatory.

Bobby shrugged, and examined his half of the pendant more carefully.

Harry leaned in to his new wife and picked the coin from its case, holding it out in front of her. They broke it together, smiling at one another.

'Come here,' he said, gently turning her shoulders so she was facing away from him. He took hold of the necklace and Angela leaned her head forward so that he could fasten it. The gold chain slipped down as he clicked the fastener shut and the half coin rested on her chest, moving with her breath. He felt a rush of affection for her, then, and turned her back towards him for a kiss.

Harry pulled away from the kiss and stood up. He put his own pendant on. He was a married man now. He waited for it to kick in, the feeling of being married, but he didn't feel any different. Well, that didn't matter, he supposed, so long as the next time he saw Big Pat Walsh he walked away with the keys to the Loggerheads tucked neatly in his sweaty palm.

October 2017

PHASE 1: Extract, then refine the DNA, and accelerate with a polymerase chain reaction.

Forensic Science Research Lab, University of Nottingham

There was something unsettling about how still and quiet the university campus was at night, the darkness of the lake and the lack of people. It was only around eight but this part of campus was deserted and very dark. Sian parked and juggled with the keycard, trying to lock the little Citroen, not quite used to its 21st-century features. With only one working foot, she couldn't drive her own car but, with a note from her doctor, she'd been allowed to hire an automatic. She swivelled, using her crutches for balance and checking behind her, scanning the lakeside and the paths.

Sian used a second keycard to open the front door of the laboratory building and the corridors lit up ahead of her, more eerie than walking into darkness. The way the lights flashed on and off on timers made her feel like she was being followed and she kept checking behind her as she walked. She finally reached her office and dumped her backpack, switching on the computer. It whirred into life, the fan making a loud noise that was preferable to all the silence.

Sian took the amaretto bottle out from her bag and placed it on her desk. She smiled at how this would look, were anyone here to see it, but she'd come here this late for a reason. Besides anything else, she wasn't even back at work yet after her accident. She really shouldn't be here at all. The login box appeared on her computer, so she put in her credentials and watched the screen go blank. There was still time to change her mind and throw the sample away, burn it; lots of time as her computer loaded up her user profile But she didn't do any of that, instead walking over to her cupboard and pulling out sterile scrubs, and a mask and gloves, getting dressed in the protective lab clothing.

The light in the hallway flashed brighter for a moment. Sian tried to ignore it because moving around was such a hassle on the crutches but she couldn't focus on anything, worrying about being seen. She pushed herself to standing again, walking out to check if someone was coming this way. She stared down the corridor; a faulty light was flashing on and off several offices away, as if someone was stepping in and out of the way of its sensor. She leaned against her office door and breathed. The lake stretched away from the window in front of her like a huge, glassy black shadow.

The sudden sound of her mobile ringing cut loud and violent through the quiet of the hallway and Sian nearly fell off her crutches. She found her balance again and pulled the phone from her pocket. It was her mum. She didn't know how to deal with Ruth right now, so she didn't answer, shoving the phone back. She turned around and hobbled back to her desk, picking up the amaretto bottle. She was going to get to the bottom of what was going on, somehow, because she didn't trust the police to do that. She wasn't sure exactly how she'd do it herself but she knew that getting a DNA profile from the tissue before she lost her nerve was the first step. She packed things up in her backpack and picked up her crutches, heading to the lab with purpose.

The windowless lab was darker than the lake and Sian imagined the light flicking on to reveal someone standing there, waiting for her. She pushed open the door to an empty room and rolled her eyes at herself, but her skin still prickled and her heart beat faster. She checked up and down the corridors one more time, using the torch on her phone so she could see further. Science was hard-coded into her DNA as clearly as her eye colour but she still believed in intuition, except that her version had a sensible explanation. There were smells, sounds, particles, tiny changes in the quality of the light that you weren't consciously aware of but your subconscious understood on a deeper level. It was instinctual and about survival and, right now, all of her warning systems were going off. But she knew that being here late at night with a tissue sample she'd stolen was sending her into a hyper-vigilant mode.

Sian placed her crutches down carefully then settled on to a high stool, reaching for a pair of disposable gloves. She strained the amaretto from the bottle and retrieved the tissue with a sterile pair of tweezers, examining the tiny strands of flesh. She cleaned the sample with strong ethanol and placed some into a mortar, adding the extraction buffer and grinding the mixture together. She tried to forget what her sample was, and how she'd got it, pretend it was cheek cells or a drop of blood. She transferred the paste she'd made into a vial, and then to a water bath.

The routine was soothing. She added reagents and buffers with micropipettes and tipped vials to mix up her solution. She found a classical album in the lab's CD player so put it on. She preferred obscure 60s and 70s bands herself, the music her Uncle Rob had introduced her to, but it least it wasn't cheesy 80s pop. She popped the vial into a water bath and waited. She tried to surf the web on her phone but got too shaky, and walked to the laboratory door and stared up and down the corridor, her head sticking out from the frame like a meerkat. Then she came back and placed the vial into a centrifuge, spinning the liquid incredibly fast to make its components separate. She repeated the steps and added new chemicals to promote various reactions and extractions.

The process was slow, with many stages, and it couldn't be rushed. She would be here until the early hours of the morning and wasn't quite sure yet how she would explain this to Kris. She might have to get drunk, pretend she'd been out drinking. It was a shame she'd had to throw that amaretto away. Then again, there was ice-cold 100 per cent ethanol in the lab, one of the reagents she needed towards the end of the extraction process. The younger students on her MSc course a few years back had joked about how wasted they'd be able to get on that, but none had tried it – well, as far as she knew.

Finally, Sian had a milky white pellet of DNA in the bottom of a vial. She flicked the tube and held it up to the light to examine it. It looked so innocent, and yet it was the key to everything. They said character was fate but Sian disagreed; DNA was what drove the world. Those codes and sequences did more than decide what colour your eyes should be or make you prone to certain diseases. Your every decision, every supposedly random turn of your life, was there, in that chemical chain. She had no idea what she'd do next, when she had the codes that this small piece of human tissue held, what she would even compare it to without access to the police database, but she had faith that everything she needed to know was here, inside this pellet.

It was time now for the polymerase chain reaction that would accelerate whatever DNA had been left in the old flesh so that she had a chance of getting a profile. She removed a small amount of the pellet and put it into a PCR tube, adding the Master Mix solution and loading up the machine. This bit always reminded her of doing the clothes washing. You simply had to add all the right powders and liquids and then turn the dial to the cycle you wanted to run and the machine would do the rest, heating the liquid to one set temperature, then the next, to encourage the reactions you wanted one after another.

The machine clicked on. It would need to run for several hours. She poured the agarose gel she'd prepared into the tray to set. She leaned against the counter top and reached for her crutches, wondering if it would be safe to leave the gel out like this. She looked at her watch. It was almost ten and she couldn't imagine anyone else would be in the labs this late but wasn't sure she could take the risk.

Sian poked her head out of the doorway again and the lights came on in three sections down the corridor. Everything about being here was making her edgy and she didn't think she could stand it for another three or four hours. She could at least go and have a quick drink somewhere while the pubs were still open. She leaned on her crutches and locked the door, looking up and down the corridors and out at the lake for the least sign of life. Everything was still but, for some reason, that made her feel even more keenly that someone, somewhere was watching her.

PHASE 2: Wait. For ages.

The Hemlock Stone pub, Nottingham

The Hemlock Stone was a typical chain pub, with smart upholstery and menus on every table; the kind of place her uncle would have hated. As Sian walked in, she realised it was worse than she'd feared, with vaguely witty quotes stencilled on the cream finish above the bar, and some kind of Halloween-themed quiz going on. Still, there were people here, and the buzz and chatter around her as she headed through the door was comforting.

It was slightly tricky to negotiate her way to the bar past people who'd had a few drinks, or were not looking, and Sian had to stop more than once. When people noticed her on her crutches, though, they moved aside, and one guy even tried to clear a path through the others. She made it to the bar and asked for a gin and tonic.

'Which one?' the barman said, indicating a shelf full of different brands and specialities.

Sian stared up, bewildered at the choices. 'Gordon's,' she said, after a moment. And there it was, her uncle's voice in her head: *It's mine, not Gordon's.* She missed him badly, everything about him, his daft jokes and all of his silly sayings. She closed her eyes as the barman reached up for the bottle and she begged the air around her to make it so her uncle wouldn't turn out to be a murderer.

Sian turned with her drink and almost bumped into the man standing behind her. With a start, she realised it was the family liaison officer who'd spoken to her at the Loggerheads the day before: *call me Jonny.*

'Hello, you,' he said, his voice warm. His complete lack of surprise at seeing her there made her feel like he'd been expecting to meet her. Had he been following her? Had it been his eyes she'd felt all evening, just out of reach but watching? That was surely paranoia.

'What you doing here?' she said.

Jonny Breen laughed, and pointed at his pint with his free hand. 'Much the same as you I'd imagine.' He grinned, and raised his glass. 'Cheers!' he said.

Sian moved to walk past him but realised that there was no way to walk off on her crutches and carry her drink. She stood still, wondering at her predicament for a moment or two then tried to tuck the drink in underneath her armpit.

'Hey, c'mon, let me take that for you,' Breen said. He smiled again, his eyes lighting up, and he took the glass from her before she could protest about it.

Sian looked at him and didn't return the smile, thinking that there was something about him that made you think he knew that smile was charming. She refused to be taken in by it. She hobbled behind him on her crutches, cursing her injury and how it'd left her vulnerable.

He put her drink down on a table and sat down there too. 'Can I join you?' he said.

'Looks like you have,' she said. She threw herself down in the seat opposite him to show her annoyance but he didn't make to move.

When Sian had settled herself and looked up again, she saw him staring at her with a smile dancing all over his face. She felt like checking her clothes for spilled food or pen marks. 'What?' she said.

'You're after acting weird, like you think I've been following you or something.'

'Well, have you?'

'Of course not!' Jonny's voice went high with amusement and he was shaking his head. 'This is my local, by the way.'

'Okaaaay,' she said, but she wasn't appeased.

'I'm not your enemy, you know, Ms Love. In fact, I just so happen to have been tasked with looking after you. Though I get the impression you're a little hostile to being looked after.'

Sian didn't know what to say to this, disturbed by how accurately he'd sussed her. She stared at him, and reached for her drink. 'You don't know a thing about me,' she said.

'Don't I? Let's see.' He pulled on his thumb, as if using it to count. 'You were quite a senior police officer, DCI, promoted to that rank at the same time as Wilkinson but you left the force after a breakdown.' A finger. 'You've worked in forensics for about ten years, in commercial companies but the last while you've been a researcher at the university just the other side of the roundabout.' His index then ring finger. 'You're from Nottingham originally but studied at Cambridge University. Hang on, what's that they say? You "read" Chemistry there.' His pinkie. 'And you're forty-six this July, although how the fuck that's possible to look at you, I haven't a clue.'

Sian stared back at him, not sure whether to be impressed or appalled. 'Well, you've certainly done your homework.'

'Some people incite you to find out more.' That smile again, the one that made it look like his lips were itching.

'Are you flirting with me, Detective Inspector?'

'Maybe. Y'know, just liaising a bit.'

'Not very professional.'

Breen shrugged. 'I'm sorry, Ma'am,' he said. But his eyes were still dancing. 'You grew up round here,' he said.

'Is that on my file, too?'

'You'd be surprised. But no. I'm just having a little guess. You strike me as a bit of a woollo gell.' He was referring to Wollaton, the nice suburbs that surrounded the pub and, if it was a guess, it was an extremely lucky one.

Sian nodded. 'Kind of, I suppose. Just up the road in a housing association place.' She pushed the lemon into her drink with one finger. 'Used to be Balloon Woods before, but the new houses were OK. Hardly posh like most of the places round here, though.'

'Ah, yes,' he said. 'I remember the Balloon Woods. That place with all the damp maisonettes and lifts that smelled of wee, where they used to send anyone mad, bad or too poor to know they deserved better.'

'Yeah, that'll be it.' The tiniest of hissing sighs. 'But, like I say, that'd all been knocked down when we moved there.' She wondered why she felt so strongly about making this clear. All these years later, there was still that scent on her skin, that mark that said she had once been poor.

'So,' she said, 'where did you grow up? In Ireland? It would explain your weird accent.'

'Charming,' he said, 'but, yeah, actual Ireland 'til I was about ten, just in the countryside near Dublin. Then Bread and Lard Island, for my sins.' This was an old nickname for West Bridgford, the poshest part of town.

Sian was staying there with Kris but didn't say so. She didn't need to tell him anything. He shouldn't have approached her at all, in the pub like this. 'Did you live on bread and lard?'

'No,' he said. He reclined against the banquette, his arms spread wide and his grin a little wider. 'I'd like to pretend, but, to be fair, we had the good life. I can't complain about my childhood.' He paused, as if considering it. 'Well, not about the food, anyway.'

Sian didn't respond to what was an obvious hint for her to ask something deeper. She found that she liked this guy despite herself but she didn't trust him and had already let herself get far more drawn in than she was comfortable with.

'I'm surprised, being honest, that we didn't know each other back then. Nice Irish *cailín* like yourself, now.'

'Ooh, all posh with your Gaelic there,' Sian said. 'Hardly an Irish Colleen.' She deliberately used the anglicised version of the word in as flat a Nottingham accent as she could muster. 'My dad's Welsh.'

'Yeah, but we all know being Irish is held on your dominant genes. You only need one parent for the thing to take over your entire family.'

'OK, a DNA joke.' She shook her head and looked down at her drink but she was smiling. 'You're good,' she said, pointing a finger at him. 'Very, very good.'

He leaned forwards towards her, as if he were about to tell her a secret. 'Do you mind me saying?' he asked, without waiting for an answer, 'but you have the most beautiful eyes. All dark and exotic.'

Sian laughed and quickly brought her hand to her mouth to stop herself spitting out her drink. 'Dark and exotic?' She coughed, and tried not to laugh again. 'What am I now, a Bounty Bar?'

His mouth was doing that thing again, that tickle at the edge like he was about to grin. But you could overuse a nice smile and he was pushing cheesy. He was exactly the kind of man she'd have gone for in her twenties, all that sparkle and trouble in his eyes but even if there hadn't been Kris to consider, she'd learned to know better regarding men like that.

'How's the investigation going?' she asked.

He burst out laughing, a warm, musical sound. 'Subtle,' he said.

'Well, what's the point in messing about? And you are my family liaison officer. Sooo-o.' She swilled her drink then looked right up at him. 'Liaise.'

'I've not much to tell if I'm being honest there. They've worked out it's a man and a woman, and not a lot else.' His eyes danced. 'They're not so quick at our place, as I'm sure you know well.'

She nodded. 'Time of death?' she said, then smiled. 'OK, I'll accept a ten-year window.'

'I can do just a tad better than that. Early to mid-70s. The forensic archaeologist was a bit vaguer but we could date the shoes,' he said. 'Did you know your uncle well? Spend much time at that pub?'

Sian put down her empty glass, thinking it hadn't taken her long to polish that off. 'Am I being interviewed under caution?'

They smiled at each other and he tipped his pint up with a wink.

'Another?' he said, pointing at her empty glass.

'No,' she said. 'Thanks.' A shake of her head as if to shake off the idea. 'I need to get home.'

'Ah, come on, then. Surely you'll have one?' His eyes were positively gleaming now.

Sian stood up and reached for her crutches. 'Maybe in another life,' she said.

'You go carefully now,' he said. 'We don't want any more injuries, do we?'

Sian half-waved and continued towards the door. She hesitated, and managed to lean on her crutches and open it towards her, then head out into the car park. She walked as quickly as she could manage towards her hire car, thinking about his last comment. Was she imagining it, or was there the merest hint of a threat in those final words?

Dragging in her crutches and bashing them on the metalwork, Sian squeezed into the car and shut the door, flinging the sticks on to the passenger side. She breathed, examining the reflections of the streetlights in the glass of the windscreen then checking every mirror. She'd had too many experiences with too many bad men, and she had probably got it wrong. But she pressed the button that locked the car doors just in case and reversed out of the space too fast, just missing the wall at the edge of the car park before pulling off fast enough that the tyres slipped and squealed.

PHASE 3: Use an agarose gel and electrophoresis to separate the DNA fragments and display a 'profile' that can be compared to others.

Forensic Science Research Lab, University of Nottingham

Sian's phone buzzed into life on her desk and she jumped like she'd been caught doing something she shouldn't. The word KRIS flashed up from her screen. Guilt crept up her throat, stinging like bile. She grabbed the phone. It was just after two in the morning.

'Hey,' she said.

'Where are you Sian? I've been worried.' His voice had an edge to it. Not anger, but something close.

'I went out for a drink,' she said. She cast around, scrabbling for something to say that would be convincing. 'With Ginny,' she said. Ginny was her sister-in-law and a close friend from university, but it had been a very long time since they'd been out drinking together.

There was a long pause on the other end of the line, making Kris's breathing sound heavier than it was. 'Drinking? You know there's a big deposit on that car, right?' A sharp intake of breath and his voice hardened. 'I'm not even convinced you should be driving!'

Sian cleared her throat. 'I have a doctor's note, Kris. If the DVLA, car hire people and insurance company are all OK with that, you should be too. I came off the codeine, and I don't need to use my left foot in the auto.' She paused for breath, realising she was building into a bit of a temper with him at having to explain this again. 'Anyway, I only had one gin and tonic,' she said.

'It doesn't sound like you're in a pub,' he said. 'It's very quiet.'

'I'm not there now.' She scratched her nose and pulled a face at herself in her blank computer screen.

'Sian, are you at the university?'

She sat back in her chair, appalled at how easily he'd read her. She didn't answer for a moment, then realised there was no point pretending. 'Yes,' she said.

The line rustled with sighing. 'Just be careful, OK? I mean, really fucking careful.' Another sigh. 'You promised me you'd stop doing stupid things.'

'Yeah, well maybe we have different ideas about what's stupid. Like, for me, it's leaving anything to Dodgy Dominic and his lackeys.'

A moment's silence and the line was filled with that weird white noise. Then Kris spoke again, more gently. 'You going to be much longer?'

'No,' Sian said. 'An hour maybe?'

'OK.'

They said goodbye and the line went dead. Sian was suddenly very aware of being alone. Not even the cleaners would be in for another few hours. There was something powerful and yet deeply unsettling about the idea of having the building to herself. The PCR cycle was due to finish very soon and she could finally look at getting a profile for that DNA. She stood up, forgetting for a moment about the bad left foot and wincing. She reached for her crutches and headed back towards the lab.

A movement made Sian stop and glance up, just in time as her colleague Claire flew out of a door a metre in front of her. Sian was startled, her whole body moved by the shock, and she put too much weight on her foot again and let out a yelp. Claire stopped and turned towards her.

'Oh, hello, you. You all right? Sorry to frighten you!' Claire had the typical accent of Sian's colleagues, that posh private school tone that she'd almost decided to imitate herself when she first went to uni.

'It's OK. I just didn't expect to see anyone.' But Sian realised that the lights were on all the way down the corridor and that she should have realised she was no longer alone. So much for intuition.

Claire smiled. 'Me neither!' she said. Then, as if she'd suddenly remembered, her voice changed. 'Are you OK? I heard about what happened. Well, saw it. On the news.'

'I'm fine,' Sian said. 'Well, apart from this.' She indicated down at her plastered foot. 'Anyway, what you doing here at this odd hour? I don't usually see you around.' She was trying to make it seem as though working late in the lab was completely normal for her.

'Oh, you know.' Claire's voice was sing-song. 'When you have some gels running and you know you won't be able to sleep for fear of someone knocking them over or doing something stupid. It's really old DNA. I don't know how much more I could get.'

'Yes, of course,' Sian said. Claire's research was about very old bones, archaeological finds, rather than the more practical, crime-focused work that Sian did. She'd probably have useful advice for Sian on her current little project, if it'd been the kind of thing that it was feasible to talk about. They walked towards the lab together, Sian feeling awkward at slowing her colleague down. As they got closer, she remembered that the amaretto bottle was still sitting in plain view in her workspace. She tried to think of something she could say about it. There was no way she could get back to the lab before Claire and if she tried to rush and get there first, she'd only look more suspicious. She'd have to pretend she'd been drinking in the lab and make a joke of it. But Claire suddenly stopped walking.

'You know what, I forgot my iPad,' she said, slapping a hand against her forehead. 'See you in there.'

Sian headed into the lab and shoved the amaretto bottle in her rucksack. She assembled the gel tray for the final process. She turned off the PCR machine and retrieved her sample, washing and preparing it. Then she added the buffer solution and put the samples in the well. A couple for the test DNA, as well as a reagent blank and a positive and negative control for comparison, so that she could tell the procedure had worked the way it was supposed to. She might be breaking the law but she wasn't about to be sloppy about the science.

There was still no sign of Claire and Sian had a moment of wondering what the other woman was doing here. Perhaps she had something to hide, too. But the weird encounter with Jonny Breen had sent her spinning, and now she was being silly. She set the machine up and checked the electrodes and connections, ready to start the electrophoresis. Comparatively speaking, this part would be fast. She would stand over and watch it, just in case Claire or anyone else came to look too closely. All that was left to do once this was finished was to get the gel under the UV and take a snapshot.

There was a gentle buzz as Sian switched on the unit. She watched, checking that everything seemed in order. She knew that the fragments of DNA would be moving already, pulled towards the anode because of their negative charge. She looked into the box at the clear liquid and the gel underneath it. You wouldn't think anything was going on there to look at it. She took off her safety goggles and took a step back, suddenly feeling very hot. For the first time since starting the process, she wondered if she really wanted to find out the answers at all.

The door to the lab swung open. Claire walked in, humming to herself, as if she'd forgotten she was not alone. She smiled through the humming at Sian and walked over to her own workspace. Sian stared down at her gels. There was no way Claire could even guess what she was looking at but, still, having someone else witness what she was doing made her nervous. She hoped her colleague would not start asking any difficult questions.

Sian smiled over awkwardly at Claire a few times as the gels developed, and she took the photographs she needed with her iPad and emailed them to herself. It was weird to see the profiles at last; they were just lines in the gel and meant nothing without a reference point. As ever, Sian would start with her own elimination profile. After that, she had no idea. She printed the photograph and lined it up against the lab card with the photo from her own DNA, the way she had so many times. She felt her heart beat faster and the skin on her face begin to flush.

At first, all she could think was how had she been so stupid? She was never sloppy, hadn't contaminated a sample since she was a student. But no matter how she adjusted the pictures, there were too many matches. It had to be a contamination, it was the only explanation. Despite all her care with the gloves and the brand-new scissors, all the crawling around in the cellar had been too much and she had somehow touched the sample and left traces of her own DNA there.

'Shit!' Sian's voice was sharp and scared as she realised that this wasn't the *only* explanation. It was just that the other was a total headfuck.

'You OK?' Claire said, looking up from her gels through the thick plastic of her safety goggles.

'Yeah,' Sian said, her voice like a sigh. It wasn't the first lie she'd told that night by a long way but it was easily the biggest.

September 1970

All I Have To Do Is Dream

The Loggerheads pub

The Loggerheads was packed. It was a big night for Harry and his Midnight Roses, now he had the two sisters in the line-up. The band hadn't played in public yet with the new singers so there were still questions to be answered about whether they were good. They'd sounded good in rehearsals. No; more than that, they'd sounded great and he could see them now, on the hit parade, both girls tall in platform shoes, eyes panda-lined with kohl.

They were on in ten minutes and, although Marilyn was gliding around the room with a drink in her hand, glowing with the attention she was getting from the waiting crowd, there was no sign of Angela. Marilyn didn't exactly look much like Harry's kohled vision of a star but she did look stunning. She was wearing a figure-hugging black dress and those red heels, like a movie star. He had no idea why she dressed that old-fashioned way, and even less about why it drove him so crazy.

Marilyn walked over to Harry and planted a kiss on his cheek. He could feel the lipstick linger on his skin. 'It's gonna be a great night, Harry.'

He smiled, and asked her the question he always asked the girls. Angela would usually just shrug and blush but Marilyn had a different answer every time. 'What would ye do to be famous?' he said, with a playful shrug.

'Why, just about anything, sir,' she said, in a breathless American accent. She was imitating a movie star, but he wasn't sure who. Her eyes widened and her lips parted and he thought that, yes, she probably would. She leaned in closer as she took a drink and he could smell that scent, the Lily of the Valley. He had bought a bottle for Angela but it didn't smell the same on her.

His wife needed to come downstairs. Harry nodded to Bobby then walked over and slapped him on the back. 'Just gony fetch my wee wifey down,' he said.

Bobby rolled his eyes and said, 'Good luck, feller.' Then he pointed at Harry's face. The lipstick. Harry grabbed a bar towel and wiped his face clean. He now smelled of old hops, but it was better than trouble.

Pushing his way through the crowd and then opening the hatch to the bar, Harry walked through to the back room and towards the stairs. He glanced up as he swung around the banister at the bottom. And there she was; standing at the top of the stairs. She looked tiny and vulnerable and tanned next to the white dress she was wearing. He could see her chest moving rapidly as she breathed and the half coin that he'd given her on their wedding day, moving with her breath. This and her wedding ring were the only jewellery she wore and she was barefoot, like Sandie Shaw.

'You look cracking,' he told her. 'My wee smasher.'

She smiled and blushed, looking shy the way she always did. Part of her charm and just wait until the crowd saw that then heard her voice. They were going to love her.

'You ready?' he asked her.

Angela nodded her head vigorously and then they walked together, hand in hand. The band was tuning up. Bobby was messing on the drums and playing to the crowd, being silly. Paul Parker, the bloke who'd moved into Harry's council house once he'd taken up residency at the pub, was a half-decent bass player, and had joined their ranks.

Two mics stood waiting for the girls at the front and the sisters hugged before taking their places. One final bit of tuning and the band was ready.

The crowd were deadly quiet as they waited for the music to start. Angela stared at Harry with those big, deep blue eyes and he prayed that she wouldn't crack, lose it at the last minute with stage fright. That was the real question about the band, whether Angela's nerve was up to it. Marilyn was grinning into the crowd, a total natural on stage, and she winked at a bloke who shouted 'hey gorgeous'.

Harry nodded to the men and the first chords of 'Waterloo Sunset' by the Kinks floated into the room.

Angela swayed slightly at the microphone, her eyes closed. She looked like she was pretending to be somewhere else. She opened her eyes wide and started to sing, but her voice wasn't carrying. She looked afraid. She made eye contact and Harry gave her his biggest smile. She smiled back, her face brightening then she turned towards the audience looking like a different person.

His young wife straightened up and that voice she had was in the room. She sang as rich and deep as good coffee, the kind you get in those espresso bars. Harry smiled and leaned back into his guitar, making it gently weep. Better than the Beatles and they'd be bigger too. There was no longer any question in Harry's mind about that.

It was OK. He had chosen the right sister. Everything was the way it was meant to be.

Let's Work Together

The Loggerheads pub, the same night

Pat Walsh nodded at Bobby O'Quaid, who spotted him across the bar and was straight over to the Guinness pump to pour him his usual. Harry McKenzie had asked for a meeting again. Which meant he wanted something. That was fine as far as Pat was concerned because folks who wanted something were useful.

'Bobby Q,' Pat said, taking his pint. 'Thank you most kindly, sir.' He took a sip and tipped the pint at Bobby like a salute. 'You weren't at all bad back there,' he told the barman. 'Not bloody bad at all.'

'Ta,' Bobby said. 'Just make sure you tell Mac. He hasn't talked about owt but tonight for weeks.'

Pat nodded, and raised his glass again, heading over to Harry Mac the Lad, who was holding court at a table in the corner. Harry had one arm around that pretty wife of his and another around her even prettier sister, and Pat took one look and was glad he wasn't in Bobby's place. Well, there were places Bobby got in that he wouldn't mind getting into, he didn't mind admitting. Those curves. And that tiny waist. He reckoned he could get his big hands completely round it and, yes, he would definitely like to try.

Harry spotted him across the pub and stood up, swaying. He raised his pint towards Pat. 'Did you see us?' he said, almost singing the words. 'Did. You. See. Us?' turning each word into a sentence.

'Yeah, Harry, I did. You smashed it, mate. Totally smashed it.'

Harry nodded vigorously, grinning and holding his pint aloft 'We did, aye. Has Bobby seen you all right for a drink? Would ye like a wee dram with that, pal?'

Pat shook his head and nodded towards the back of the bar.

''Scuse me, my lovelies,' Harry told the women, kissing each one before staggering after Pat and towards the back room.

As the door closed behind them, the sound of loud music and drunk people was muted. Pat gestured with a hand to invite Harry to sit at the table. His Scottish friend was weaving and couldn't keep eye contact without dancing, first one way, then the next. He was ugly drunk.

'Y'know, we need a bit more recognishion,' Harry said, slurring his words. Pat had heard he was obsessed. That he shouted loudly about the band and how famous they were going to be whenever he got drunk, whether or not anyone wanted to hear it.

'You'll get there,' Pat told him. 'Give it time.' He tried to sound reassuring, like he was patting a dog.

'Oh, we're gony get there, no doubt about that.' Harry waved a hand dismissively across his face. 'Fuck getting there.' An expansive grin lit up his face. 'I'm no aftay getting there, Patrick. I want to be there! And word is that ye're the man who can.'

Pat frowned. He'd helped Harry get the pub and now he wanted more. That was typical but Harry was right. He was Pat Walsh and he could get anything.

'I can always help,' he told Harry. 'For a price.'

'Wha, money?' Harry's face had screwed up into a scowl. 'Depends how much.'

'Come on, Harry, my lad, you know that ain't my currency for favours.' Pat sat back and took a drink. The Guinness tasted good, and it was partly because it had cost him fuck all. 'My kind of people are kind to each other, if you catch my drift.' He tapped his nose, conspiratorially.

Harry was nodding.

Pat looked Harry up and down and considered this. 'The next round of that telly show, what's it called. *Opportunity Bollocks* or whatever. Coming here next month. Let's put it this way, the Midnight Roses are gonna walk that round.'

Harry grinned, showing three gold teeth. 'You betchya we're gony.'

Pat leaned forward and took hold of Harry's face, his right cheek, squeezing skin between his fingers like an uncle with a toddler. 'And you, me old mucker, you're going to help me out with a favour or two in return.'

'Oh aye?' Even in his drunken state, Harry was wary enough to be measured in response.

'Yeah. There's something that comes straight to mind, now I think about it.' Pat put down his pint and gave Harry a grimace of a smile. He grabbed the till roll and a pen off the table. Then he wrote down a name and handed the paper to Harry.

Pat watched as Harry read, suddenly doubtful the bloke could focus after the skinful he'd had. Harry's eyes were blank for a moment. Then they filled with understanding. Harry nodded and Pat knew he would be getting what he wanted. Harry and Pat, they spoke the same language.

Don't Cry Daddy

The Loggerheads pub, two weeks later

It was cold outside. Angela had always been a bit nesh and she was shivering all over. She was glad to get back inside to the warmth of the Loggerheads. She took off her coat and found her hand moving, by instinct, towards her stomach. She needed to watch that. It would be a bit obvious if she made that gesture in front of anyone else and she wasn't sure yet, that she wanted it to be obvious. That she wanted it. She'd only been married five minutes, well, married to Harry, anyway. And there were options these days, weren't there?

As soon as she'd had the thought, it seemed evil. She knew her mam would think so. She wasn't sure she could be a mother and the idea of having a child she was responsible for terrified her. It didn't fit with this life, with the band, with gigging at pubs and drinking with Harry. It didn't fit with Harry at all, now she thought about it, and that was the thing that had been giving her sleepless nights this last week. The Midnight Roses was Harry's baby, and Angela wasn't sure he had room inside him for another.

Angela could hear the sound of the band rehearsing as soon as she opened the door to the public bar. She stopped and took a breath then she walked through the pub and towards the back room. She smiled as she walked in, and Bobby lifted a drumstick to wave.

Harry was tuning his guitar and barely looked up at her. 'Ye're late,' he said, talking to his plectrum.

All the air went out of Angela and the vague half-thought she'd had of kissing him lightly on the lips and then telling him her news was gone. She would keep this to herself, for now. Until she was surer.

She didn't want to take any risks this time. She'd been pregnant before, and it hadn't worked out.

'What we starting with?' Paul asked Harry.

'We need to do our own songs for this yin,' Harry said. 'Let's start with "Angel Baby".' He looked up finally, and smiled. This was the song he'd written for Angela. For a moment, the softness and warmth coming from him soothed her, and he looked like a potential dad. Then that cleared, and there was just that cool, cold blue in his eyes and his determination as he struck the first chord.

Angela wandered over to her microphone and waited for her cue. This was one of the tracks where Harry mostly sang, and he sang this one to her. Her job was to sway, and smile, and look pretty, and then add a harmony in the chorus that even she realised made the song rise above its status. It was the one part of their set that made her wonder if Harry was right, if they might actually make it and be famous.

Harry leaned forward, bending over the guitar and staring at strings as if they were betraying him. She wondered how he'd feel about the baby growing inside her. He might see that as a betrayal – of the band, of their life together. She hadn't done it on purpose, though. She knew he would never beat her up then kick her in the stomach so that the baby died, the way Jack had, but she couldn't see him as a dad. Rocking around the clock with a pint in his hand, but not holding a baby, rocking it to sleep.

Angela started to sing. She was hesitant and quiet, and she saw the frown hit Harry's temples. She closed her eyes. She didn't like displeasing Harry, not at all. She realised that all of her doubt about having the baby was tied up with this. There was a part of her that would have liked to be a mum but it wasn't strong enough, not really. She wanted to keep Harry happy far more than she wanted the baby. This idea terrified her.

Angela let her eyes flicker open then sang, her voice and mind clearer now. She tried to forget about the baby and thought about the music instead, let herself get lost in the song where she'd been sent from Heaven for Harry. She would deal with the baby thing another time.

November 2017

FATAL

The Embankment, River Trent, Nottingham

The sky was beginning to lighten, turning an indigo blue above the black snake of the River Trent. Sian sat in the car and stared at the printouts in front of her; the photograph from the gel she'd processed with the DNA from the body and, next to it, her own elimination DNA profile. She lined them up again and there was very little doubt in her mind what she was looking at. The thing about DNA was that, unlike human witnesses, it told the truth. It was just which truth it was telling you that you had to work out sometimes.

Pulling her phone from her back pocket, Sian brought up the recent call list. The missed calls from 'Ruth MUM' sat there in red text below Kris's entry. She could just ring her, tell her exactly what she'd found and ask her to explain. But what would her mother tell her? The truth? Forty-six years of experience told Sian otherwise and she didn't want to hear another lie from her mother, didn't think they could wear that between them.

It had begun to rain, the water gently thudding against the car roof. Sian picked up her rucksack from the passenger footwell. She needed to pull herself together and finish the clean-up operation. She emptied the contents of her bag on to the seat beside her. She put her purse and pens and all the items that weren't part of the problem into the glove compartment of the car. Then she put the amaretto bottle and the lab equipment into the rucksack. She'd squeezed the gel into an old glass jar and put the lid on as tightly as she could. She had used the less toxic dye with disposal in mind, even though it was expensive and she'd have to explain why she'd needed it. Still, she'd rather have been caught than dispose of something as nasty as ethidium bromide in an improper way.

With her rucksack on her back, Sian took her crutches and got out of the car. She walked over to the river bank. Standing at the top of the concrete steps that led down to the river, she felt unstable again, so she put down the crutches and sat down. She heard a movement in the trees behind her and turned sharply. A bird shot out. She shook her head at her own jumpiness and slid herself down the steps. She stopped a metre or so from where the water came; she wasn't supposed to get her cast wet.

Steadying herself by leaning on a higher step, Sian got to her feet. She took her rucksack and threw it, overarm and as hard as she could, into the water. It landed with a dull shush about a third of the way across, and sank, the weight of the bottle and jar and other equipment she'd stolen doing its job. Sian wobbled slightly, and sat down harder than she wanted to.

There was a noise from the road behind her – footsteps. Sian turned and they got faster, pounding the concrete like the sound of running. Had someone been watching her? She got on her knees and tried to crawl up to the top of the steps as quickly as she could. On the grass bank, she grabbed her crutches and tried to rush, tripping over herself and almost falling. She heard the sound of a car engine then there was a flash of headlights. The car pulled off with the kind of screech a clutch makes when the driver is in too much of a rush to bother with silly things like biting point, the tyres skidding.

Sian stood and leaned against her hire car, her breath coming in short. She was being followed. She had experienced this before and knew what it was like. Was it him again? The ex whose name she tried not to even think about, in case she conjured him up like some demon in a mirror. Her heart beat faster just thinking about him and she tried to persuade herself that he really had been scared off, somehow, by Kris and the others. She couldn't spend the rest of her life worrying he'd turn up again in the shadows the moment she let her guard down.

Loading her crutches in first, Sian got back in the car. She pressed the red button that locked its doors and tried to get her breathing back to normal but then she glanced over and saw the DNA printouts again. She'd eliminated all of the other possibilities and, by the Sherlock Holmes conjecture, the one that remained, mad though it was, had to be the truth.

The DNA that Sian had tested brought up a mixed profile. The remains she'd found were a man and woman who had died together and laid there for years in the cave behind her Uncle Rob's cellar, one rotting into the other, until everything they'd ever been was merged. But the partial match against her own DNA was more than a coincidence and it was not contamination; she knew it wasn't, in her gut. She wanted to persuade herself that there was a chance that this was something as simple as a mistake, but Sian wasn't that great at self-deception. One of the bodies she'd found was a close relative, most likely a parent, and when she added that to the other things she knew about her life, it was obvious what she'd found.

Sian had done enough paternity work in the commercial lab and she knew what this looked like, knew the sums. The probability that she was wrong about this was so small as to be negligible. She had finally held her biological father's hand. Unfortunately, he was dead and mostly skeletal, having been hidden for years in a cave behind her uncle's cellar. Sian had known for a long time that her family were capable of hiding things from her, but this? Her actual genetic father's remains? It was more than she could process.

Her hands were shaking so badly that she found it hard to insert the card that started the car. She was struck again with a conviction that her life was going wrong, that it was spinning towards tragedy and there was nothing she could do about it. Her belief in this only got stronger the more she tried to resist the idea. She had the sense that everything she did, no matter how well intended, every single action only sealed her fate further, faster, towards the crash that was written into her DNA.

FLAW

Central Police Station, Nottingham, the next day

Sian folded her arms across her chest as she sat in a plastic bucket seat in the police station reception. Meadows had rung early that morning saying that she needed them to come in and Sian was worried about what they wanted to discuss. Kris reached for her hand and she let him take it; she was bored of all the waiting. Why had the young sergeant asked them to come in at ten if she wasn't able to see them before half past? Sian pulled her hand away from Kris so that she could look at her watch again. Was this some kind of game?

The sound of the main door opening made Sian glance up. Her mother walked in, and her brother, Tom. It felt like the floor was moving and the room was spinning. Sian nudged Kris and he looked up, his eyes widening as he saw the rest of her family.

'Did you know they were coming?' he whispered.

'No,' Sian said. She watched as her mother glanced in their direction and said something to her brother, who looked over and waved nervously. The pair headed to the counter to announce their arrival. 'If we've been waiting for those two, I'm going to kill someone,' Sian whispered.

Her mother and brother finished chatting with the charge officer and were directed to sit in the waiting area with Sian and Kris. They walked towards the row of seats. Tom strode ahead of his mother and, when he got close, he held his arms out to Sian for a hug. She got up and let him take hold of her and he squeezed, tighter than she would have liked, but she was glad to see him. She pulled away. 'How's Ginny?' she said.

Tom shrugged. 'Fine,' he said. 'Says I need to get you guys over for dinner soon, that we're not seeing enough of you these days.'

'OK,' Sian said. She wasn't convinced that her old uni friend was that keen, though. Her sister-in-law had not been happy at all back when Rob died last year and his will left absolutely everything to Sian. 'Sounds good,' she said, keen to move the conversation on before Kris realised she'd been outright lying about meeting Ginny, that night at the university.

'Hello again, Sian,' her mum said.

Sian nodded a hello and sat down before her mum could attempt to hug her.

'Meadows call you in too, then?' Kris asked.

'Yeah,' Tom said, taking the seat next to him. 'Do you think they've found something else?' He paused then cleared his throat. 'Something incriminating?'

Sian's mum pulled a face as she sat down. 'Don't be so dramatic!' she said. 'It was probably just an accident or something. I doubt that anyone even knew they were there.'

Sian's eyes were narrow and she tried to keep the emotion out of her voice. 'Dead bodies stink,' she said. 'It would have been impossible for good ole Bobby Q not to know they were there. Did he never go down into the cellar? In a pub?' She wasn't about to let her bloody mother get away with anything, not anymore.

Her mum was sitting with her hands folded neatly on her lap, her face tight. 'Your Uncle Robert was a good person,' she said.

'That's not what you said when they read the will,' Sian said. She watched her brother's face, saw him struggle not to laugh. He'd not cared less himself about his uncle leaving everything to Sian, assuming, like she did, that Rob knew she needed his help more than lovely Tom ever would. Her mother, though, had gone mental and Sian was not expecting her to see the funny side now, either.

Ruth half-smiled. 'You're funny,' she said. 'But you always had your dad's evil sense of humour.'

'Whoever the fuck that was,' Sian said, hammering home at Ruth's point for her. Kris elbowed her lightly in the ribs but she saw him bite his bottom lip to stop himself smiling.

A door opened behind them and the young FLO, Lizzie Meadows, walked into the waiting area with a warm smile. She approached the group. 'Hi Sian,' she said. 'And this must be your mother, and Thomas?'

'Tom,' he said, standing up, then holding out a hand and smiling. Meadows shook his hand. Kris got up too, helping Sian to her feet, and the four of them followed the family liaison officer through several doors, which she unlocked, and then relocked behind her. This aspect of police buildings had always bothered Sian, making her feel trapped and claustrophobic. They came to a meeting room and Meadows opened the door and directed them inside. Sian had to make an effort not to tense up her whole body as Meadows closed the door and disappeared in the other direction, locking them in.

DCI Swann and DI Jonny Blue Eyes were both sitting at the table, waiting for them with a pile of folders and printouts. Breen smiled up at her and she remembered his smile from the night before, dancing all over his face like he knew all of her secrets. What was he doing here, anyway? Why was he sitting next to Swann like that if he was the family liaison officer? So much about him added up to trouble.

'You OK?' Kris asked her, an arm on her shoulder.

'I'm fine,' she said, trying to smile. They sat down together and Sian leaned her crutches against the edge of the table. Tom and Ruth sat down too. There was a jug of water and some glasses in the middle of the table but nobody moved to touch them.

'All right,' Breen said. 'Well, we've asked you for this meeting to give you the information we have so far and, also, we're after asking for a little help from you, too.'

Sian folded both arms across her chest and felt herself close up. She remembered her uncle's motto about not talking to the police, the jokes he'd made when she'd joined the force about her consorting with the enemy. She was beginning to understand why he'd felt that way.

Swann looked professional, a hand territorially hovering above a folder right in front of her. She opened it and took out some papers, then tapped them with a slightly mannered carefulness. 'We believe that the remains we've found in the cellar could belong to a pub landlord and his wife who disappeared in the early 70s.' Her voice was crisp and businesslike. 'They were members of a rock band who were fairly well known locally.'

'As I mentioned to your good woman yesterday, the forensic archaeologist has only helped us to a certain extent,' Breen said, gesturing towards Sian but with his eyes on Kris. She felt a flush rise at the back of her neck. He grinned at her; she was sure he was deliberately trying to make her feel uncomfortable. 'She was somewhat vague about when these people were likely to have died, but we've dated them from belongings we found with them, including clothes and jewellery.'

'Jewellery?' Ruth's voice was soft and scared. Sian shot around to look at her. Did she know about the pendant? Was she expecting it to be there?

'Wedding rings,' Breen said, looking at Sian's mother for the first time. 'Matching rings in a heavy white gold that was quite unusual for the time, and would have been expensive.' He looked back down at the folder. 'There were several metal chains and pendants on one of the bodies, including a Mizpah pendant.' He pushed a photograph across the table. Sian had not noticed this pendant amongst the tangle of metal on the second body; she tried to work out what it meant that there were three of these love tokens. She tried to transpose the photo and bring to mind her uncle's coin and the one she'd taken from the other body, trying to work out which ones fitted which. 'We think the other person must have had a similar piece of jewellery, as they come in pairs,' he said, 'so this was perhaps taken away, at some stage.' He glanced down at the picture then looked right into Sian's eyes.

Sian went cold all over but she was determined not to let it show. She held Jonny's eyes. 'OK,' she said. 'Or maybe not. It could have been lost, or thrown out the window in a row. It could be that whoever he shared the other half with wasn't the person you found next to him in the cellar.'

'Interesting that you should say "he",' Jonny said. 'Why would you assume that?'

Sian shrugged. 'I saw all that jewellery when I found them. It looked like men's jewellery, sovereigns and the like.'

'Okaaaay.' Swann stretched the word until it almost snapped. Then she looked up from her notes and held her head slightly to the side. 'Do you think your uncle knew they were there?' She directed the question at Sian but Ruth sat back in her seat as if to move away from the very idea.

'No,' Sian said. She felt Kris's leg nudge her under the table.

'Did your uncle ever say anything that makes you think he might have known? Any other family members make suggestions about funny goings-on at the pub?' It was Jonny now, asking the questions in his sweetest voice. You wouldn't think he was trying to get them to pin this on a dead man. Not that this idea surprised Sian. Blame the dead guy; doesn't matter if it's not true, no one gets hurt and you're one case up on your solve rate. Standard Dominic Wilkinson policing policy.

'No,' Sian said. 'I can think of nothing like that.' But she turned from the police officers and glanced under her lashes at her mother, a very meaningful look.

'Mrs Driscoll,' Swann said. 'Do you remember anything your brother said about the pub? About the people who used to run it?' She paused as if it had suddenly struck her. 'Did you know the Loggerheads and the Cliff Road area in the early seventies? Did you ever go and watch the band?'

'Yes, I watched the band,' Ruth said. 'Once or twice.'

Sian turned sharply and glared at her mother; this was more than she'd ever told Sian about the band.

'I knew them all slightly, although I'd moved away with my husband by then and was living in the flats at Lenton. But I met the landlord, that Scots bloke. And his wife. My brother was pals with them. But I don't remember Rob saying anything that struck me as odd about the pub.' She was shaking her head.

Sian wanted to embarrass her mother and quote all the things she'd ever said about the Loggerheads but she tried to keep all of that from her face and stared benignly across the long table. There were lots of ways of talking to the police, and she didn't want to engage with any of them right now.

'And Marilyn? Your brother's wife. Did you know her well?'

There was a special kind of silence in the room, then. The two officers waited with their eyes wide, and Sian and Tom turned to look at their mother too.

'Mrs Driscoll?' Breen's voice seemed to sing the syllables of Sian's mother's name.

Ruth shook herself, as if waking from a dream. 'Sorry,' she said. 'No, I never really got to know her.' She tried a smile but it didn't reach her eyes. 'I didn't like her. She was...' She struggled for the right word. 'She was flighty. Thought a lot of herself.'

Sian watched her mother as she failed to make eye contact with either of the officers and scratched at her neck. She couldn't be sure that she was lying but talking about Marilyn O'Quaid was making her uncomfortable.

The officers took heavy breaths, and then Swann glanced at Breen, who seemed to nod.

Swann cleared her throat. 'You see, we can't seem to find anyone who knew them very well. Rob's wife Marilyn, or Harry and Angela. The whole street seems to have had a memory bypass.' She stared at Ruth. 'Which is strange since they ran the pub and were in a popular band. I'd have thought they'd have been the subject of quite some fascination on a small road like that one.'

Ruth was rolling her eyes. 'Harry and Ange were all over the place. They often disappeared for weeks on end so it wasn't much of a surprise when they eventually didn't come back.' She made eye contact with Breen and gave him her most winning smile. Even at nearly seventy, she had a way about her that men responded to and Sian bristled at the sight of her using this. 'They weren't my kind of people at all. Like I say, they were always off places, and arguing, and splitting up, and getting back together. It was pretty chaotic at the pub when they ran it.'

'And your brother and his wife?'

Again, Sian noticed her mother bristle.

Ruth swallowed. 'Like I say, I didn't like her, but they got on fine as far as I'm aware. It was all a massive shock to Bobby when she ran off'

'Oh, so he's Bobby now,' Sian muttered.

'We still have a few possible means of identification to follow up,' Breen told them. 'DNA and the like. There are a number of living siblings from the Callaghan brood, so there's work we can do there.' He glanced across the group then his eyes landed on Sian. 'And there are a few anomalies picked up in the post mortem that we need to investigate further.'

Sian shivered. They had discovered the sample she took and they would soon discover, too, that one of these people was related to her; as an ex-officer, her DNA was on record for elimination and would come up as a partial match. She glanced at Kris, who was doing a good job of keeping his face straight, true to his word. She got the distinct impression that Breen knew exactly what she'd done. She wondered if he had been following her last night and remembered the sense of threat she'd felt as they said goodbye at the Hemlock Stone.

'Anyway,' Breen said, 'we've a little something for you.' He reached into an evidence bag on the desk and pulled out a set of keys. 'We've done with your place,' he said, 'and these things. They're not relevant so you can have them back. Mostly old photos and clippings from back in the day, when your uncle was almost famous.' He hand-ed her the keys and two sealed bags.

Sian put the bags on the floor.

'Look,' Swann said, 'I need to be completely honest with you. We have a lot of evidence already and some fairly clear leads. It's all look-ing pretty obvious and we expect to close the case very quickly. And I have to warn you, the result is probably the one you're not going to want.'

Sian frowned. 'So much for professionalism and keeping an open mind. You're going to pin it on my uncle.'

Breen laughed, as if the idea were ridiculous. 'Course we're not going to *pin* it on him. That's not how we work here!'

Sian was rolling her eyes. 'Why are you even in this room, Detective Inspector? And on the FLO team too, way below your pay grade. What's that all about?'

'Sian–' Kris's voice cut across hers like a warning.

'No, it's OK. Happy to address your concerns,' Breen said. 'It's been a while for you, Sian, since you were a police officer, and things change. You can blame austerity. There've been a lot of cuts.'

Sian snorted. It wasn't like he was going to admit it but she knew. She'd known it as soon as she was introduced to him and heard his rank; he was dodgy like the rest of them, as bent as his boss Wilkinson. 'Whatever,' she said, rolling her eyes. 'But if you think I'm about to sit back and let you pin this on my uncle, you are very, very wrong.'

'No one's trying to pin this on anyone,' Swann said. Her voice sounded oh so reasonable. 'But we do intend to close the case fairly swiftly. There's nothing to see here, quite honestly, and things are usually exactly what they look like. There's no way your uncle could have missed two decaying bodies sealed into a cave behind his cellar, as a publican, is there? We can't spare your feelings about that.'

Sian folded her arms across her chest and shook her head, her mouth tightening. Even though she'd told her mother the same thing, she knew this wasn't Rob. She knew her uncle. He was what they'd call a 'bogger' round here, cheeky and mischievous, and prepared to cross a few lines, but he wasn't a murderer. They had no real evidence but they intended to pin it on him, anyway, because that was easier than finding out what had really happened. Well, she wouldn't let them do that to her uncle and she would find out the truth herself, before they had the chance to close the case and slur him.

FAULT

Kris's house, West Bridgford, that evening

The sound of the TV had become a drone. Sian had been sitting with her leg elevated, flicking through Netflix for the last few hours. She'd tried walking without her crutches earlier. It had taken her a while to take her first step, focusing, trying to remember how walking worked. It had felt strange and her balance was off but she'd managed to take the four steps from the sofa to the armchair, then back again. Now, though, her foot and leg were very sore.

Elvis sat up in his basket, his ears straightening like antennae. Then he barked, and ran into the hallway. The next thing Kris was on his way in, back from work. He was fussing the dog, who was dancing around him, and Sian smiled. You can trust someone your dog likes.

'Hey up, duckie,' he said, making Sian smile. His London accent was even more obvious when he spoke 'Nottinum'. He threw his coat and car keys on to the sofa. 'You reet? Need owt?' Still doing the accent.

'You could fill up my water bottles,' Sian said. He had set her up with lots of drinks and snacks before he'd left to get back to his shift The awkward thing about being on crutches was carrying anything around the house. Sian could cook or make herself a drink, but she couldn't carry anything to her chair, not even a glass of water, as she had no free hands when she was walking.

Kris dashed into the kitchen then was back with more water for Sian. 'I'll take Elvis out now, and then how's about a bottle of wine and a takeaway?'

'OK,' Sian said. She didn't do junk food very often but a bit of comfort was what was needed at a time like this. And wine would be nice too. Things had felt very tense with Kris after the police meeting that morning and then he'd had to go straight off back to work.

'OK, then.' Kris reached on to the shelf behind him and grabbed a pile of menus, handing them to Sian. 'Peruse these and decide what you want.' He reached for the dog's lead and Elvis shot up from his basket, his tail going crazy as he paced around Kris's legs. Kris clipped on the lead and then the two of them were gone, faster than Sian was expecting.

The house was very quiet. A feeling of melancholy settled in the centre of Sian's stomach. She badly wanted to walk her own dog. Patience didn't come naturally to her, but she was having to learn it, her body no longer under her control. She was fed up with the sound of the TV and flicked it off, reaching for the laptop instead. She opened it up and logged in, then googled the family tree website she'd read about earlier that day.

Genealogy websites were getting more interesting. You could send off your own DNA and find matches you didn't know about. This was bringing people together, adopted children and their birth mothers, for example, but it was also driving families apart. Sian had already decided that she would send for a test herself, look for clues that would unlock her own puzzle a little further. For now, though, she found the website and signed up, setting up a free trial that would give her access to the older census records, as well as births, deaths and marriages.

Sian searched the database for Harry McKenzie. Of course, that was not his actual name. Was he Harold or Henry? She tried both and came across lots of matches. That was no good. She tried Angela and this was a little more helpful; it wasn't a very popular name for that generation although there were still too many to narrow it down. She did a more specific search on Angela's maiden name and weddings and the results were less than a page long. She couldn't find a wedding with a Harold or Henry McKenzie that had taken place in Nottingham. Maybe they'd never been married? It was probably commonplace, back then, to pretend to be married so that you could live together without being vilified.

There was a loud bang in the hallway. Sian jumped to her feet with her hands raised, ready to fight. Her bad foot collapsed underneath her and she grabbed for the mantelpiece, scratching her arm on the edge of the wood in the process. The front door had been slammed open and a breeze chilled the room.

Sian took a deep breath, trying to regain her composure. Perhaps Elvis had been a pain, pulling after a cat as Kris tried to bring him indoors. He was a good boy and didn't do that kind of thing to Sian but, then, Kris wasn't his 'real' dad. Except no answer came from the doorway. A spike of dread shot up Sian's throat. There was no panting sound, no feeling of her dog being back in the house. She was suddenly sure that this wasn't Kris and Elvis and all the possibilities of who it might be were dancing in her head. That name came to her, the one she tried not to think about. The ex.

Time slipped again, the way it did for Sian when adrenaline kicked her. She was somewhere dark and musty smelling, held so tight she could barely breathe. She didn't know where she was or who was holding her. The air was ripped open with the sound of an explosion, such a shock that it stopped her breathing. Then the sound of a baby wailing. She sucked in air and told herself it wasn't real.

Sian closed her eyes and took deep breaths, trying to ground herself in reality. She'd had this flashback before but didn't remember the event in real life. She opened her eyes again.

Detective Superintendent Dominic Wilkinson was standing in the doorway of the living room, like he'd been conjured up. Sian caught her breath, letting out a sharp sound.

'Hello, Ms Love,' he said.

DEAD FLOWERS

Dominic knew how to use her name, how to make it sound like something to fear. Sian sat down, almost falling back on to the sofa. She felt sick, and her head was fuzzy.

October 1970

Sugar Sugar

The Loggerheads pub

The world was nicely blurred and fuzzy, the way Harry liked it. Angela looked exhausted and was nursing her half of stout like she didn't want to have a thing to do with it. She'd been tired a lot recently and he could see that the performing and attention were wearing her thin. But this was important; it was their big chance. He walked across the bar to where she was sitting and put an arm around her.

'Y'OK, hen?' he asked her, with a light brush of his lips against her forehead.

She sighed and leaned in against him. 'Yeah.'

'Go bed, if ye like.' He rubbed her cheek as he spoke.

Angela smiled up at him. 'OK,' she said. She kissed him, and then disappeared through the bar hatch, the door into the back room slipping closed behind her.

Harry surveyed the room. Bobby was frantic at the bar; two of the barmaids had had to go home for various reasons, and it was just Bobby and Paul working tonight. Marilyn was holding court with a group of men in the far corner and Harry didn't like the look of it. He wished Bobby would keep her under control but, if his pal couldn't, then it would have to be his job.

Harry sauntered over. 'Hey, lassie,' he said, to Marilyn. 'Come and have a wee chat with yer brother-in-law.' He stressed the last words as if to make the point that she was married.

Marilyn frowned then turned from the men. She headed towards Harry, the hands of one young fella in the air around where she'd been as if he was about to grab hold of her, stop her from walking away. Harry couldn't blame him. His sister-in-law was more than easy on the eye; in that tight dress, he'd defy any man not to want to do more than just look.

'Looked like ye were in need o' rescuing,' he said.

Marilyn smiled, her mouth tense at the edges. 'Thanks, my lovely. You know what those boggers can be like!' She flipped a hand as if dismissing such things and followed Harry to the other side of the bar.

'We'll have a wee nightcap,' he said, grabbing a bottle and two glasses. He gave Bobby a slap on the back as they walked through to the back of the bar. His pal half-turned, saluted Harry. And then they were heading through the hallway at the back of the pub, towards the kitchen.

Marilyn sat down at the table, running a hand through her hair. She gave Harry a nervous smile, and watched him pouring drinks. When he put down the bottle, she picked up her glass and started to sip, leaning back in her chair.

'What about Saturday!' Marilyn said. She threw her head back and closed her eyes, looking like she was lying back in a hot bath. 'I love it, Harry,' she said, 'the crowds, the shouting. When they sing along!'

Harry smiled. 'The music?'

She giggled, loudly. 'Course, the music, Harry!'

He refilled their glasses. The sound of the clink was a gentle percussion.

'I could sing some of the songs, Harry, you know.' She took a sip of the whisky and offered him a cigarette. He took it from her, and she lit it for him with a wink. 'Sing the lead for one or two.'

'Ye could, aye,' he said, taking a drag. And she could, but she wouldn't carry it nearly as well as Angie. You didn't have to tell people everything, though. One of the things Harry had learned as a wean.

They smoked and drank. She filled up the glasses again with a smile. 'What's your favourite?' she asked. 'From the set.'

Harry shook his head. 'I couldnay pick one,' he said. 'But "Waterloo Sunset" reminds me o' the first time I heard yer sister sing.' He took a big gulp of whisky. 'So that's special, ye get me?' he said.

Marilyn flicked ash from her cigarette. She tried to smile but it didn't reach her eyes.

'Are ye jealous of Angie?' he said.

'No!' she said, a tad too vehemently. 'I love my sister.' Her voice sounded like acting and she gulped at her drink.

'O'course, hen.' Harry tried to sound neutral.

Marilyn finished off her drink and slammed down the glass. 'Bedtime,' she said, grimacing, then pulling off a smile. She stood up.

Harry stood up too. He grabbed her by the wrist. 'Ye need to behave yoursel, hen.' He could hear the growl in his own voice and saw her shock.

She opened her mouth to speak; Harry was half sure what she would say and didn't want to hear it. He squeezed her wrist harder. She twisted and pulled, trying to shake off his grip, so he squeezed harder and bent her arm back. Her musky, lily-toned scent seemed to fill the room until Harry thought he might choke on it.

'You're hurting me, Harry.'

Harry didn't let go. He could feel how tight his mouth had gone and suddenly wondered why her behaviour bothered him so much.

'Harry!' Her eyes flashed at him, defiant, but he could see that she was trying hard not to cry.

Harry pulled her closer and her back arched. She looked up at him like a starlet in an American film. In that tight-fitting dress and with those high heels, in the half-light of the kitchen, that was exactly what she looked like. Harry stared at her and, for a moment, it felt like anything could happen. He let go of her arm. His breathing had turned heavy.

'Get yersel tay bed.' Harry closed his eyes. But when he opened them again, she was still there, staring up at him through her eyelashes like she was waiting for something.

Travellin' Band

The Loggerheads pub, the following week

Angela held her breath all the way from the car into the pub, feeling thrilled and terrified and excited, her heart beating fast and her face flushed. There was a cheer as they barged through the doors of the Loggerheads and Harry and Bobby walked in, their hands in the air, being patted on the back and congratulated by everyone they passed. It hadn't taken long for the news to travel the couple of miles from the Commodore Club where the competition had taken place. They had won the Nottingham round of *Opportunity Knocks* and were going to be on the telly! She didn't think she'd ever seen Harry so happy, not even on their wedding day. Not even on their wedding night.

They jostled into the Saturday night madness of the pub and Angela's hand went instinctively to her belly, again. Someone would notice, and soon, if she kept doing that, but she couldn't help it. She knew she should tell Harry but that was the only thing that scared her more than the thought she was about to be on the telly, watched by thousands of people.

Bobby elbowed his way to the bar and shouted back to the rest of the band, asking what they wanted to drink. Angela asked for a mild and black. She'd heard that the dark beer was good for your baby; lots of iron, although she found it bitter and hard to drink. The cordial helped. Bobby's sister Ruth and her husband, Davey, came over to say hello. Ruth's long red hair shone under the pub lights. It was weird how Ruth looked just like Bobby except with those piercing blue eyes. She was so beautiful that Angela couldn't help staring. The couple made their excuses to leave, Harry nodding and winking at Davey, making some comment to him about enjoying married life.

DEAD FLOWERS

Harry cleared a table 'for the lassies' and Angela sat down opposite Marilyn. Her sister was glowing, always so much happier and more comfortable with the attention than Angela was. Harry came back with a tray of shots. Angela wasn't sure about getting drunk, but he pushed one into her hand, insistent. She looked at the amber liquid and decided, why not? It wouldn't harm her to have a little fun, loosen up, as Harry often suggested.

'To the Midnight Roses, who are gony be bigger than the Beatles!' Harry said, raising his glass.

They all knew the right response to this by now. 'Bigger than the Beatles!' they chanted together, clinking their glasses with Harry's. Harry didn't even like the Beatles, but he liked how famous they were, fancied some of that for himself and wasn't afraid to say so.

Bobby got up and shouted to someone he'd spotted on the other side of the bar. Harry followed and the two men were talking and laughing loudly in the crowd. Angela and Marilyn were alone at the table.

'Do you think it'll really happen? That we'll be famous?' Marilyn asked. Her eyes were wide and chocolate brown, her bleached blonde hair was arranged in that pinned short style that the women in Hollywood had favoured about twenty years ago. Angela took in all of this and realised for the first time: being famous was something that really mattered to her sister.

'Harry says so,' Angela said. As she looked at her drink, her stomach roiled. She took the smallest of sips and it settled slightly. 'I think it'll be all right in the end.'

'And if it's not all right, it's not the end,' Marilyn finished, waving her hands in a flourish with the words. This was one of Harry's favourite sayings.

They shared a smile, and Marilyn proposed a toast, off-guard for a moment as she lifted the glass. Angela saw something broken in her eyes. There was a lot of make-up to cover it up, but she saw through that as clear as the gin and tonic in her sister's glass. Something wasn't right. The way Marilyn was reminded Angela of the time she'd had some problems at school, when she was little, and the doctor had given her tablets for her nerves. Something had happened to Marilyn whilst Angela's attention had been elsewhere.

Marilyn raised her glass higher then, and smiled that Hollywood smile and it looked real, but that was what Hollywood was about, wasn't it? Making acting look real. Angela had a moment of wondering if her sister was pregnant too; they'd done so much together, meeting Harry and Bobby, then getting married, that it would make a weird kind of sense.

'Are you all right?' Angela asked her.

'Of course.' Her smile broke for just a moment then she was beaming again. 'Of course, I'm all right. It's not the end.'

Angela sipped her drink and glanced towards the men, who were being patted on the back and had too many drinks to carry. Marilyn had got the saying the wrong way around and hadn't realised. Angela had noticed, though. She stared at her sister but Marilyn was intent now on her glass, on disposing of the drink inside it like she was starving for it. Angela thought she had never seen anyone need a drink so much.

November 2017

DISHONESTY

Kris's house

Sian stared up at Dominic. She wondered what she could say that would persuade him to leave. But he walked closer and held out both hands.

'I'm not going to hurt you, Sian,' he said. But she'd heard this line before and she didn't believe him. Dominic had been there; he had helped on several occasions when her ex had wanted to 'persuade' Sian to do as he said.

She edged away from him on the sofa. 'What do you want, Dominic?'

'I just want to talk to you.' His eyes glinted as he spoke. 'I need you to listen to me.'

'Kris will be back soon,' she said.

He smiled a broad and knowing smile, and Sian had a flash vision of Elvis and Kris dead in a ditch somewhere. She tried to shake away that image, told herself she was being paranoid. Dominic was a bent copper but he was still a trained detective. If he'd been doing any killing he would be dressed differently, with gloves and shoe covers, everything possible to avoid leaving any evidence.

'I've come to talk to you about the post mortems. Certain, shall we say, anomalies.' He sat down on the armchair opposite her. 'Do you have any idea what might have happened to the bodies before my team arrived?'

'No, not a clue,' Sian said.

'I think you might,' he said. 'I don't know what you're playing at, Ms Love, but I intend to find out.'

'Is this an interview under caution?' she said. 'If so, I'd like my solicitor present.'

'OK, so you want me to arrest you?' he said.

Sian shrugged. 'You shouldn't be turning up at my door like this, on your own and unannounced. Just walking in off the street.'

'Well, to be fair, your door was open and swinging in the wind. Hope your dog's all right.' Sian flinched; Dominic had a way of making everything sound like a threat.

'Are you going to arrest me?' she said.

Dominic smiled. 'Now, why would I want to do that? You haven't done anything wrong, have you?' He leaned over Sian, coming close enough that she could smell the soap on his skin.

'No,' Sian said, 'I haven't.' She tried to keep the fear out of her voice. She stared at the clock on the mantelpiece and away from his grey-blue eyes.

'Look, Sian, we know each other better than this. I've come here to do you a favour, OK? So that we can both do each other a favour, really. There are bigger men than me who are bothered about this case and you need to be a good girl and stop digging so that we can clean this one up quickly.' He cleared his throat. 'Otherwise I might have to look a little closer at why there were such bizarre anomalies at my crime scene and then I might well have to make some arrests. Understand?' His face clouded over and he swallowed, as if it hurt him to say the next bit. 'People we both know are involved and have asked me to say something. Mutual friends.'

Sian nodded. Bile spiked her throat; it burned and she had to cough it away.

Dominic leaned over, close enough that she could smell his breath; a sour sweet mix of old alcohol and chewing gum. 'Nice to see you again, Sian.' His voice was level, professional even. 'I'll let

Gary know that you're doing well. He's always asking after you.' And there it was, conjured into the room, the spirit of her ex-boyfriend. Even though Sian knew that Dominic was saying this to freak her out, her breathing came in fast and she felt lightheaded.

Dominic got to his feet and walked to the door. Sian hardly dared believe he was leaving. But then she heard the sound of the door closing. She took deep breaths, sucking in air as if she'd just been pulled out from drowning.

CONFESSION

Kris's house

Sian heard the door go again and jumped out of her skin, surfacing from some very deep thoughts and memories. She held her breath for a moment, thinking how this could be anybody at all, but then Elvis gambolled in and jumped on her, licking her face the way he always did when she was upset. She petted her dog and tried not to cry with relief. Kris followed behind him, throwing his keys into the bowl on the shelf.

'OK, Love. You decide what you want?' he said, walking straight out of the room and to the loo at the back of the house before she could actually answer.

By the time Kris got back, Sian had managed to regain most of her composure. 'I'm saying curry,' she said. 'A veg vindaloo with boiled rice.'

'What you been up to while I was gone, then?' Kris asked.

'Oh, I did six marathons and found a cure for cancer,' she said. She could hear a shake to her voice.

Kris half-laughed and sat on the chair opposite Sian, exactly where Dominic had been. 'What's wrong?' he said.

'I had a visit,' she said. 'From Wilkinson.'

Kris reached for her hand. 'Here?' He held tight on to her. 'You're kidding me?'

'No,' Sian said. 'Not kidding. He told me to lay off, like that's a surprise. Pretty much threatened to haul me in about taking the sample if I didn't do as I was told.'

'Well, you kind of played into his hands there. Taking that sample. Exactly what I mean about "stupid things".' He let go of her hand and sat back.

'Sure,' she said, the word she used when she was only half-conceding. But, yes, she could see Kris's point. Then a sick thought washed over her and she had to suck in a big breath. 'He must have been watching the house, waiting for you to leave,' she said.

'Maybe,' Kris said. 'He knows I live here. He's not far away, just up on Muster's Road.'

Sian considered this, thought about the idea that he could come back again anytime he liked, so easily. 'Maybe we should go back to the Loggerheads. Now.' She was on her way to her feet and Kris stood up, grabbing her.

'Calm down,' he said. 'He's not about to murder us in our beds. Let's get some food and, if you really want, we can go later.'

Sian let Kris sit her back down. He reached for his phone and the curry house menu, opening up an app to make his order.

'What do you think of this Jonny Breen bloke?' she asked him as he typed.

Kris glanced up, raising one eyebrow. 'What do you think I think? Weird rank for a FLO and then he's almost interviewing you all; family meeting my arse.'

'Quite.'

Kris reached into the carrier bag by his feet and produced a bottle of white wine. 'Shall I crack this open?' he said.

Sian nodded and waited whilst he went into the kitchen, coming back with glasses and the open bottle. He poured them both a good-sized glassful and handed one to Sian.

'He's bent as fuck,' Kris said. 'So, tell me. What else has he done?'

'He turned up at the pub, when I was there the other night.' She paused, thinking about exactly what to say that didn't sound crazy and completely paranoid. 'I dunno. I felt all night like someone was following me. And I think they were. I think it was probably him.'

'Is that when he told you about the forensics? He seemed weird when he said that, as if he was expecting some kind of reaction.' Kris swilled around the wine in his glass.

'Yes,' she said. 'He was being weird that night too. Kind of flirtatious in a way that's hard to pin down. And he came out with this list of things about me like he'd been reading my police file'

'He'd read that anyway, wouldn't he? Part of the investigation.'

'That doesn't really make me feel much better.' Sian scratched at the side of her nose then rubbed at her face with both hands. 'Something really fucked up is going on here and they want to tick this one off as being my uncle, as quickly as they can. I have no clue what his motive was supposed to be, but I don't believe it. No. I know it wasn't him.'

'What would he say about it, Sian?'

Kris had met Rob, just once or twice and after the Loggerheads had closed for good. They'd got on well and Sian knew he'd got enough of a sense of him to know the answer to this question. 'He'd say, fuck it. That it didn't matter.' She shook her head. 'He'd come out with one of his sayings and then grin, telling me to keep safe and that you can't harm the dead.'

'And so? Isn't it best to just leave it like he'd tell you to?' He sighed. 'Yes, it does look dodgy, but if no one's going to get hurt, not really hurt, what's the big deal?'

'My uncle can't defend himself,' she said.

'Sure, but he wouldn't care.'

Sian swallowed. She realised she had to tell Kris everything if she wanted to keep him on her side, even the stupid things she'd done. 'I tested the DNA and got a profile'

'I guessed that. And?'

'Kris, I need your help to sort this out. My head's a mess, and someone big's involved in all this. Wilkinson mentioned Gary, but I think he did that to scare me. But it's still someone big.' Sian took a gulp of wine trying to wash her ex's name away, then put down her glass, pulling at a loose piece of thumbnail. She'd had no idea when she got together with Gary Bolton that he was one of the biggest crooks in Nottingham. Now, she was half-sure he'd only wooed her in an attempt to recruit another dodgy officer. 'One of the people down there was my father, biologically,' she said. 'The DNA was my DNA. Well, a big chunk of it was, anyway.'

Kris stared back at her, his eyes wide.

'Will you help me find out what's going on?' she asked him.

Kris hesitated. Then he looked Sian right in the eye. 'Only if you promise that you won't keep anything else from me. OK?'

Sian nodded, and saw that he was waiting for her to say it out loud. 'I promise,' she said. What was it her uncle used to say about promises? *They're like noses, duck, made to be broken.* Sian tried to be truer to her word than that, but she knew this would be a challenging situation.

'OK,' he said, his voice quiet. 'Look, you might still not like the answers you get.'

'I know,' she said. 'I've thought about that but I still want to know the truth.'

Kris looked very serious. 'Yes,' he said. 'You do. Honestly, I think that's nearly always your biggest problem.'

SCANDAL

Kris's house

The coffee machine was whirring and spitting. Sian propped herself up on her crutches and poured two mugs full as Kris walked into the room.

'I made you coffee,' she said, nodding down towards the work-top, unable to pass the cup to him and stay balanced. Kris's eyes were focused on his iPad, his face very worried-looking. 'What's up?' she said.

Kris handed her the device and grabbed a cup, scraping a chair out from the table and flinging himself d own into it. All the noise and sudden movements were making Sian edgy. He nodded down at the screen. 'See for yourself.' He took a loud slurp of his coffee.

Sian leaned against the counter and looked at the screen, a news app screaming headlines at her. ARE PUB BODIES OPPORTUNITY KNOCKS PAIR? In another paper, shorter, simpler OPPORTUNITY KNOCKED? She clicked through the links, reading the pieces. The articles were accompanied by an old photo of a drunk-looking but handsome man with a thick moustache. He had his arm around a woman who had hair stacked on top of her head in a beehive and heavily kohled eyelids that made her look sleepy. Sian stared at the photos. She couldn't imagine her mother with this man, not even the young, beautiful red-headed version of Ruth she'd seen in old photographs. 'Bloody hell,' she said. 'I guess that's daddy.'

Sian was staring so intently at Harry McKenzie that she almost missed something more worrying; a smaller insert picture on one of the articles was of her and Kris coming out of his house a couple of mornings before. She looked up at Kris, a coldness spreading through her chest.

'How the fuck did they get this address?' he said.

Sian looked up from the phone screen at Kris. Gary might see these and be able to work out where they were. This put them both in real danger.

'I won't let him bully you again, Sian.' Kris's face was set and his mouth hard.

Sian didn't like being bullied, either. She had said as much, once, to Gary, telling him she'd rather die than be pushed into doing the dodgy things he was asking of her. That was when he'd made sure she understood that it could be arranged. She could still see the view from the motorway bridge, feel the world spinning around her, hear the violence of the speeding cars as they rushed along below her. PTSD made you experience time in a fluid, non-linear way, holding you back in the past whenever it wanted to. Sian let go of the worktop and the room was spinning.

'You OK?' Kris said. It sounded like his voice was coming from a very long way away. 'Sian?' He stood up and touched her arm.

Sian shivered. 'I'm fine,' she said. 'We need to go to the Logger-heads.'

Kris nodded.

Sian looked again at the picture of Harry, pinching her fingers outwards on the screen's surface to enlarge it. She couldn't tell for sure in black and white but his eyes were bright and clear in a way that made her think that they were blue. She looked at Angela too. There was something nagging at her about this woman.

Kris took hold of Sian by the shoulders. He kissed her on the forehead. 'We'll deal with this together, right?'

Sian didn't answer, still intent on the screen.

'Sian?'

She looked up at Kris. 'What if my uncle did it, after all?'

Kris shrugged. 'Then we find out and you know,' he said. He made it sound so simple.

She passed the iPad back to him. 'Does that look like a person who could be my biological father to you?'

Kris held the phone close to his face and examined the picture carefully. 'No,' he said, 'not really.' Then he shrugged. 'To be honest, though, I don't look much like my dad at all.'

Sian looked at the pictures. She had expected to recognise her 'real' father when she finally saw him but nothing she could do made this image feel like anything other than a photograph of a complete stranger. She zoomed in on Angela, though, and she looked familiar. Sian felt like she knew this woman, although she couldn't remember how. She just felt it, in her bones, like a sickness.

November 1970
Everything Is Beautiful

The Loggerheads pub

Harry was driving too fast again, making the car skid and screech along the road. Angela felt sick but was thankful that he hadn't yet turned into Harry the one-eyed bandit.

'It's gony go great,' Harry said. He nodded back towards the boot of the car. 'With them beauties. Best in the shop.' He was grinning.

Angela wondered about the new equipment he'd bought, whether it was wise. She'd tried to talk to Harry about it but he'd brushed her off. He'd done the same to Bobby, when he'd said that he'd rather use the drum kit he was used to. Harry had pointed out how good they'd look with The Midnight Roses on the kit, and the picture of rambling, blood-red and black flowers that wound around the name. And it did look good; it was hard to argue with him. It was always hard to argue with Harry.

'Will we have time to practise?' Angela said. She cleared her throat.

Harry laughed. 'Wut? Ye was there the other night, hen. Who needs practice?' He turned the wheel sharply, and pulled up outside the Loggerheads, the car mounting the pavement with a screech. 'A few pints and a wee dram for good luck, that's all the practice we need,' he told her with a wink.

Angela climbed from the car. She was wearing a floaty green top and flared jeans, and had been to the hairdressers to get her hair done in a beehive. She'd struggled to fasten the jeans and had left the top button undone. The baby was beginning to make itself known, kicking its feet at the real world outside Angela's belly. But Harry hadn't looked at her properly for weeks now, had hardly held or touched her, and he hadn't even noticed. All he seemed able to focus on was the band.

The pub was buzzing. Men she knew and some she didn't patted Harry on the back as they walked through. Bobby was standing in front of the bar, messing with a TV set, trying to get it to tune into the right channel. The screen buzzed with static then a picture sharpened and emerged from the dots, then static again, as he moved the dial. Finally, the picture cleared to an advert for Nimble bread, which meant ITV, and a cheer went up.

Harry ordered a round of about ten whiskies, which he passed around with a big grin. He held his aloft and then they all downed their drinks. Angela managed to avoid drinking hers, taking the tiniest of sips; alcohol, and especially whisky, was giving her terrible heartburn these days. She was worried about the competition and about being on TV. She was already finding singing much harder, the tight ball of new life inside her pushing against her diaphragm and making breathing more difficult.

Harry passed more whiskies round and Angela took one. She smiled and raised her glass. Harry looked away and she tipped the contents of the glass on to the floor under the table. This felt like the story of her life right now. She was hiding, right in front of everyone, and Harry was enjoying himself and looking in the opposite direction.

Black Night

Pat Walsh's house, West Bridgford, Nottingham, the same night

Big Pat Walsh walked out on to his balcony to take a better look at the commotion that was going on by the river. Just upstream before the Trent bent out of sight he saw a crowd of football fans. Forest, he could see from the red scarfs with the trees embroidered on them. Two men were having a fight and one hit the other so hard that he fell into the water, which turned red around him. His mates waded in to get him out, and tried to stem the flow of blood, which was pouring out of his nose. Pat smiled. He remembered fights at the Arsenal when he was a lad. It was something he'd enjoyed.

'Are they after starting yet?' Kathy called through. She was fussing in the kitchen over something.

Pat walked back in and sat down, putting his feet up on the smoked glass coffee table. 'Not yet,' he said. 'Five minutes.'

His wife came through with a tray of snacks and two more beers. 'Oi!' she said, nodding down at his feet. He moved them and she placed the tray on the coffee table then rubbed at the marks left by his shoes. He reached for her hair; strawberries and cream. He was a lucky man with a beautiful wife and lovely home. He'd do well to remember that.

Kathy flicked his hand away and gave him a piercing bad look. 'You keep your dirty feet off my table!' But as he stared back and widened his eyes, she grinned and let him kiss her. He pulled her down on to the sofa with him. The presenter with the plummy voice was talking about the acts they had on tonight. He described the Midnight Roses as a 'little bit country, a little bit rock-n-roll' and

Pat added, out loud, 'a little bit rolling drunk'. Kathy laughed and he caught her beautiful green eyes with his.

The Midnight Roses had been drunk when they left the pub, to a man and to a woman too. That bothered Pat. It wasn't professional. There was a gang at the pub he'd noticed were whispering about Harry and the band and they weren't saying good things. They'd love to see him fall but, then, people always loved that, didn't they? Pat didn't care either way, really. He'd already had his payment so what did he give a fuck for?

This magician was up first, a Geordie-sounding geezer. He was pretty good but kept telling everyone they'd 'like it', which put Pat off. He'd make his own mind up, ta. Pat and Kathy watched, taking the mick and laughing about the tricks. Pat tried to come up with theories about how they were done and Kathy laughed at his ideas. But then the act was over and the Midnight Roses were on the screen. It was weird, seeing them like this on the small screen, a bit like being in a dream.

The camera came in close on Angela and Pat knew right away that something was wrong. Her eyes were lined with smudged mascara. She sometimes forgot to smile with all the nerves but this was different. She looked tragic. And Marilyn looked much the same; all smudged make-up and sadness, which was out of character for the younger sister. She was usually all summer's day and sunshine. Pat sat up so sharply he spilled some of his beer and Kathy rushed out to grab something and clean it up.

'Hurry up!' he shouted after her. 'You're missing it.' But she was back seconds later, cleaning the spill but staring at the telly.

The band fired up but their timing was all over the place. The drums looked good with the band's name and that picture of crawling roses, and Bobby was keeping good time, albeit without his usual flourishes. The electric guitars, though, were making a weird grating sound that wasn't very musical. Angela kept looking back, uneasy, as she waited for her cue.

The girls came in singing on the wrong beat. Marilyn was out of tune. Even Angela struggled to hold the notes and kept turning to look at the others. Harry was the main singer on this one, though, and he was worse than the ladies, the slur of being drunk very clear on his voice. It was the 'Angel Baby' song. Pat could just about make that out, but it was almost unrecognisable.

'They're dreadful,' Kathy said.

Pat smiled and repeated what she'd said, making fun of her accent, and she play-slapped him. He never got bored of the way she spoke; the Dublin accent was much sexier than the Nottingham one. But it was hard, being married to one woman, even a woman as lovely as Kathy. Pat shook his head and took another sip of beer and tried to forget all the ways he'd let his wife down. It would never hurt her, he was determined. She would never find out. The presenter came back on and the music was faded out. Hughie Green did that thing where he widened one eye and pushed the other eyebrow down. 'Not quite what we were expecting,' he announced, in that posh boy way he had about him.

'You're not kidding,' Pat muttered. He put his arm around his wife but his mood had fallen. Although he couldn't have given tuppence for what happened to Harry, whether the Midnight Roses rotted in the ground, he'd realised something he'd not considered before. There would be trouble with Harry now. He would need handling. For the first time, he wondered if what he'd asked for from Harry had been a big mistake. There had already been some unforeseen complications.

The clapometer said it all and as the camera panned, Pat saw that even the band weren't cheering for themselves. They just stood there looking sad and tragic. There would be the postal vote, yet, and the full result would only be announced in the next episode. But there couldn't be any doubt in the mind of anyone who'd watched their performance that the Midnight Roses had just crashed out and they'd done it properly, with some panache. Big Pat Walsh had given them the opportunity of a lifetime and, when it came knocking, they got themselves tight as bastards and fell on their arses.

Harry Fucking McKenzie. What a twat.

November 2017

TROUBLE

Kris's office, Meadows Police Station, Nottingham

Kris's office building always made Sian feel transported back to the 1970s with its cord carpet tiles and scruffy magnolia walls. It was a low-key station, though, which meant her presence wouldn't attract the kind of attention it might have elsewhere. Sian swung on the black office chair, using the button under the seat to move it up and down. Kris came through the door holding two Styrofoam cups of coffee. 'Here you go,' he said. 'Medders station's finest.' He was doing his best Nottingham impression again.

Kris handed her sugars and sweeteners. 'You might find these make the mudwater vaguely drinkable,' he said. Sian pulled a face at the idea, and then at the taste of the overheated, bitter coffee, which burnt the inside of her mouth. Kris reached into his inside pocket and handed her a sheet of paper. 'The login,' he said. 'This is from before, when we were working on making sure Gary would never come knocking again and needed to make sure we didn't leave a trace.' Sian's ex had, unsurprisingly, stalked her for several months after they broke up, until Kris and a couple of Sian's colleagues managed to 'persuade' him to stop. 'It gives you anonymous access to quite a bit locally. Not everything, but a starting point,' Kris said.

'HOLMES?' Sian asked. This was the main police database and investigation tool, holding extensive records about murders, missing people and criminals and by far the most useful resource.

Kris shook his head. 'Sorry, no, and not DNA, either. Which I know you could do with. I'll see what I can find about rustling up something anonymous there but don't hold your breath.'

'Where did you get this from?' Sian asked him.

Kris kissed her on the forehead. 'I have a meeting, so I'll see you in an hour or two,' he told her. 'And I promised not to reveal my sources.'

Her uncle's saying about promises was almost on Sian's lips, but she decided that Kris wouldn't like it. She watched him leave and then shuffled on the chair over to the door, using the catch on her side to lock it shut after him. She opened out the piece of paper he'd given her and stared at his computer screen. She wasn't sure about doing this, even with an anonymous login. Every action leaves a trace and that was never truer than of an action taken on a computer. But what other choice did she have?

A loud knock on the door made Sian sit up and hold very still. Whoever it was waited a moment or two, then knocked again. They tried the door. Sian held her breath. What if they had a key? But after turning the handle and pushing on it a few times, they gave up and walked away.

The visitor had spooked her and Sian took her laptop from her bag instead, opening it and placing it on the desk in front of her. She logged in and connected to Wi-Fi via tethering on her phone. Then she went to the genealogy website that she'd signed up to. She'd sent off for a DNA kit from the site but wasn't sure about using it. It seemed silly, paying out seventy quid when she knew more about DNA than the labs she'd be sending her sample to. They added a couple of solutions and a computer chip to identify a few standard genetic markers and she wasn't even sure that the test would give her any answers that she hadn't got already. She'd need to have a bit of luck and find some relatives who'd tested themselves too.

Sian had found out more about Harry and Angela through the site, though. In fact, it was frightening how much information was there. Like, she knew that Harry's parents hadn't quite been married when he was born. That would have been a huge scandal back in 1928. He'd been quite a bit older than Angela and older than Sian's mum too, the snake. She remembered what her mother had said, about the pub being a chaotic place. She couldn't imagine Ruth as part of that chaos but people changed a lot as they got older, she supposed.

More settled now, Sian switched on Kris's monitor and entered the credentials he'd given her into the login window. The computer whirred and clicked, and then the tools she needed appeared. She found the local case files and opened them, reading them in a rush and closing each one quickly. The police investigation had now officially identified the bodies as Harry and Angela McKenzie but Sian wasn't convinced. The evidence that pointed to this being Harry and Angela was mostly circumstantial. They'd disappeared from the same pub where the bodies were found, of course; then there was the jewellery and the shoes. Sian never would have called an ID based on this stuff.

Sian pulled up another case file and looked through the notes. They had run some DNA on the bodies but were waiting for the results; mitochondrial on the bones and a standard police profile on the mummified remains. She couldn't help smiling at the idea that she was ahead of them. There was other forensic information too; the archaeological reports, which suggested a range of ages and some ideas about place of birth for each person, as well as the very rough estimates of time of death that Breen had already communicated with her. Sian read through the results. She'd been a bit unfair in her uncharitable thoughts about Dominic's haphazard ways. The places and approximate dates of birth matched, which was almost evidence. He'd sent off for a mitochondrial DNA test on one of the younger

Callaghan sisters, who had come forward, although it would be a good while before that came back.

There were documents, too, about the tenancy of the pub, oldfashioned sheets from the brewery that had been filled out on a typewriter with duplicate paper. Harry had become landlord in 1970 and the pub had been signed over to her uncle, Robert Malcolm O'Quaid, in July the following year, just two days before Sian was born. Seeing the date on the form in the smudged and leaky courier font made Sian shiver. She wished that forensics had been able to give a bit more of a clue about the times of death because she really wanted to know if they had happened before or after her uncle took over the pub.

Sian opened a second forensics file and started to read. This included some information from the post mortem. The suspected cause of death was gunshots, as she had assumed the moment she'd seen the keyhole in one of the skulls. Then a detail she had not been expecting; it made her sit back so sharply in her chair that she almost fell off it. She minimised the window and tried to get her head around what she'd just seen, and what it meant. The female remains held yet another secret in the chemical composition of the bones, which showed signs of a recent pregnancy and birth. There was no sign of the baby tangled up with the remains. Had it lived? Did Sian have a half-brother or sister somewhere in the world? A shock ran up from her stomach and into her throat at the thought of this.

A rustle from behind made her jump. Sian turned, and saw a piece of paper being slipped underneath the bottom of the door. She stared and sat, frozen in the chair, for several moments. Finally, she got her nerve up and shuffled the chair over to the doorway, leaning down to pick up the paper. There were two neat sentences written in a smooth, black ink at the top. It looked like writing from a fountain pen.

DEAD FLOWERS

I know you're there Sian, the message said. *And I've a friend who needs to talk to you.* Underneath this the name *Jack Donnelly* and the address of a care home was scrawled, in blue biro and entirely different handwriting, old-fashioned and cursive.

Sian hauled herself to standing on her crutches and pushed the door open slowly. She peeked out, looking up and down the corridor. There was no one there but why would there be? Whoever left the note had plenty of time to walk away. Sian closed the door and locked it tight, sitting down on the office chair with a bump. She looked down at the piece of paper. *Jack Donnelly?* There was something familiar about the name but she couldn't work out why.

DOUBLE

Beeston Care Home, Nottingham

Google Maps wanted Sian to take the A52 but she knew better than her phone and cut through campus and out of the traffic. A few minutes later she was across the roundabout near Beeston and the bossy female voice was telling her to turn left. She drove into a busy car park, with vehicles already blocking others in. She put her car in the least offensive place she could find then locked it and headed to the door on her crutches.

'Hi,' she said to the receptionist.

'Hello!' came the enthusiastic reply with a huge smile. The girl was very pretty, dark skin with make-up perfectly contoured and fake lashes framing her big, brown eyes. 'Can I help?'

'Hopefully,' Sian said. 'I'm here to see Jack Donnelly.' Then, an afterthought. 'Am I OK to leave my car like that? It's the silver one.' She pointed.

'Oh yes,' said the girl. 'No problem. Just sign in over there and put your reg number. I'll come and find you if anyone needs to get out.' She was refreshingly cheerful, but not in an irritating way. Sian warmed to her.

The girl told Sian all of the door codes and pointed her in the direction of Jack's room. Not the best security she'd come across. What if she'd been an old gangster friend set on revenge? She hadn't had to show ID or prove any connections or anything.

The corridors were dark and murky and smelled of overcooked food. Sian passed an office, the door flung out into the hallway, patient files splayed open on a chair. This place needed closing down! She found the room. There was a picture of

Jack Donnelly with the name of his nurse and key worker in case she hadn't seen him for years and needed to make sure she was assassinating the right man. He looked very old and frail and she didn't recognise him.

'Hello?' she said, hesitant, stepping around the open door. For the first time since getting the note she had a moment of misgiving. It was careless, coming here. But she came closer to the bed and looked at the man lying there, and realised he was no danger to anybody.

The frail old man pushed himself up in the bed slightly. 'Ay-up,' he said, 'it's you.' A cough. 'Put the kettle on, duckie.'

Sian looked around the room for a kettle and didn't see one.

'C'mon, duck, get mashing!'

He thought she was somebody else. Dementia, probably. She wasn't sure what to do. Both her father and uncle had died suddenly and she'd never had to deal with anyone in this kind of decline. Weren't there rules about it? She had a vague recollection that you were not supposed to contradict someone with Alzheimer's but she didn't even know if that was the same thing as dementia.

'Hello,' she said. 'Mr Donnelly?'

He seemed to wake up then, scan somehow back to the realities of his present. 'Hello,' he said. 'Hang on, you that gell? The one they was sending to see me?'

'I think so,' she said, wondering who 'they' were.

'He left you a note,' the old man said. He was suddenly strangely lucid. 'On the chair.' There was a large, very padded wheelchair across from the bed. It crowded the tiny, dark room. Sian squeezed her way through and, sure enough, found an envelope with her name on it.

'You look just like her,' Jack said. His voice had taken on that dreamy, thoughtful quality that goes with nostalgia. 'Bloody hell, you don't half. You're her double.'

Sian was pretty sure he was still mistaking her for someone else. 'Whose double?' she asked him.

'Your mam, of course,' he said, laughing, as if she were thick not to realise who he meant. 'A sight for sore eyes,' he said.

Sian stared at him for a moment, wondering if he might have known Ruth. He looked blankly back at her without a hint of recognition and she realised that it wasn't that. It was just the dementia, playing tricks on both of them. Then his face changed, mashed itself into a ball as he started to cry. 'I wish I'd been better,' he said. 'Been good to you.' His voice was laced with regret and it was the saddest thing Sian had ever heard. He wiped at his face and let out gentle, quiet wails. 'I'm sorry,' he said. He carried on talking but it was hard to make out what he was saying through the sobs. There were more sorries, and he seemed to be apologising for something specific he'd done to her.

Sian was overwhelmed with sympathy for him. She walked over to the side of his bed and leaned her crutches against it, reaching for his hand. 'We don't know each other,' she told him, her voice quiet and gentle. 'You haven't done anything to me.' It seemed more important to put his mind at rest than worry about contradicting him.

'No!' he said, suddenly angry. He bashed her hand away. Then he stared at her, and reached out, taking hold of her by the wrist, hard, and pulling her close. He was surprisingly strong. His mouth set in a tight, hard line and carried a hate that was utterly familiar to Sian, the kind that had a weird, messed-up love at the back of it. 'Fuck off telling me what's what,' he said, his voice hard and nasty. 'You don't get to tell me owt.'

His eyes were a dark pit of nastiness. Something about the set of his mouth made her feel like he might bite her. Sian tried to pull away but he pulled her closer. 'Get off me,' she said. Then, louder, 'Get off.' She twisted her arm and then pulled it hard away from him, getting herself loose and having to grip the side of the bed to stop from falling. She grabbed her crutches, rushing from the room and into the hallway, pushing past a nurse with a trolley full of meds.

In the car park, Sian leaned against her car. For the first time in years, she badly wanted a cigarette. But she was done with cigarettes just as definitely as she was done with men like Jack Donnelly. He might have lost most of his faculties but he hadn't lost who he was, not at the core of him. And she recognised that, even if she didn't know him. She wondered if he had known her mother, if that had been more than old age and confusion. Perhaps an old boyfriend? She couldn't see it, though, couldn't imagine Ruth having had anything to do with a man like Jack. Her mother had always been far more sensible about these things than Sian was. And anyway, no one ever told her she looked like Ruth.

Sian's breathing and heart rate began to slow back to normal. She remembered the envelope. Pulling it from her pocket, she ripped it open. The message was short and very slightly cryptic, written in the same blue biro and old-fashioned, cursive script as Jack Donnelly's name and location on the other note.

Be a good girl and leave the rest of the skellies locked in the closet

The attempt to code the message was hardly sophisticated. Sian was being warned off, probably by the same person who had sent Dominic to speak to her. Jack Donnelly was incidental, just an old man they could leave a note with who would not remember afterwards. Sian stared at the perfectly formed letters, wishing she could decode the twist and fall of the handwriting. She was convinced that everything anyone created, even a little note like this one, contained their DNA, imprinted in a deep, elemental way. She just needed a way to profile it.

TAKE

Loggerheads

Kris pulled up outside the Loggerheads and pulled the handbrake on hard. 'You ready for this?' he said.

Sian nodded and handed him the keys. She opened the door and placed her crutches down, pushing herself from the car.

Crime scene tape still decorated the front door of the Loggerheads in a massive X. Kris pulled it off and unlocked the door. Sian pushed it open and swung through and down the hallway, remembering how you used to have the choice of left to the public bar, or right to the lounge, back when she'd first visited the place as a child. She took big gulps of air and tried to swallow down the nostalgia.

The police had boarded up the cellar and told her not to go down there for now. That suited Sian. She didn't imagine she'd ever go down there again, given a choice. She came down the hall and to the back of the building. There was a lot of dust in the hallway near the downstairs bathroom, from where they'd taken down the stud wall. The hall opened up now straight into the old skittle alley, barely changed since Sian was a little girl, its red and green paintwork dull with old dust.

Kris had gone into the kitchen and Sian heard the sound of the kettle warming up. She walked in and let herself drop heavily into one of the fold-out chairs. She leaned against the pasting table and let her head fall into her hands. She wasn't enjoying the way they'd cut the place up, disturbed everything. It didn't feel like the Loggerheads she knew anymore.

Kris placed the bags containing her uncle's belongings on the worktop. 'Are we going to look through this stuff, then?'

Sian nodded. 'I suppose,' she said. She'd been putting it off for days, even though there was no way whatever was in the bags could be worse than what she'd found downstairs.

Kris pulled the nearest towards him and tipped it up on to the table, carefully emptying its contents, some loose, some wrapped in evidence bags.

'Their usual consistent approach, I see,' she said.

Kris gave her a bad look, but carried on unpacking the bag. Sian picked up and examined the objects he'd put on the table. There were some old tapes and records, cine recordings too. She wondered what might be on them. There were photograph albums and loose Polaroids. Some of the photos were black and white but the Polaroids were colour. There was the odd landscape but most of the pictures were of various combinations of the four people who had lived at the Loggerheads together, her uncle and Marilyn, Angela and Harry. Kris emptied the other bag and rifled through the items, too.

Some of the Polaroids looked like wedding pictures. The women were wearing white dresses and carrying small bouquets. Sian didn't recognise the place the photographs had been taken. Then she saw a shot of Harry kissing Angela in front of an anvil and realised. It was Gretna Green. No wonder she'd struggled to find their wedding records on the genealogy website; they hadn't got married in Nottingham. They'd run away together. But why would they have done that? They were old enough to get married, weren't they? She tried to work it out. Had they all been twenty-one? Was that the age you had to be, back then?

'Bloody hell, your Auntie Marilyn was a looker!' Kris said, handing her a picture.

Sian took it from him and held it out. She certainly had been; a real beauty with curves and a smile that lit up her face. Angela was pretty too but like a faded version.

'Hang on.' Kris's face had become very focused, like he was trying to work something out. He looked up at Sian and held out a photograph. 'You need to look at this.'

She took the photo from him. It was a shot taken here, on the back stairs, although the hallway looked more closed in then, like there was an extra wall somewhere. Angela was standing about halfway up the stairs, looking shyly down at someone, waving an arm across the front of her as if to say 'no pictures'. She was wearing a simple dress and no shoes, her eyes kohled and her hair loose around her shoulders. She was tiny and very slight, but the resemblance was undeniable nonetheless.

Sian looked at her mug of tea, at the kettle. She remembered what it said in the police report: that Angela had given birth not long before she died. She gripped her mug so hard that it slipped, so she placed it slowly down on the table.

'She looks like you,' Kris said.

'I know.' Sian's words crossed with his; she'd known exactly what he was about to say. She could have pulled out a dozen snaps of herself at that age, from university, shortly after, where there was a resemblance. She'd been bigger than Angela, even then, and her hair had been shorter, a slightly darker blonde, her eyes brown rather than Angela's deep shade of blue. There was one picture, from a fancy-dress party with a sixties theme that Sian had gone to when she was doing her master's degree. She'd worn a bright yellow minidress and platform heels, and make-up just like this. If you'd have put the photos side by side, they'd have looked like sisters.

Sisters shared 50 per cent DNA on average. About the same as a mother and daughter. Sian realised just how massive her assumption had been when she'd found the matches between her own DNA and the mixed profile, like the simplification in the O-level Biology class that had caused so much trouble. Sian had been so sure she'd found her father in the cellar of the Loggerheads because she'd known all her life that he was missing from it. But she had underestimated Ruth and the lies she was capable of.

'She doesn't just look a bit like you, Sian,' Kris said, as if he was worried she hadn't got his point.

'I know,' Sian said. 'I see it.' She stared at Kris. She hadn't found her father in the cellar at the Loggerheads Pub. She'd found her mother.

February 1971
Mama Told Me (Not To Come)

The Loggerheads pub

Pat was sitting in the corner of the Loggerheads enjoying his usual quiet pint. He'd been at the Loggerheads every night this week, and he knew it'd been noticed. He'd seen Harry's face flatten and his nostrils flare when he realised Pat was keeping an eye on him. But Harry needed managing. He'd thrown out the wrong people a couple of times lately, and not politely; drunk enough he'd have been chucked out of any other pub himself.

Angela brought a drink over with a tight smile. 'From the hubby,' she said. She leaned over to put the Guinness down and he felt the firm curve of her belly as it brushed his upper arm. She was having a baby; he'd have put money on it. He smiled politely and raised the glass in Harry's direction, who had the courtesy and common sense to nod back, even if he didn't look happy. Then all attention turned to the main door, where a row was erupting. Pat grabbed Angela by the wrist. 'Sit down with me a bit, sweetheart,' he said. He didn't want a pregnant woman in the middle of a load of trouble. Angela glanced towards her husband and looked unsure. But then she sat down.

'How you feeling?' he said. 'You got the sickness and all that?' He was scanning the whole room as he talked to her, looking over her head.

Angela blushed. 'I don't know what you mean.'

He looked at her dead on. 'Yeah, you do. Now, you need to stay here with me. Because something's kicking off.'

She tried to stand up, her eyes wide with panic, looking around for a way out.

Pat held her by the arm firmly. 'Stop,' he said. 'Sit here with me. I promise I'll look after you.'

Angela looked terrified, but she did as she was told.

A couple emerged from the fracas; a tall man pulling along a short, very slim woman with blonde hair, dragging her by the hand like she was a reluctant kiddy on the way to school. The girl was attractive. Looked a bit like Twiggy. He watched them cross the bar to shouts and jeers from Bobby, who clearly wanted them out.

Angela followed Pat's gaze, turning to see for herself what was going on. She saw the woman first. 'That's Sue Hill,' she said sounding almost pleased. 'Went to school with her. Haven't seen her in years.' Then she got a view of the bloke her friend was with and her hand shot to her mouth as she let out a sharp sound.

Pat grabbed hold of both her hands and pulled her back round to face him. 'Look at me,' he said. 'What did I tell you?'

'You don't understand—'

She didn't have time to explain whatever it was he didn't understand, as a loud shout came from behind the bar in a gruff, slurred Scottish voice. 'Ye fucking barstarrrdd!' Harry had climbed on to the bar and was pulling off his shirt. 'I fucking warned ye, pal!'

Then the lights went out. Another fucking power cut. There were shouts and squeals all around the bar, and Angela sucked in air like she was struggling to breathe.

'It's OK,' Pat assured her. He still had hold of both of her hands.

'It's not,' she said. Her voice was low; she could barely get the words out. 'That's my husband.'

'I know. But Harry can look after himself,' he said.

'I don't mean Harry.'

Pat understood her right away. 'I see,' he said. 'Well, this is a development.'

'He can't get to me.' The words came out in a rush. 'Don't let him get to me.' Angela blew out and sucked in air several times. Her hands had gone sweaty and Pat could feel the panic coming off her like heat.

'What did he do to you?' Pat said. Goosebumps prickled the skin on his arms. If this was what he thought it was...

Angela let out a wail. 'My baby!'

'Did he hit you?' Pat asked. 'Did he beat you up?' He heard Harry screaming obscenities and the wet thump of a hard punch, a yelp of response from someone. He hoped the drunken twat had landed it on the right person, in that state and in the dark like this.

Angela was crying now and managed to wail out a weirdly musical 'yes' between sobs. Then she took some deep breaths and got control of herself again. 'He killed my other baby,' she said. And then she let out another sob.

Pat pulled her closer and held her to him. 'I'll put the fucker in hospital.' His voice was a dangerous whisper. 'You stay right there.' There were shouts and bangs coming from the bar, getting louder and too close for Pat's liking.

'No!' She was swallowing the words. 'No!' Her voice sounded hoarse. 'Don't leave me.'

The lights came back on. Harry McKenzie was on the floor in front of the bar; knocked out or passed out, it was hard to tell which. Angela's other husband was standing with a broken glass in his hand but Bobby had hold of both his forearms, holding them behind his back and stopping him from moving anywhere or doing anything.

'Come with me,' Pat said. He had to pull her to her feet. 'I promise I'll make sure you're OK.'

Angela let him lead her across the bar, his arm around her shoulder. Her legs looked like they were giving way on her. He took her through the bar hatch and into the back room, then sat her at the table. 'Stay there,' he said. 'What's your husband's name? The other one?'

'Jack,' she told him. 'Jack Donnelly.' Her head dropped into her hands.

Back in the public bar, he walked over to Bobby and the bastard he had hold of. The tiny woman he'd brought in with him was still standing right in the middle of it all. She didn't even look scared; very tough or mental, probably both. He remembered that Angela had told him her name. 'Sue?' he said.

She nodded, her arms folded tightly across her chest.

'You're going to get the fuck out of here now, OK? I won't ask you twice.'

Sue opened her mouth to argue and then looked into Pat's eyes and something she saw there changed her mind.

'Yeah, you are,' he said. 'And if you know what's good for you, you'll have fuck all to do with this low-life bastard no more.' He turned to look at Jack. 'If he's in any state to have anything to do with anyone when I'm done with him.'

Sue looked from Pat, then to Jack, and she scampered off, as instructed.

Pat nodded at Bobby Q. 'You can let go of him now, go out back and sort out your sister-in-law. She's in shall we say a bit of a delicate state to have to deal with all this trouble.'

Bobby's eyes widened and Pat saw that he understood.

'This cunt's mine now,' he said, with a grimace.

Bobby let go of Jack's arms, and the bastard fell to the floor, dropping the glass as if he'd never planned to use it. He looked up at Pat and the big man smiled back down at him. 'You're in trouble now, sonny,' he said. And he rolled up his sleeves ready to make good on that promise.

I Hear You Knocking

The Loggerheads pub, two nights later

Harry was leaning against the bar chatting to Paul and Les Parker. Bobby was out of earshot, serving someone over the other side. 'Aye,' he said, gesturing at the tables around them. 'Been in every night this week, like some kinday fucking guardian angel. Thinks I havenay noticed.' He puffed up, and wiped at the top of his collar like there were crumbs on it. 'I isnay putting up with him. Big Pat, my arse. He's no the big man in my pub and he'd do well to remember that.' Every time he thought about Pat, his arrogance, thinking he needed tay step in to sort out that fucker Donnelly, he felt the bile rise and sting in his throat. 'Dirty sod has a few secrets he wouldnay want me talking about, ye get me?' Harry patted the side of his nose with one big finger.

There was a general turn of heads around him and Harry twisted to glance in the same direction himself. Marilyn strode into the public bar, back from God knows where with God knows who again. She was dressed up in that black dress and fur coat, those red shoes that she got married in. She was a sexy woman and he wasn't surprised to see men turn to look. He turned back to his pint with some effort. Sometimes, when he saw his sister-in-law dressed like this, he had this weird but overwhelming feeling that she'd be the death of him.

Angela walked over on the other side of the bar, holding on to her tummy and taking deep, heavy steps, acting like the baby was weighing her down. He didn't understand; she'd always been skinny and was barely showing yet. 'I'm going to bed, love,' she said.

Harry nodded and leaned backwards over the bar to give her a peck on the cheek. He heard the door go behind him as she headed upstairs and tried not to think about what things might be like in a few months' time with a baby here. He couldn't see himself as a father. Something about what those old women had said to him had stuck. Maybe it'd help if Pat Walsh hadn't found out about the baby before he did.

With a shiver, Harry turned to see Marilyn sidling up to him at the bar. She leaned forward, throwing the tiniest of kicks backwards with her left leg and shouting for her husband's attention, demanding a drink. Bobby poured it but looked grudging. Marilyn took her gin and tonic and turned from the bar, leaning against it and looking out into the room. Her eyes were narrow and she looked far, far away.

'Penny for 'em,' Harry said, turning to look out at the pub himself.

His sister-in-law undid her fur coat and leaned back, tipping the drink up. As her coat flapped open, Harry noticed she'd put on a bit of weight. It was subtle, but her stomach was slightly rounded and she was a little fuller at the hips. He wondered if she was in the family way too. But Bobby wouldn't have served her gin if she was. Unless he didn't know.

Marilyn sighed. 'Do you ever think about what coulda been, Harry?' Her voice was odd. Sleepy and misty, like dreams, but fake. Like acting. He wondered if she was imitating someone from a film. Marilyn was in love with the pictures and came back with a new leading lady in her head every time there was a big movie out.

'All the time, hen.' Harry swilled round the dregs in the bottom of his pint glass.

Marilyn smiled, and turned towards him. She leaned in. Conspiratorial. 'It's never too late,' she said. 'You're a long time dead.' She was definitely imitating somebody.

'I'm gony be if I'm no careful,' he said, with a wink and a smile, thinking about the liberties that Pat Walsh had taken. He never should have given him what he wanted; now he seemed to think he was in charge here.

"Scuse me you two.' It was Bobby's voice. He came between them and placed fresh drinks in front of them. Harry jumped. Even when he realised it was just Bobby, the fear stayed with him; a coldness all over. The death of him, those words came back.

Then Bobby was away dealing with someone the other side of the bar.

'I could sing, you know.' Marilyn was making her voice sweeter still, as if to prove her point.

'You did sing.' Harry supped his pint and licked foam from his upper lip. 'It didnay work out.'

'I could be the lead singer, though.' She turned towards him and put a hand on his arm. 'I could.'

'Marilyn, please.' He gently removed her arm and placed it on the bar.

She leaned back against the bar, pouting.

'You should get yersel upstairs. Don't ye got jobs to do and such?' Harry asked her. He felt out of control around his sister-in-law and didn't like that feeling.

Her pout grew bigger. 'Women don't have to do all that stuff anymore, you know.'

Harry shrugged. He wasn't sure he did know. 'I didnay have you down as a women's libber,' he said.

Marilyn didn't reply, but tipped her drink and narrowed her eyes. Perhaps that was a reply – of sorts.

Harry stared out at the pub. Was this it, all there was? This pub? The odd pint? Weans and nappies and then a stroke or heart attack and the end of him? Surely there had to be more to life than that? He wanted to scream.

DEAD FLOWERS

'I could be your lead singer,' Marilyn said.

Harry's breath quickened. The way she said 'your' made it sound like so much more than singing. And he looked her up and down and had to admit that it was tempting. They could run away, set up somewhere new. Start another band.

'You know I'm a good girl. I work hard and I'm prepared to do what it takes.' She paused and took a drink. Then she turned towards Harry and looked at him full on, held his eyes with hers. 'I've done all the things you asked me to.'

There was a stand-off. The pair looked at each other and Harry had to make an effort not to grab her and kiss her, hard and raw, here in the bar in front of her husband and all of their regulars. Right then, he wanted her so badly that he didn't give the least shite what any of them thought, even Bobby. He took one big deep breath. Made himself still and thought about all the things that were important in life, and that he'd royally fuck up if he did what he wanted to.

Harry turned away from Marilyn and stared out into the bar, deliberately cold, purposefully ignoring the pure lily-scented draw of her. 'Yer no good enough,' he said, his voice iron. It was the bare truth of it, and he wasn't talking only about her singing any more than she was.

Marilyn recoiled like she'd been slapped. Just for a moment, the mask lifted on that disguise she seemed to wear, and he saw the pain of all of it in her eyes. But she needed told, that was the problem. She was the kind of woman that needed told.

Marilyn held his gaze. Her eyes narrowed and he saw hate there; pure, unbridled hate. The strength of emotion Harry had only ever felt for people he loved. He tried to swallow that idea and repeated those words again, the ones that he was sure were true.

This woman will be the death of me.

Marilyn grabbed her drink and swivelled on one heel, stomping through the bar hatch and to the other side, then slamming the door before heading upstairs. Men's heads turned again at the sound but they looked away quickly and awkwardly. All except Bobby, who glanced at the door, then at Harry, then at the door again, eyes brimming with concern.

Harry closed his eyes, blinking the room out of existence. He couldn't help thinking he'd made a very big mistake indeed.

November 2017

HEART

New build housing estate, East Leake, Nottingham

This was Sian's idea of hell; the big estate full of similar looking houses where her brother and Ginny lived. The more she thought about Tom and his 2.3 children and steady job in finance, the more she wondered how she could have ever imagined that she was related to him. Sian parked across Tom's drive, getting out and leaning against the car for a moment. She hadn't even worked out what she would say to Ruth when she saw her and steeled herself for how seeing her mother might make her feel after what she'd found out. Sian limped down the front path; she'd finally managed to learn to walk again without the crutches, but the cast on her foot still made progress slow and difficult. She rang the doorbell and waited. She would usually have knocked and walked straight in but she needed the extra minutes to compose herself before she saw her mother.

Tom opened the door. 'Oh, hello,' he said, kissing her on one cheek, then the other. 'Come in.' He looked past her and down the street as if he were expecting someone else.

Sian did as she was told, removing the trainer from her good foot and placing it with the neat line of shoes in the porch. 'Is Mum in?' she said.

'No,' he said. 'She's actually gone to stay with a friend for a couple of nights. In Sheffield.'

'Oh,' she said. 'OK.' She felt her jaw and stomach muscles release, surprised at how tense she'd been. Probably for the best,' she said.

'Probably.' Tom smiled. 'Would you like a drink? Ginny's just putting the girls to bed. Tea, coffee, something stronger?'

'Driving,' Sian said. 'But a glass of pop or something?'

'Sure,' Tom said. He disappeared into the kitchen.

Sian walked over to the smart beige sofa and sat down. She always worried in this house that she might spill things and leave stains. It was so beautiful, so perfect, and she was so good at spilling things and ruining everything. How they maintained this level of cream-coloured perfection with twin toddlers and a ten-year-old boy was beyond her.

Tom returned with a glass of cola, which he handed to Sian. She should have asked specifically for something colourless; lemonade, or even water. She took a deep sip from the glass then placed it down carefully on the coffee table.

'While Ginny's not here, Tom, this isn't exactly a social call.' She cleared her throat. 'Not just a social call, anyway.'

Tom's blue eyes looked vivid against all the cream and white in the room. She saw that all too familiar frown twist up the middle of his forehead. It always made her smile.

'It's about mum,' Sian said, thinking curse him and his blue eyes, his *real* parents.

'What about mum?' Tom looked worried.

'She's not sick or anything.' It was Sian's turn to frown. 'Well, not as far as I'm aware. Mate, you are always going to be the one giving me that kind of news. How can you not know that?'

The smile on Tom's face was tight and he still looked worried. 'OK,' he said.

'I don't think she's my real mum.'

Tom stared at her, his face dancing with thoughts as he tried to make sense of what she'd said. 'You what?'

'You heard me.'

'Sian, if she wasn't your mum, you'd have found out years ago. You must have had your birth certificate along the way. To apply for a bank account. Passports.'

'That's the thing. It's her name on all the forms and official documents but I have good reason to believe it's all lies.'

Tom's frown was cutting deeper and he was shaking his head. 'You're starting to sound a bit mad,' he said. Then, backtracking slightly, 'You know, paranoid.' He couldn't help but be nice, even though Sian could see he was feeling very uncomfortable.

'David's name's on my birth certificate too, you know,' she said.

'You could still call him Dad, being as he brought you up.' Tom sounded offended on his deceased father's behalf.

'It's Dad's name on my birth certificate. And we know he's not; at least, not the man who provided the sperm.'

'Sian!'

'Sorry, but how else should I put it? I'm just trying to be precise.' She swallowed. 'Look, this is hard to explain, really, but I have a good reason to suspect that it's neither of them, my biological parents. A really good reason.' She paused for breath. 'A scientific reason.'

'I thought you'd sorted this out years ago.'

Sian shrugged. 'Not really. Mum never would tell me the full story, and something new has come to light.'

'To do with the bodies they found?' Tom said. He'd made that leap rather quicker than she was expecting.

Sian took another sip of the ice-cold cola, buying enough time to consider her options. But she didn't like lying to Tom. 'Yes,' she said, finally. 'But I'm not going to go into details. You just have to believe me.' She made eye contact with her brother. 'Please.'

'Fine,' he said. He'd always had a way of making this word sound like the ultimate concession.

'Listen,' Sian said, quietly. 'Please. Will you talk to her? Find out? I don't think I can cope with trying to catch her here again.'

Tom looked at Sian in a deeply appraising way. 'You probably shouldn't ambush her, anyway.'

Sian was startled by the bang as Ginny dashed into the room, coming through the door in a rush somewhere. 'Oh hi, darling,' she said. She vaguely air kissed in Sian's direction and then ran through to the kitchen, calling back, like an afterthought, 'I hope you got your sister a drink, Tommy!'

Ignoring his wife, Tom stared at Sian. 'I'll try,' he said. 'But I can't promise I'll get anywhere with this.' He ran a hand through his dark blond hair. 'She's not going to take this well if you're wrong.'

'I know.' Sian leaned back and reached for a cushion. She was beginning to feel more at home despite the perfection around her. 'But I'm not wrong.'

'Rule one, Sian is always right. Rule two, if Sian is wrong, see rule one.' A light danced in her brother's eyes as he recited the motto his mother had made up when she was younger. Sian had used to laugh along but she found she couldn't any more.

Ginny's head appeared around the door, her tastefully highlighted hair swinging as she talked. 'Sianey, can I get you something? A V and T or a glass of wine?'

Sian shook her head, and motioned at the glass in front of her. 'I'm driving,' she said.

'Oh, never mind that.' Ginny waved a hand dismissively. 'I'll make you my perfect under the limit voddie and slim, you'll be fine. Honestly.'

Sian shrugged and thought that at least the drink was colourless. 'Sure,' she said. 'But take it really easy on the vodka. My car is hired and I can't afford—'

'Oh, trust me, darling, it's fine.' And Ginny was off as quickly as she'd arrived.

'Whatever you do, don't drink the whole glass,' Tom told her, with a smile.

Sian smiled back. 'Mate, I knew Ginny for two years before you even met her.'

Tom grinned.

Ginny returned with the drinks. She handed Sian the glass of clear liquid with a conspiratorial wink. 'You can get a taxi,' she said. 'I'll pay.'

Sian took a sip and realised she would have to unless she left it at that one mouthful. It was almost strong enough to make her cough and left her throat feeling pleasantly warm.

'Stay for dinner?' Ginny said. Her demeanour was considerably warmer than the last time Sian had seen her, but perhaps the sting of Rob's will had worn off for her by now. Ginny, after all, was from a very posh family and didn't need the money. It had been the principle of the thing, she'd said loudly, just after the will was read. The extra little gift that had been left for Sian to find in the cellar of her inheritance had probably changed Ginny's mind.

'OK,' Sian said, thinking that it would be nice to spend some time with Tom and Ginny. She looked nervously at the pair of them, wondering if they felt at all the same way about her.

BREAK

Loggerheads

The taxi swung over to the pavement at the side of the Loggerheads. Sian paid and climbed out. She wasn't too drunk, despite having consumed a number of Ginny's lethal cocktails, but she caught her cast on the edge of the kerb as she got out and stumbled slightly. The taxi sped into the distance, as if the driver couldn't get away fast enough. Suddenly, Cliff Road looked dark and lonely. Sian pulled her keys from her coat pocket and reached for the door, unlocking it and slipping into the pub. She hoped that Kris was still awake.

Elvis piled over, sniffing her then heading towards the kitchen when he realised she wasn't carrying anything edible. Sian smiled at his optimism as she walked in and saw him sitting like a good boy by the cupboard where she kept his treats. She placed her bag down on the table and found him something chewy and chicken-flavoured from the cupboard. He ran off to hide in a corner with it.

She heard the stairs creak as Kris came down to find her. He walked into the kitchen wearing just his boxers and looking mussed up.

'Hey,' she said, leaning in to kiss him.

Kris lightly kissed her back then moved away, his face very serious.

'What's wrong?' she said.

'Sit down, please, Sian. I need to talk to you about something.'

Sian held on to the pasting table as she lowered herself on to a chair, her eyes not leaving his face.

'Dominic Wilkinson came to see me this evening when I was on shift,' Kris told her.

She swallowed. 'OK,' she said.

'He says he's not messing around anymore. He threatened to arrest you if you didn't stop.'

Sian laughed then, a dark, bitter sound, and she leaned back in the fold-out chair. 'At least he's got the balls to come out and say it now,' she said.

'He mentioned Gary again. And other people, higher-ups, some proper gangsters.' Kris ran his fingers through his hair. 'I don't think we should mess about with this, Sian. I don't think your uncle would've wanted you to put yourself in danger.'

She pushed herself to standing, carefully, to avoid putting too much pressure on her foot in the cast. Then she went looking in the kitchen cupboards for something strong to drink. She needed something to wash away the feeling that hearing her ex-boyfriend's name had left her with. She found a bottle of vodka and some tonic, and pulled two glasses from the cupboard without checking that Kris wanted one. She noticed that there was a bunch of flowers in the sink.

'What are those for?' she asked.

Kris shrugged. 'Dunno. Someone left them on the doorstep.'

Sian poured the drinks and handed one to Kris. Then she walked back over to the sink and picked up the bouquet, removing the plastic from the outside. They were white lilies; wide open and beautiful with massive stamens and an intense musky smell. She breathed them in and found all sorts of memories came with the scent; bizarre, elemental feelings that made her feel nauseated and sad. 'Funeral flowers,' she said, looking for a card.

'They're pretty,' Kris said. 'It was nice of someone.'

'You're such a beacon of optimism.' Sian meant this as a compliment but it sounded sarcastic.

'I'm worried about you,' Kris said.

'You're not allowed to worry about me,' she told him, digging into the flowers for a card. 'You can be concerned...' She trailed off as her hand found a small black envelope and she pulled it out. She opened it. It was a simple card, black on one side and white on the other so that a note could be written there. Perhaps these weren't for her at all but had been sent to the Loggerheads by old friends of Harry and Angela who'd read about what had been found here in the papers. But then she saw the writing, that familiar, old-fashioned style written with a blue biro:

I know about all the things you love.

'Sian, are you OK?' It felt like Kris's voice was coming from a long way away and, for some reason, she couldn't reply.

Sian reached for her bag and pulled out the note she'd been given at the care home to compare it. The scent from the flowers was becoming overwhelming, foggy and cloying. It was getting up her throat and stopping her from breathing.

'Sian!' She was sure the voice was Kris but where was he? Outside or in another room? She couldn't see him, but she could hear his voice.

Sian was in another room too. In another time and place, one that was really confusing. The dark air smelled like the lilies she was holding. There was a voice. It screamed. *No!* The sound filled her up and vibrated through her. It was her uncle's voice and he sounded really frightened.

March 1971
He's Gonna Step On You Again

The Loggerheads pub

Angela's legs were aching and she longed to sit down. She could hardly wait until eleven when the bar closed so she could tidy up and go to bed. Going to bed had become her favourite thing in the world. Sleep was wonderful. She knew she had a shock coming when the baby did because her mum had told her that often enough the first time she'd been pregnant.

Harry was settled on a table in the middle of the room with Paul Parker and some other blokes Angela didn't know. He looked up and raised a finger when she caught his eye, and she nodded back at him. Angela poured a pint of mild and a lager and lime for Paul and took them to the men, her eyes filming over with fatigue.

Angela put the pints down heavily on the table and pushed out a smile. 'Anyone else?'

Harry nodded around the table and the men called out orders. Angela hoped she would remember them all. As she headed back to the bar she heard Harry's voice, proclaiming what a good girl she was. She didn't feel good. There was a hot acid feeling in her stomach towards Harry that made her want to hurt him. She had dreams and visions of carving knives and heavy objects, and Harry, dead on the floor. She wished she could stop it, but she couldn't.

When Angela returned to the table, she placed the drinks down and the men ignored her. Not one turned in her direction and she felt invisible. She stood a while and listened. Harry was waxing lyrical about Pat, again. He was waving his arms around and his accent was getting thicker, 'Ah've been let down one time too many,' he said. 'I cannay continue like this, ye get me?' He glanced around at the men fixing each of them with his eyes, one after another, as if getting together a gang for something. 'We need tay stand up to the bastard,' he said. 'Show him he cannay do what the fuck he likes round here.'

Angela stared. She didn't like Harry saying these things about Pat. He'd told her himself that there were two things she needed to know about the big man, and that the first was you didn't talk about him. Besides, Pat had looked after her when Jack came looking for trouble again and she didn't understand. Harry should have been grateful but was angry, instead telling everyone that it was *his* job to protect his wife.

'He's full o' the proverbial,' he said, his accent stretching that last word. 'He promised us this and that and the world on a spoon, and he hasnay come up with the goods.' He gestured with his pint, as if holding a beer amplified his point. 'He insisted on all that new gear and wouldnay listen to reason on it. That fucked us, that did.' Angela couldn't believe the outright lie, even coming from Harry. The things he said were usually half true, at least.

Harry carried on, full of ire and blackness towards the man he'd once seemed to worship. As Angela stood listening, something changed. His eyes brightened and widened and his voice lowered and she saw all of the men get closer, tighter to him.

'I ken all the fucker's dirty little secrets,' he said. His face twisted into a smile that looked demonic in the half light of the pub. He lowered his voice further still and told the men something, but Angela couldn't make out what he was saying.

Harry glanced up then, and noticed Angela staring. 'Are'ye alright there, hen?' he said. The words were friendly enough, but Angela could hear the menace in them.

'I'm fine,' Angela said.

'Aye, ye'are.' Harry said. He narrowed his eyes and leaned back with his pint.

Angela took the hint and turned, walking back to the bar. She was shaking as she walked away. She'd never felt scared of Harry before, but she did now.

Would he beat her up like Jack used to? She didn't think so. Would he bring other kinds of trouble to her door? Well, that was a different matter.

Angela cupped two hands over her baby bump and rubbed. The baby kicked and she smiled. She'd do anything to protect the little child growing there. The little girl, she'd convinced herself. Her mam had always wanted a granddaughter. She'd a name saved for one and everything, and told all her daughters that she wanted them to call the first-born girl Sian. Angela hadn't seen her mother for over a year but the name was still there, in her head, although she wasn't totally sure she'd use it.

For a while, Angela had told herself that Harry would keep them safe, her and the baby. He'd protect his little family from anything that threatened it. But she was no longer sure that he wasn't the biggest threat to them both.

It was too late, now, though. The baby would be here soon enough, whether Angela was ready or Harry was fit or not. Her time would come around the way these things did, and the idea of being single with a baby was worse than the idea of being with Harry. Angela couldn't see any way out at all.

Another Day

The Loggerheads pub

Bobby slammed the door and stormed downstairs. His wife was impossible. She'd got worse lately, all hot and emotional from the inside out, and he just didn't know what was going on with her. How had he ended up married to her? Bloody Harry McKenzie, that was how; he never should have listened to the bleeder.

It was quiet downstairs, the punters all finished and gone off for the night. Bobby wished he could go off from this place. Moving in with the other three had seemed like a grand idea back when Harry had suggested it, but now the place felt like his punishment for something. Only he couldn't think of one thing he'd done bad enough for this.

He lit up, taking a deep drag and putting the fag packet down on the table in the back room. He heard the low rumble of voices from the public bar and realised that Harry hadn't quite finished in there. Who was he talking to?

It was dark in the bar, the lights all switched off, but there were two voices; Harry's Scottish growl and the unmistakable cockney of Big Pat Walsh. Bobby's skin cooled and crawled as he realised who Harry was talking to. Big Pat staying behind after closing time could not be good. This was not their usual kind of lock-in.

'All right,' Bobby said, flicking on a light.
Pat held up a hand, his eyes screwed up against the brightness.
Harry was gazing at the table in a trance and didn't flinch.

'Not so bad, Bobby Q. Just telling Harry how we need to watch for people giving me a slagging.' Pat had his usual pint of Guinness in front of him but he wasn't drinking. 'I've heard that there are a few folks what have been, see,' he said. 'There's all sorts of rumours doing the rounds and, some of it, well, it's not very nice, Robert my friend. Not very nice at all. The kind of crap that would get me in a lot of trouble with the missus. You know anything about any of this?'

'No,' Bobby said. 'I haven't heard owt like that.' He balanced his fag on the side of an ashtray and poured himself a pint. He walked over and sat at the table with the other two. He offered the packet of cigarettes round. Harry and Pat took one each and then Harry got out his lighter; a big, heavy silver one with a Scottish flag on the front.

'See, I've heard different,' Pat said, blowing out smoke from his first drag. He gritted his teeth and made a sucking sound. 'Very different.' His eyes met Harry's. They gave the impression of something hard and immovable.

Harry gestured at his own chest, looking incredulous. 'Ye talking about me?' he said. Pat nodded in response and Harry's eyes grew wider and wider. 'That's just rubbish!' He held his cigarette in front of him and waved it from one to the other of the men sitting with him. 'Ye tell me who the fuck said that. I'm no having nay bastard spreading shite like that about me.'

'See,' Pat flicked ash then took another drag, turning his head to the side, 'I heard different. I heard you ain't very happy with me. At all.'

Harry laughed, nervously. Bobby stared at him; had Harry been saying stuff? Because he'd known Harry a fuck of a long time, and he'd never seen him look as shady as he did right now. He wouldn't put it past him to be so stupid, but he'd not heard any of it himself, and that was strange if it was something Harry was saying.

'I heard,' Pat said, his voice rising like a song, 'that you ain't at all bothered about what I hear. That you've told a few folks round here that I can bring it on, that you're waiting.'

Something on Harry's face changed. Hardened. Bobby didn't like the way this was going at all. Harry was going to get them both killed, and their wives upstairs too. Bobby's argument with Marilyn felt silly now and all he wanted to do was go up and hold her in his arms, be there to protect her.

'Now, listen pal,' Harry said, putting his pint glass down firmly on the table. 'I don't wanttay get a wee bit nasty here, but I will if I need to. You get me?'

Pat looked at Harry, a half-smile dancing on his lips. Harry was getting into it now. He gesticulated as he spoke. 'Frankly, this shite pisses me off. People trying to stir things up between us.'

'Harry—'

But Harry didn't give Pat time to say whatever was on his mind. He banged the table, hard, and stood up. 'If ye're gony believe any auld bollocks you're tellt by whatever shower of shite's saying this, then that's yer look out,' Harry shouted.

Pat stood up, his height making him look like he was unfolding. 'Oh yeah?' he said, towering above the both of them.

'Aye,' Harry said, almost on tiptoes in an effort to get into Pat's face. 'That's right.'

'Guys, guys.' Bobby stood up and tried to get between them but Pat pushed him out of the way like he was made of paper.

'I wouldn't get in my face, Harry, if I were you. If I knew what was good for myself.'

'Ye wouldnay, eh?' Harry didn't move.

'I hear that's not all you been saying. I hear you've been spreading nasty, dirty little rumours too.'

'Oh aye?' Harry stood defiant for a moment, his mouth set in a tight line. Then he nodded, and stepped back, holding up both hands in a gesture of surrender. 'Ye're gony have tay excuse me, pal. But I'm offended by all this ye been listening to. That ye pay these trouble merchants any mind at all!' Harry sounded truly slighted. 'Now, thing is, there's two lassies up them stairs and one of them with a wean on the way, and we don't want nay trouble. Not any of us, do we, eh?' Harry's voice was almost a whisper but Bobby thought he heard the edge of a threat there.

Pat stared at Harry as if he couldn't believe what he was hearing. He took a step closer again and the two men were kissing distance from each other. Pat's eyes looked set to bore holes right through Harry's head and Bobby prayed he hadn't got a gun with him to follow through on that. Then Harry held up both hands and stood down a second time.

'I didnay say a fucking thing,' he said. 'Not a dickie bird about ye. Never.'

Pat held up both hands in a conciliatory gesture. 'All right,' he said. 'All right.' He looked Harry straight in the eye. 'The person what told me is usually straight as a die and I've no reason not to believe him, but all right.' He sounded resigned, worn down by Harry's insistence.

'Well, mibbe ye need to have a second think about who ye listen to,' Harry said. 'Ye get me?'

Pat looked dubious. But something that Harry had done or said must have put enough doubt in his mind. He nodded. 'Fine,' he said. 'But if I find out this is more bullshit, I'll be back. And next time, I won't be asking no questions.'

Harry nodded at that. He lit another cigarette. 'That'd be well within ye rights, aye.'

Pat Walsh grabbed up car keys and stood up. 'No questions,' he said, to Harry, pointing a finger at the space between his eyes. Then he looked across at Bobby. 'You're my witness, right?' Bobby nodded back at him.

Harry was all smiles as he let Pat out of the pub and Bobby noticed that the big man had barely touched that Guinness. He picked it up and started drinking it himself.

The door closed behind Pat and they both heard the sound of his car starting. There was the growl of the engine, and then the sound as it disappeared into the night.

When the room was silent again, Harry raised a glass. 'To getting tay that bastard first,' he said, with a grin and a wink.

Bobby couldn't help but smile back and raised his glass for the toast but he found it difficult to swallow Pat's Guinness. Something had passed between the two other men back there, something that Bobby didn't know about. Whatever it was, they were both keeping it secret from him, and he didn't like that one little bit.

November 2017

DOWN

Loggerheads

Sian opened the door. Her brother Tom stood there, looking up the street, then he realised the door had opened and turned towards her.

'You look a right mess,' he said.

'Thanks,' she said. She opened the door to let him through. 'I am.'

'Kris rang mum. She's beside herself but I told her I'd sort it.' He frowned and looked down at his phone. 'Just going to message her and let her know that you're OK before she comes over herself!' He looked down at his phone and typed, using both thumbs like a teenager. He looked up at her again. 'Where is he, anyway?'

'Night shift,' she said. 'Come in. I'm getting cold.'

Fifteen minutes later, Sian was drinking hot chocolate on the sofa and had managed three bites of a Marks and Spencer's sandwich Tom had picked up on the way. The TV was on, playing episodes of *Friends*, something that her brother knew calmed her. He'd fed and let out Elvis too, and the dog had been for a good bark and was now settled in his basket. Tom sat on the chair with his feet up, watching her. She couldn't help thinking that he looked much more like himself here in the scruffy old Loggerheads than he did surrounded by all that white and cream in his own house.

'I'm going to run you a bath,' he said.

Sian nodded and then looked at the TV screen. It was safe there. It was still the 20th century, and New York City was small, quaint, hand-painted with all the right prints on the wall and a coffee shop with a sofa and six people who would do anything for one another.

Tom's head appeared around the living room door. 'The bath needs a clean,' he said.

'Everything here does,' Sian said. 'You should see the cellar!'

He shrugged and went off to look for the right equipment. He was back ten minutes later to tell her the water was running.

'I'll go up in a minute,' she said, knowing that Tom would be kind, and wouldn't nag her. Wouldn't make her go anywhere until she was ready to.

'It's weird being back here,' he said.

'Tell me about it.' Sian stared at the screen. One of the characters was dressed up as an armadillo and she couldn't help but smile.

Tom picked up the remote and flicked off the television. 'I spoke to mum,' he said.

'Right.'

'She's being weird about it,' he said. 'Says she's not going to talk to me; that it's not my business.'

Sian felt her lips curl into a very strange smile. 'Sounds about right,' she said. 'If she can't lie, she ain't talking.'

'Sian, come on.'

She straightened the cushion behind her. Her fingers itched for the remote control, desperate to watch comforting TV again rather than talk about this. 'Did you ask her? If she's even my mother.'

'I did.'

'And?'

Tom looked concerned, angry even. 'She said it was between you and her and that if you wanted to talk about it, you needed to go and see her.'

Sian let out a short, bitter laugh. 'And she'll tell me the truth? Like she's got such a record for.'

Tom shrugged. 'I asked her about me. If her and David were my birth parents. She was adamant that they were. Told me I could do a DNA test if I wanted, she didn't care. She had nothing to hide.'

Sian felt her teeth grit harder. 'That says it all,' she said.

'Well, I can see why you say that.' He reached a hand out and touched her arm. If it had been anybody else, Sian would have batted his hand away, but Tom was allowed. 'I'm not sure myself. Not anymore. I never thought I'd say that.' He looked down at the floor. 'I thought you were being paranoid. But the way she acted when I brought it up; I've not seen her like that before.'

Sian breathed in, then out. It felt like all the tension was going out of her. To be believed was so important.

'Did you DNA test the bodies?' Tom asked her.

Sian nodded, slightly disturbed that he had guessed this so easily. 'I'm pretty sure Angela's my real mum,' Sian said.

'Well, the Scottish thing would explain all the drinking and junk food,' he said.

'Bit racist!' she said. 'Anyway, she wasn't Scottish, that was Harry and I don't think he's my dad. The way the tests work out, if Angela's my mum, he can't be. Well, provided it really was the pair of them I found down there.'

They were both silent for a while, Tom looking thoughtful.

'Fancy a spliff?' she asked him.

'Jezuz, what are you, sixteen?' Tom's voice had the edge of a squeak to it. 'You still smoke that stuff?'

'Occasionally,' she said. Then, an afterthought, 'It's medicinal.'

'OK.' His face twisted into a cheeky grin and Sian felt like she had got him back, the younger man he used to be, before he started to dissolve in vodka and Ginny and perfect cream walls.

She pulled a tin from a shelf behind the fireplace and took out a joint. 'One I made earlier,' she said. She sparked up, had a few drags then passed it to Tom. They smoked in companionable silence for several minutes.

'You gonna get in the bath?' Tom asked her, eventually, his voice warm from the weed. 'Then I'll order in some Chinese and get some proper food inside you before you waste away.'

Sian laughed. 'Not much chance of that,' she said. She took one last drag and handed the dog-end of the joint to him, heading upstairs.

The bathroom door was open and the scent of bubble bath and candles leaked out on to the landing. Tom had laid out clean pyjamas and a big bath towel. The room was spotless too; much cleaner than it had been at any point since she'd moved in. She didn't deserve her lovely brother. She was glad she had him, though, even though he might not be related to her at all.

Sian undressed then climbed into the bath, balancing her bad foot over the side so that she didn't get the cast wet. The water was lovely and warm, and the bubbles held on to her like a hug. She thought about her parents; the ones who'd brought her up. Yes, they'd lied to her. But they'd looked after her, too, and God knows she hadn't been an easy child. They were good people; Ruth was a good person, despite all of the lies. Sian thought about all the harsh things she'd said to Ruth since her uncle had died. She cried then. Her tears came out hot and fierce and killed bubbles as they fell.

The tears subsided, and Sian lay there as the water cooled. She got out and sat on the side of the bath, drying her body down and wrapping the towel around herself. She stared at her face in the mirror on the opposite wall. Her eyeliner and mascara had run, and it looked like a dark smudge of kohl around her eyes, which made her look more like Angela than ever. She rubbed at her hair, trying to force it dry. For some reason, Jack Donnelly came into her head. It was the text of his name that she remembered as if it were a picture, in a modern, computer-formatted font. But that hadn't been how she'd seen his name, on that note, in the cursive handwriting. The memory that had come back was text on a screen. From where?

It all came back to Sian in such a rush that she dropped the towel and stared into the mirror, shivering. She remembered where she'd seen Jack's name for the very first time and it hadn't been on that note. It had been a marriage record on the genealogy website, one that she'd dismissed as belonging to a completely different Angela Callaghan. But what if it hadn't? What if Jack Donnelly was not random at all?

Sian hurriedly climbed into her pyjamas. She limped from the room and downstairs. She needed her laptop and to login to that site again, right away, to find out if what she suspected was true.

DIRT

Beeston Care Home, Nottingham

Even from the car park, the nursing home looked oppressive; the kind of building you knew would be far too hot inside. Sian wandered in, signing as Marilyn Monroe in the book at the door and then letting herself through with the same security code as the last time she'd visited. It was early evening and, as she walked through the corridors, she could hear a woman screaming. It sounded like the poor soul was being tortured.

The care home was dark and empty. The shouts of the woman were getting louder and Sian felt her stomach contract. She was having a visceral reaction to the place, and it made her swallow and hesitate, thinking weird thoughts about the kinds of things she didn't believe in. Then she was at Jack's door, looking at his picture. She walked into the room.

Jack's bed was empty. The curtains were closed but the window was open, a breeze sucking then blowing the chintzy material in an inhuman way. Sian walked further into the room and looked for signs of life. Had the old man died just as she'd found him? Surely she couldn't be that unlucky?

A hairbrush was sitting on a table beside the bed. It was a bit of a fallacy about hair; unless the root was still attached, it wasn't a great source of DNA. But seeing the brush made Sian wonder. She walked through to the bathroom and reached for the toothbrush; saliva was a much better prospect. Then she heard the door to the room open. She shoved the brush into her pocket.

There was a woman's voice, and then Jack's, deeper and wavering. Sian had a choice. She could hide in the bathroom and maybe get caught anyway or she could style it out. She decided on the latter, and walked into the room.

Jack saw her first. His eyes met hers and she thought she saw recognition there, but he said nothing. Then the woman looked up from putting the brakes on the wheelchair and saw her. She jumped at the unexpected sight, her jaw snapping. 'Who are you?' she said, her voice high and raspy.

Sian considered her options. The woman wasn't wearing a uniform, so she was visiting Jack. 'I'm looking for my dad,' she said. It wasn't far from the truth.

The woman's eyes widened. 'But this is *my* dad.' She looked stricken, as if she were discovering a nasty family secret. Sian knew all about that.

'Yes, so I see,' Sian said. 'Which means I have the wrong room.' The woman looked relieved, her breathing deepening. 'Thank God for that!' she said, a hand moving to her chest. 'You frightened me for a minute there.' A little, light laugh. 'Thought I had family I'd never met.'

Sian tried not to stare. Was this her half-sister? She didn't look anything like Sian, but she knew that didn't always mean that much. She hadn't considered the idea that Jack might have gone on to have another family but she suddenly realised that she might have any number of siblings.

'Phew,' the woman said.

Sian made a show of mock wiping her brow and they both laughed. Sian smiled, and left the room.

Walking back down the hallway and towards the stairs, Sian realised she was shaking and her heart was racing like mad. She tried to centre herself. She looked for the toothbrush and realised she'd shoved it straight into her pocket, brush side first. Hardly the best way to keep the sample pure. She'd almost certainly contaminated the brush with her own DNA and it would be no good for a paternity test now. She popped it into a bin on the way out.

Sian climbed into her car. She sighed and started the engine. That had been a close one. She needed to be so much more careful than this.

By the time Sian had got her breathing and heart rate back to normal and was properly focused on her driving, she noticed a car in her rear-view mirror; a smart black Mercedes. It seemed to be stuck to the back end of her hire car. She tried to look at the driver but the windows were tinted illegally dark and she could only make out vague shapes. She turned left, then right into a small road. The Mercedes was still right behind her.

Sian cut through a housing estate and pulled out on to the ring road. She booted down, accelerating and slipping right across into the fast lane. She shot up to the speed limit and then a little faster. The car was still there, in her rear-view mirror. It was definitely following her. Her heart started beating faster again.

The road was unusually quiet for the time of night. Sian wondered if there was a big football match on the TV. She thought about where to go, how to lose this tail. The wrong turn here and she might end up on an industrial estate somewhere, on a lonely road near factories and warehouses that were closed for the night. The retail park was a better idea.

Pulling off at the next exit, Sian took the left from the round-about faster than she was intending, and she had to work to keep control of the car. The black Mercedes was still on her tail. She tried not to panic. She headed up into the main car park and towards B&Q. She drove around the car park. Checking her mirror, Sian could see no sign of the black car. She pulled over into a parking space near the motorbike shop, which was closed.

Sian sat in the car, staring out of the windscreen. She could feel the pump of her heart and did some breathing exercises to try to slow everything down. This was ridiculous. Who the hell did she think was following her? Jack Donnelly? Or Gary Bolton, the mad, bad ex?

The name set fireworks going in her head again. Sian closed her eyes. She heard the screech of tyres and didn't know if it was real or imagined. She opened her eyes and looked into the rear-view mirror. The Mercedes had pulled up behind her and skidded to a halt. She saw the door open. A man got out, tall and dark in a suit and heavy black coat. She couldn't see his face. She held her breath as he walked like a shadow towards her.

May 1971
There Goes My Everything

The Loggerheads pub

Bobby stretched his hands out to Marilyn in a gesture that was almost pleading. Her mouth opened and closed, and he saw spit lining her lips, tiny droplets flying from her mouth across the room. She was screaming, her voice loud and harsh, but he was focused on her twisted-up face, and on her mouth, and he didn't take in any of the hurtful words she said. He'd become the master of removing himself. Marilyn hadn't been herself for ages but since she'd given birth to a baby, a surprise to them all, she'd become an unfathomable, emotional wreck and Bobby had no idea what to do to help her.

'What's wrong with you!' she yelled. Then, not getting a reaction, she got closer and closer, her teeth gritted like she wanted to bite him. She bashed her arms on his chest in percussion to the screaming. 'What! Is! Wrong! With! You!'

Bobby put one hand on each of her shoulders and held her, lightly. 'You need to stop this,' he said, making an effort to keep his voice gentle and level. 'I'm just trying to understand it, duck. Why you never said you was pregnant.' Their little girl had come suddenly, and early enough she'd needed to stop at the hospital. All of this had taken the wind right out of him and he didn't know what to think. 'You need to calm down and talk to me.'

'You what?' She spat the words with some venom. 'You don't get to tell me what to do, you bloody bastard.'

Won't Get Fooled Again

The Loggerheads pub

Harry was carrying around a small bin and emptying ashtrays into it. He could hear the sound of banging doors above him. Those two at it again. He was beginning to think they should go their separate ways but he knew Bobby would never do that. Not with a wean here. She'd kept that pregnancy quiet and Harry was pretty sure he knew the reason why. He just hoped Bobby didn't find out.

The door shot open and Bobby followed it. Harry took one look at him and knew something serious had gone down between them upstairs. Bobby didn't take any shite but Harry had never seen him look so loose and out of control.

'What's a matter?' Harry said, putting down the bin and walking towards him. But things were worse than he'd realised. He held both hands up and got closer to Bobby and the face on him; he looked ready to lift his fists and punch Harry. The shorter man was on guard and ready to punch first if necessary. But Bobby gritted his teeth and held himself, and Harry read it correctly but kept just out of reach all the same, so that his pal would have to lunge for him to land a punch.

Bobby tried to open his mouth to say something then his face crumpled. He swallowed, and pulled himself together. 'Marilyn says it's yours.'

Harry stared dumbly in Bobby's direction. What was his? He didn't get it. But then he looked at the state of his friend and he knew. The little bitch.

'Away and shite,' Harry said. 'She didnay say that.'

Bobby stepped towards him. His face was red and wet from tears. 'I thought you were my best friend,' he said.

Harry put one arm on each of his pal's shoulders. 'Aye, I am,' he said. He held Bobby up, made him look right at him. 'I am, Bob, pal. Ye and me.' He cleared his throat, then made a fist with one hand and struck his own chest. 'Brothers.' He felt a sharp, hard pain in his throat and swallowed it. 'I swear it on me auld ma's grave,' he said, striking his chest over and over again. 'I wouldnay do that. I truly wouldnay.'

'Then why would she say that?' Bobby's words were warped by tears. 'Why would she say that, Harry, if it weren't true?'

'Damned if I ken anything about wimmin.' He shrugged. 'Why do they say any o' the shite they say?' he said. He slapped Bobby on the back. 'Come on, pal. You know that's pish.' He really stressed that final word, put all of the power of his emotion into it, and it sounded convincing, even to him.

Harry slipped through the bar hatch and grabbed a bottle of whisky from the back, two glasses. He took them over to a table and sat down. 'Join me for a wee dram, man.' He made it sound compulsory.

Bobby sat opposite him. 'Why would she say that?' he said, again.

Harry poured them both drinks and put the bottle down firmly on the table. He felt in control now. Say it like you mean it and persuade yourself; that was the secret to talking round anyone. 'I have-nay the first clue why the fuck she'd say something so nasty,' Harry said. 'The only thing I can think is that it had something to do with the other night.' He took a sip from the whisky, savouring its ashy bite.

'What went off the other night?' Bobby said. He stared into his own glass of whisky. Finally, he took a sip, and pulled a face with the burn of it.

Harry sighed, and sat back in his chair, as if preparing himself for the reveal. 'Look, she came tay see me. All full of this pish about being lead singer for the Roses. But I wasnay having it.' He was shaking his head. 'She isnay a singer, we both ken that, not a lead singer anyway. Yer lassie is easy on the eye, but that isnay enough to carry a band.' Harry did his best to look serious and tragic and sad about it. 'I tellt her it wasnay happening. I guess I may have tellt her a bit harsher than I'd meant to.'

Bobby stared at him. He looked like he wanted to believe it, but he wasn't quite there yet.

'I tellt her she wasnay good enough,' Harry said. 'That was a wee bit cruel. I could see I'd really upset the poor lassie and was sorry straightaway, but she stormed off afore I could make it right.'

Bobby narrowed his eyes at Harry. 'You sure that's all what went off?'

Harry nodded, reaching a hand to Bobby's shoulder. 'Between ye, me and that wall, I've heard ye pair at it hammer and tongues. It isnay going well, eh?'

'No,' Bobby admitted. 'It's getting worse since she had the baby.'

'Well, that isnay a surprise with her all hormonal.' He let out a small, bitter laugh, waving a hand like he was conjuring up the idea. 'That post-natal whatnot they talk about. It can send 'em a bit mental, eh?'

Bobby nodded. 'Yeah,' he said. 'I heard it can.'

Harry rubbed the space between Bobby's shoulder blades in a circular, comforting motion. He could feel the tension slip out of his pal.

'So, you reckon she's lying to get you back for saying she weren't a good singer?' Bobby said.

Harry leaned in closer; like he had a secret to tell. This always worked. Bobby leaned closer too and the atmosphere changed between them.

'Naw, more than that,' Harry told him. 'She's lying to get tay us both. Me, for saying she isnay good enough to be lead singer. And ye for making her fat and sad down tay the wean.' Harry shook his head and rolled his eyes. 'Ye'd be surprised at what wimmin can end up getting into their heads!' he said. He shook Bobby by one shoulder in an encouraging way.

Bobby finally smiled, although it looked like an effort. 'You promise me this is the truth?'

'I'll swear it on my own life. On the life of my wean in that belly up there!' Harry said, pointing up the stairs.

'OK.' Bobby looked finally convinced.

The two men downed their drinks. Harry poured some more and held up his glass for a toast. They clinked glasses and Harry tried to drown the blackness that was welling in his stomach. He'd gone too far. You didn't make promises on things like that. No matter what you were promising, even if it were true, you never made promises on a wean's life.

November 2017

DARK

Retail park, edge of Nottingham

The dark figure loomed over Sian's car then a hand rapped on the window – one, two, three. She looked up and saw a familiar face; Jonny Breen. Sian sighed, and rolled the window down.

'Hello, Sian,' he said.

She stared at him, folding her arms across her chest and waiting for his next move.

'Can you get out of the vehicle, please?' he said,

'Oh, come on!'

Jonny just stood there, looking serious. He opened the door and gestured for her to get out. Sian really didn't want to leave the protection of the metal and glass but Jonny was a police officer and held all the power here. She gripped the steering wheel and let her head drop in frustration. Then she turned herself, placing her bad foot down first and getting up with some effort. Breen grabbed her by the arm and pulled her to standing.

Sian pulled away from him. 'Get off me,' she said.

'Now, now, Ms Love. Calm down. I know you've been through the mill the last while but please don't give me any reason to feel I need to arrest you.' His voice was teasing, almost flirtatious.

'Get to fuck,' Sian said. 'I've done nothing wrong.'

Breen smiled, raising one eyebrow. 'You were driving rather erratically back there,' he said.

'You were following me!'

He grinned, wider, looking pleased with himself. 'Yeh, I was. Because you were driving erratically!'

Sian had to make an effort not to roll her eyes, a gesture she knew would not go down well. She realised that she was in trouble here, in danger. 'What do you want from me, Jonny?'

'DI Breen to you, thanks, young lady,' he said. 'I just need to make sure that you're OK for driving, because your road behaviour was so erratic back there.' He glanced down at her foot. 'Should you really be operating a car with your injury there?'

Sian rolled her eyes. 'I have a doctor's note. I had to get one before I could hire the car.'

Breen leaned closer to Sian and her hands squeezed into fists involuntarily. His lips curled. 'Just checking your breath,' he said. 'Have you had a drink?'

'No,' she said, her voice tense.

They stood there for a moment or two, their eyes locked.

'If that's all, officer,' Sian said, 'I'll be getting on my way.' She lunged for her car door but before she could get it open, Breen punched her in the stomach.

Sian bent double, a searing pain underneath her lungs. She couldn't breathe. Jonny pushed her to the ground and held her down and she felt like she was suffocating. She gathered herself, got her breath back and held still for a moment. His right leg was pressing into her face and she pulled back just enough and bit him on the thigh as hard as she could. He recoiled, shocked, and she wriggled free. He came after her. She punched in his general direction, hitting his shoulder then the side of his face. Then she kicked out with her cast and caught him on his right kneecap. Her foot and leg shook with pain on impact but Jonny stepped back and yelped, so it was worth it.

'Bitch!' he said, bearing down on her. He pushed her to the floor again and bent her arm behind her, twisting it hard. She let out a squeal. 'Yeah, wanna play with the boys? Eh? Like this?' He held her down then twisted her arm even harder. Sian's eyes were watering and she thought he might break a bone or dislocate something if he pushed much harder. 'Hold still,' he said. 'Just fucking stay there.'

Sian let all of her muscles go limp and this surprised Breen so much that he nearly let go of her. Then he caught up with what was happening and grabbed her harder.

'Sian Love, I'm arresting you on suspicion of attempting to pervert the course of justice, resisting arrest and assaulting an officer. You do not have to say anything, but it may harm your defence if you do not mention now something you later rely upon in court.'

Sian heard the words she knew so well, that she'd said so many times herself, echoing in the car park around her. She was in trouble now, and it was her own fault for being so stupid. Kris had warned her from the very beginning but she had carried on doing stupid things anyway.

Jonny shoved her upright and roughly pulled both arms behind her back to handcuff her. He dragged her over to the unmarked car and Sian felt her bad foot collapse beneath her, her leg going under and her knee scraping across the concrete. He pulled her head down by the hair as he loaded her into his car. So much for 'necessary force'. But so much for all the rules with Dominic and his team. Hardly news to someone who'd left the police force to get away from all of their crap.

Jonny Breen crouched by the back door of the Mercedes still holding on to her by the hair, like a threat. He was grinning and his eyes looked haunted. 'I do love a girl in handcuffs,' he said, with a leery smile.

Then he pushed Sian hard and slammed the door shut and that was it. Sian knew – she was Dominic's property now.

GRAVE

Bridewell custody suite, Nottingham

Sian's stomach cramped and she bent forward over the table. She was in a side room rather than the cells of the custody suite because they had not booked her in. Officially, she was not here, which was far more worrying than a proper arrest. They'd left her handcuffs on, too, which wasn't normal. They were just trying to make her feel scared and uncomfortable and she refused to comply, taking deep, calming breaths. She hadn't eaten for hours and the dirty emulsion on the walls swirled, and bulged, and moved. Some kind of optical illusion but she couldn't shake it.

Sian sat up sharply at the sound of the door, the sudden movement sending her lightheaded. Wilkinson and Breen walked in and sat down at the desk opposite her. Dominic gave her that weird smile he did, his lips turning up just at one side. She sat down where she'd been told to. Dominic formally introduced himself and Breen, as if they'd never met before.

Sian sat with her cuffed hands on her lap and glared at both men. 'I want someone informed of my presence here,' she said. 'And I want a solicitor.'

Dominic sat back in his seat and chewed on a pen. He nudged Breen. 'Ex-police are the worst,' he said.

Breen looked up then, and the two of them exchanged a meaningful look.

Dominic leaned forward, a smirk on his face and his elbows wide. 'The PACE act states that the right to representation and the right to have someone informed of your arrest can be withheld where an investigating officer has reason to believe it would prejudice the case, or lead to flight of further suspects or further loss of evidence relating to an offence. And there's already issues with evidence in this case, with things being tampered with.' His smile had disappeared and his voice had gone formal. 'In order for these rights to be withheld, this must be authorised by a person of rank, superintendent or above.' He kept his gaze level and dispassionate, fully aware that they both knew he had the authority to do this to her.

'That senior officer cannot be the SIO investigating the case,' Sian said.

Breen spoke this time. 'She does know her stuff, guv.'

'Yeah,' Dominic said. 'Thing is, though, Ms Love, I'm not the investigating officer in relation to any charges we might decide to bring against you to do with your conduct relating to the crime scene in the ex-licenced premises at 59 Cliff Road, or the assault you carried out on my detective inspector here. I'm only SIO in regard to the murders someone committed at said premises. And you're not a suspect for those, strangely, given that you were at most a toddler when they happened.'

'So,' Breen said. 'No lawyer. No notification. Not yet. You have to help us first and then we'll see what we can do.'

Sian's hands were becoming numb. She wriggled them around in the cuffs to try to get the blood to flow and shifted in her seat. 'I doubt there's much I can help you with,' she said.

'Really?' Breen was sitting back in his chair now, smiling to himself like he knew all the secrets in the world. 'See, a guy I know called Gary Bolton says something different.' There was innuendo in his voice. 'He's well connected, Mr Bolton, in the local criminal underworld. And apparently a very close associate of yours, too.' Breen looked down at his notepad as if checking something then back up at Sian. 'Very close.'

Sian tried not to shiver. She knew that Dominic knew her well enough, that he'd had Breen bring this up to unnerve her. She turned to look at him and he glanced away as if he wasn't even interested in this part of the interview. 'I had no idea about him,' she said. 'I thought he was a businessman.'

'That's an interesting way to put it. A "businessman".' Breen made air quotes with both hands.

Sian turned sharply towards him, her voice hard and level. 'For clarity, I thought he actually owned and ran a business,' she said.

The two officers exchanged glances. Dominic nodded at Breen to continue with his questions.

'Did you take a tissue sample from human remains you found in your home, at the former Loggerheads pub on Cliff Road?' Breen said. He held his pen ready, as if to make notes in his book.

Sian stared at him. 'No comment,' she said.

'No comment, she says,' Dominic echoed. 'Write that down.'

Breen grinned at Dominic and scribbled in the book.

'Did you interfere with any of the evidence from the crime scene at your home, previously known as the Loggerheads public house, at number 59 Cliff Road?' Dominic asked her.

'No comment.'

'There's a shocker.' Dominic was shaking his head.

'Did you steal a piece of jewellery from a body in the cellar of your home, and fail to report the crime scene for several hours so that you could rifle through the belongings of these poor, unfortunate victims, perhaps to protect a family member, now deceased?' Breen stared at Sian and waited for an answer.

Sian felt her breathing quicken. They knew that she'd hurt herself. They knew that this was why they'd not been called to the scene quicker. It was very hard not to blurt out the facts but she also knew that was the trick they were playing, trying to get her talking, and she wasn't about to fall for that. She glanced down at the cast on her leg. 'No comment,' she said,

'Oh, come on now, Ms Love.'

'It's Dr Love, actually,' she said.

'OK, Doctor Love, I do apologise.' Dominic turned towards Breen. 'She's commenting on that, then.' He looked at Sian in his frightening, intense way. She reckoned he rehearsed that look in the mirror. 'Come on, Doctor Love. You know how this goes. You know we'll be searching your property. We'll find the jewellery, and anything else you've taken.'

'No. Comment.'

The men exchanged glances.

Dominic stood up and straightened his blazer. 'Well,' he said, glancing at Breen. 'We did our best.'

'Didn't we just?' Jonny Breen smiled at Sian, then got up and left the room. Dominic walked around the table and put a hand on Sian's shoulder. She froze.

'Sian, you've left me with no choice.'

'No comment,' Sian said. But there was a shake to her voice and she didn't sound as brave as she would have liked.

Dominic patted her shoulder then left the room.

The door opened again nearly straightaway. The man who came in was tall, and very broad. He must have been pushing seventy but looked fit with it; like he'd kept himself in shape. His smart suit was more Kray Brothers than Brooks.

'Hello, Sian,' he said. He had the Cockney accent to match the suit.

'Hello,' she said, trying to ward off he shakes and failing.

The big man paused then gestured to the chairs as if to ask her permission. Sian nodded, and he sat down. 'My name's Pat Walsh,' he said, 'and I want a word with you.'

June 1971
I'm Still Waiting

The Loggerheads pub

Big Pat Walsh pushed open the door to the Loggerheads pub. The sharp, hard chords of 'You Really Got Me' by the Kinks announced his entrance but nobody turned to look as he walked in. The music was coming from the cave at the back, where the Midnight Roses were playing, having reformed with Harry as lead singer.

Pat walked past the bar and through to the cave at the back. He stood on the edge of the crowd, tall enough to look over heads. The room was packed and had that echoing, small feeling that you get with footage from the 60s in the Cavern Club. The music added to the feeling of going back in time. Harry 'Mac' McKenzie was singing and strutting. His voice wasn't at all bad. It stretched and strained at the edges, but he could hold a tune. There were no women in the line-up tonight; neither Angela, the one with the voice, nor Marilyn, the one with the body.

Just as well because Harry was at his flirtatious best, throwing kisses and winks out into the audience and enjoying himself. Big Pat watched Harry as he strutted to the music and pursed his lips, acting more like Mick Jagger than Ray Davies. Pat's face tightened, his shoulders broadened as he stood back and sneered. Harry sang the final line with a flourish and a tiny sense of a cadence that wasn't supposed to be there, right at the end – 'meee-yaaa!' Then the crowd cheered and he bowed and shouted, 'I'm no just a musician ladies and gents. I'm an entertainer!' before walking off the stage with the rest of the band.

Pat's frown deepened and he reached a hand across the chest pocket of his thick black jacket, patting it to check its contents. Then he turned from the crowd, and the band, and the old cave room and back into the public bar. He walked up and smiled broadly at the barmaid, a smile that lit up his face. 'Pint of Guinness, please, sweetheart,' he said.

She reached for a glass and popped it underneath the tap; the black liquid poured thickly and slowly in. 'Anything else while we're waiting?'

'Bobby O'Quaid here, my lovely?'

'Bobby Q?' The barmaid nodded her head backwards as the glass filled. 'You want me to call him over for you?'

'Nah, it's fine.' Pat leaned against the bar in an easy pose. 'He's expecting me.'

Bobby appeared behind the barmaid. 'I'll finish up here, duck,' he said.

The barmaid turned her attention to the next customer. Bobby waited for a minute or two, then flicked the Guinness tap back up and handed the pint to Pat. 'Tonight's the night, then?' His voice was calm and level.

Pat used his finger to draw a line across his own neck, his tongue flicking to the corner of his mouth. 'Indeed it is, my son. Indeed it is.'

'Right.' Bobby placed the pint on the bar. Next to it, he put down a key. 'Might as well get on with it, then,' he said.

The big man nodded. He took his drink over to a table and sat down with it. Bobby walked into the back and Pat took a long sup of beer. He sat drinking and listened to the buzz of the pub. He liked sitting there alone, with so many people having fun around him and no one taking note of him. Occasionally a voice would rise above the others like a soprano in the choir.

Pat finished off his pint and left the empty glass on the table. He walked towards the front doors of the pub. But he didn't walk through them. He headed around the far wall instead, past the entrance to the cave room. He made it look natural; an afterthought. Then he unlocked a door and walked through, closing it behind him with the lightest of clicks.

Pat sat down on the chair in the cupboard Bobby had shown him when he'd arranged all this a week ago. He placed a brick next to the door and took his gun from his pocket, held it pointed at the door. You never knew and, although it seemed that Bobby Q was at the end of whatever friendship he'd had with Harry, Pat found it was always a good idea to underestimate the honesty of anyone you did business with.

The sound of the band was muffled in here but he could hear Harry's voice, straining at the seams of the Beatles' 'Day in the Life'. Pat listened to Harry and remembered the face on him earlier; the bastard loved himself. And he had a mouth on him, too. An entertainer, indeed. 'Big' Pat closed his eyes and thought how he was about to take the smile off Harry Mac's face and half his brain matter with it. He would really get him. Get him so he wouldn't know what he was doing ever, ever again.

Double Barrel

The Loggerheads pub

The public bar was quiet now. Harry and Bobby wandered around, emptying ashtrays into the bin and picking up empties. Harry nipped through to the lounge next door then the skittle alley at the back. He crossed the yard and opened the toilet doors shouting 'ay there!' and having a quick look around. 'All's quiet on the Western Front,' he muttered to himself.

He walked back into the bar. 'Get off with yoursel,' he told Bobby.

Bobby nodded and picked up his keys. 'Bye, Harry,' he said. Then he turned back, as if he had something more to say. But, if he had, he must have thought better of it, shaking his head and heading upstairs to bed.

Harry locked the front door. He looked around the public bar; it was littered with the remnants of a really good night. The band had bloody killed it, even without Angela or Marilyn. Maybe they still had a chance at the big time with the original line-up. But even as he let the thought hang in the air around him, he couldn't believe it. Not anymore.

He wasn't ready for bed so he decided to take five minutes. He poured himself a large whisky then sat down and lit a cigarette. He savoured the moment and wondered whether he might be able to get some better gigs for the band, at least. Make a bit of cash.

There was a shuffling sound coming from somewhere. Harry wondered for a minute if they had a rat, or if Bobby had come back down for something. He stubbed out his fag and downed his drink, getting up to investigate. 'Who's there?' he shouted. His gruff

Glasgow accent was rough with the words. 'Who is it?' Just the hint of fear hiding under the aggression.

The door to the stock cupboard was flung open and there was Big Pat Walsh, standing in front of him scowling. 'You know why I'm here, don'tchya Harry?' There was something of the cowboy about him, the way he held his hips and the lift of one eyebrow.

'No clue,' Harry held out both arms. 'And I've even less of a clue how on God's earth ye got the key for that room, there.'

Pat stared at Harry then he smiled with half of his mouth. And Harry knew. *Et tu Bobby Q?*

'No more questions,' Pat said. His hand rose, slowly, and Harry saw the gun.

There were only two things you needed to know about Pat Walsh and the second was that he was a serious man. The gun was a serious gun, with a silencer. The kind of weapon someone carried if they planned to use it.

Harry stared at the gun for the tiniest moment then he turned and ran. He barged through the door to the back room, then out through the other side. He sprinted down the hallway and pushed open the cellar door, diving through and jumping halfway down the staircase, sliding down the rest and rolling on the ground at the bottom. His shoulder felt bruised as he pushed himself to standing and looked for somewhere to hide. He curled into a ball behind a barrel of ale. He sat there, shaking, realising it was a shite hiding place and that there was no way out.

Pat strode into the room, not even rushing. Harry crouched and hugged the barrel, clinging to the thing like that would help. Pat loomed over him.

'Harry!' It was Angela's voice. She was shouting but he could only just hear her, somewhere above them in the pub. 'Harry!' she was shouting louder, urgently, and moving down towards them.

Was his Angel about to turn up at his hour of most need? He felt the tiniest pang of hope then he turned to look at Pat, into those dead brown eyes.

Pat frowned. 'Fuck's sake,' he said. He stood for a moment, rolled his eyes. Then he stared right back at Harry and levelled the gun at his head. 'Nah,' he said, tutting. 'That's too fucking quick and easy.' He moved the gun, pointing it at Harry's stomach instead. 'You're a performer, are ya? Perform this, Harry, will you, sunshine?' And Pat shot him in the stomach twice, then a third time, for luck.

It's Impossible

The Loggerheads pub

Angela stood on the stairs, holding hard to the banister and shouting. 'Harry!' Why wasn't he coming? She could hear echoes and bangs below, the sound of something being hit or dropped. Had he fallen over? 'Harry!' she shouted again. She'd have to go down to him. She hoped she wasn't about to find him passed out on the floor of the lounge bar and smelling of whisky, like she had one morning a few weeks ago. She took each step carefully, slowly. Her legs and feet were covered in the fluid that had come gushing out of her and it made the stairs slippery.

Halfway down the second flight she heard footsteps coming her way. 'Oh, Harry, thank God. My waters've broken!' She leaned over the rail, glancing down. Then she stopped still. It wasn't Harry looking back up at her but Pat Walsh. She stood in front of him feeling half-naked and cold, her bump stretching her nighty taut over her belly, everything below her hips soaked as if she'd just got out of the bath.

'Angela,' he said. That same soft voice he'd used when Jack had turned up that night.

'Where's Harry?' The words came out squeaky. 'What you doing here? Where's my husband?' A bubble of fear built in her chest and then she was shouting but in a shrill, broken tone. 'Where's Harry? I'm having my baby. I need to go to the hospital!' She took another step and slipped, grabbing hard to the banister to stop herself falling. 'Where's Harry?' And then she noticed what Pat was holding. And she knew what he was doing here and why Harry hadn't come up when she'd shouted.

DEAD FLOWERS

Angela was about to scream but then she felt her insides squeeze; hard and slow they began to crush her from within. She bent double and let out a loud moan. Her eyes watered. She was sweating so badly that the liquid dripped from her skin. 'I need the hospital.' She rushed down the stairs and tried to push past Pat. 'Please,' she said. 'Pleeease. I'm having my baby. I need to go.'

The big man stood exactly where he was and there was no way past him. Angela pushed against him and tried to squeeze her way around but he was far too strong. She felt the beginning of the next crushing pain and it bent her double. She stared up at Pat as the pain ripped through her.

'Why couldn't you just stay in the bedroom?' he said, lifting the gun.

Angela stared at him. There were tears in his eyes.

November 2017

BIRTH

Bridewell custody suite

Sian stared at Pat Walsh. There was something about his expression that looked immutable, something about his eyes that made her think he was dead inside. The longer Sian looked at him, the more she realised she was right to be scared of him.

'I'm an old mate of your ma and pa's.' He stared at her, as if trying to work something out. 'You know who your mum and dad were, right? You've worked it out by now? I've heard tell from certain colleagues of mine that you're a clever gal.'

Sian sat still and gritted her teeth. Her stomach growled at her; she was so hungry that she had begun to feel sick.

'Well, do you? Have you worked out who they are?'

She sighed a breath out. The words 'no comment' were on her lips but she knew this man was not a police officer and that he wouldn't respond as neutrally to her lack of cooperation. 'I'm pretty sure that Angela McKenzie's my mum. Not sure about who provided the sperm. Maybe her first husband.'

'You're Angie's girl all right,' he said. 'I could've picked you out in a line-up. I don't think Donnelly sired you, though, sweetheart. I couldn't promise for sure, but I think Angie at least had the sense to keep away from him after he beat her to a pulp and she lost her first baby.'

Sian remembered Jack Donnelly, the way he'd grabbed her arm, the hate she'd felt from him. Yeah, this guy knew him, and he was telling the truth.

'He's getting his now,' Pat said. 'I'm seeing to that.' There was a very sinister tone to his voice and, even though Sian guessed Jack deserved to suffer, she felt a gut punch of anxiety at the implication.

'What do you want?' Sian asked him. 'Or did you come here just to catch up on old times?'

The man smiled, his face chewed in half by the grin. 'You'd be surprised,' he said.

They sat looking at one another for several moments. The silence was hard and awkward, and she wondered if he was trying to break her. She was scared, and tired, and lack of sleep and food were making her feel fluffy through to her bones. But she sat up and held it together.

'Look,' he said at last, 'you'll be surprised to know I'm actually on your side, sweetheart.' He smiled again; he had a knack of making it look like he knew secrets. 'D'ya really think it was all your police officer mates who made lovely Gary go away? Honestly?'

Sian shrugged. 'I wondered,' she said. 'I found it unlikely. I wasn't convinced he'd really gone away.'

Pat's smile slid back on to his face and he patted the table, twice, looking pleased. 'Good girl,' he said. 'Never trust no one.' He pointed one finger at her. 'Not a single person. That's wisdom, that is, sweetheart.'

'But I'm supposed to believe you're, what, on my side?'

The lightest of laughs. 'Oh,' he said, 'we got history, you and me, that's the thing.' He gesticulated towards the table, pointing down at it like it had done him wrong. 'And I don't like it, men who beat up on women. I won't have it.' His face had changed, turned serious and straight. 'Gary had it coming.'

Sian looked across the table at him. He was staring straight back at her, his gaze level and psychopathically clear. What did he mean had it coming? What had he done to Gary Bolton?

'Listen, I've got information for you. Things you're going to want to know about, to do with that history I mentioned. I shit you not, but there's probably only two people on this planet now who can tell you what you deserve to know, and I'm one of them. But I want you to take a step back, or three. Stop digging around.' His face grew more serious. 'Leave well alone.'

Sian refused to let eye contact go, as if it were a kid's game. 'Leave the skellies in the closet,' she said.

He was nodding, the tiniest of curls to his mouth.

'You left that note.'

He shrugged, neither confirming nor denying it. 'No comment,' he said.

'You had something to do with putting those bodies there,' she said.

'You wanna watch what you say.' A frown cut into his forehead. 'Might be best not to make any more guesses about anything.'

Sian considered her next question carefully. 'Are there any more? Skellies?'

'Nah.' He grinned in a very weird way. 'Not at the pub, anyway.'

Sian nodded. 'And if I do – as you say – leave well alone?'

Pat sat back in the wooden chair, as if settling down for story time. 'See, thing is,' he said, 'I was there when you was born. And your mum, Ange, I know her.'

'Knew her,' Sian said. It made her feel less afraid, correcting him.

'No, my darling. I *know* her.' He was smiling now, and leaning back looking very pleased. 'And if you promise to be a good gal, I'll give you her address.'

Sian sat up sharply. 'She's still alive?' she said.

'Oh yes, my sweet. She's still alive. And I know where she lives.' The way his voice swept in a wave over that last sentence made it sound like a threat. Sian wasn't sure if he'd meant it to, or if he'd made that kind of threat so many times that it'd become the natural tone of his voice. Pat pulled a piece of paper from his pocket and waved it across the table towards her.

Sian reached her cuffed hands to try to take the paper and Pat quickly pulled it back, shaking his head.

'Nah,' he said. 'First you gotta promise.' He leaned towards her, a smile like a grimace decorating his face. 'You gotta promise me that you'll stop digging.'

Sian considered this, sitting back and trying to stop the cuffs from chafing her wrists.

'Well, are you going to promise?'

She nodded. 'OK,' she said.

A lazy laugh. 'Nah,' he said. 'You gotta say it, Sianey.' He sounded teasing, like an adult to a child.

'Fine,' she said, 'I promise.'

He made a show of checking that she wasn't crossing her fingers and then laughed again, sounding like Sid James from the Carry On films. 'Nice one,' he said, pushing the piece of paper across the table.

Sian took it and curled her fist around it tightly. She twisted herself awkwardly so that she could get it into her pocket. Then she looked back at Pat, his face creased with smiling, and wondered how many punches it had taken to break that tough-looking nose of his.

LOVE

Canalside, Nottingham city centre

Sian rested her head against her cupped hands on the table, unable to get a wink of sleep despite her tiredness. There was no natural light coming through to the meeting room so she had no way of even guessing the time, except that she knew she'd been there hours. They'd sent a uniform in to remove the handcuffs not long after interviewing her the night before, with a cup of tea and some food. She'd drunk the tea but not been able to stomach the food, which was sitting on the table and beginning to stink the room out with its school dinner smell of cheap meat and overcooked vegetables. She heard the door opening and sat up.

'Good morning, Love.' Kris smiled from the doorway. 'Fancy seeing you here.'

Sian felt her throat tighten. Then she jumped to her feet and ran to him, wrapped her arms around him. He took her arms and straightened them away from him, examining the bruises. He ushered her back over to the table and sat her down. 'Are you OK?' he said.

She nodded, thinking that if she tried to say anything out loud she wouldn't be able to stop herself from sobbing.

'You sure?' He was searching for her eyes with his.

Sian looked right at him. 'Yes,' she said, managing to spit the word out. 'Bit of a rough arrest but I'll survive.'

'I heard you gave as good as you got,' Kris said.

'Not quite but I left my mark,' she said. 'Thanks for coming to get me.'

Kris's gaze moved up and down all over her, as if he were trying to take in every tiny detail of how she looked. 'Tell me what happened,' he said.

'Here?' she said.

He shook his head. 'No,' he said. 'Let's get out of here.'

Kris wrapped her in his coat like he was treating her for shock and took her out from the custody suite and then into the daylight. The brightness felt like assault and Sian had to shade her eyes with one hand. 'We could get a coffee over there,' Kris suggested, gesturing at one of the canalside chain bars that was open for breakfast. 'Unless you're keen to get further away from here.'

'No,' Sian said, 'it's OK. There is fine.'

The two of them strolled over and took a seat inside the pub. Kris went to order. Sian hugged herself and tried to feel warm. She was safe now but she was still shivering. She felt lightheaded and very weak.

Kris came back and placed two coffees on the table, sitting down with a flourish. 'You want to eat?' he asked her.

Sian shook her head. The idea of food made her stomach churn.

'OK,' he said. 'Tell me everything.'

Sian picked up the mug of coffee, which warmed her hands. The shaking abated slightly. She began to talk, telling him about being followed in the car and Breen's heavy-handed arrest tactics. She described the weird interview, and then meeting Pat Walsh. 'He said he was there, when I was born. Angela's my mum and she's still alive. Which I guess means Harry's my dad, after all, and it was Aunty Marilyn I found with him in the cellar.'

'Wow,' Kris said. 'Bit of a head fuck.'

Sian raised both eyebrows and took another drink. 'I'm pretty sure he killed them. He's the one behind all the notes. Behind everything.' She grimaced and shook her head. 'He gave me her address and made me promise to stop digging.'

Kris leaned back, his eyes narrowing as he considered this. 'So, you going to pay her a visit, then?'

'Yeah.' She sighed. 'I have to meet her. Ask her about what happened.'

'Have to know the truth?' He was shaking his head but looked resigned to the idea.

Sian nodded.

'OK, let's finish these drinks and do this.' He picked up his mug and considered its contents. 'Where we headed?'

'I can't drag you into this, Kris.' She cleared her throat. 'This is my problem. I need to deal with it.'

'For fuck's sake, Sian.' His voice was low but it brimmed with anger.

'Please.'

'Look, you don't even know that this is your mum. What if it's some kind of trap? What if it's a lie to lure you somewhere so they can make sure you stop digging? A permanent solution? Because if this fella has found out the least thing about you, he has to know a scrap of paper isn't about to stop you trying to get to the truth.'

Sian hadn't thought of that and stopped to consider it for a moment. 'I don't think it's a lie.' She shrugged. 'I dunno. There was something about him that seemed honest.'

'Apart from all the people what he killed!' Kris's voice was incredulous.

'I can't explain it,' she said. 'I just trusted him.'

'Then you're a fucking idiot.' Kris's voice was level now, the emotion squeezed right out of it. 'You barely trust yourself, and you certainly don't trust me. But you trust this guy? Are you kidding me?'

'I'm sorry,' she said. She stared at him, realising just how badly she was treating him.

'That's not good enough.' Kris's voice was quiet, but there was a grit to it. 'I can't help you if you won't let me. I can't protect you if you keep doing stupid things.' He cleared his throat. 'I can't keep doing this, Sian.'

Sian wanted to say sorry again but she knew that it didn't cut it. Besides, her mum had drilled into her to only apologise if you can be sure you won't do the same thing again and she wasn't sure.

'Oh, honestly, Sian. I sometimes get the impression you think you can say jump and I'll be there for you, every time. And so far I have, haven't I? Like a right fool.' He swallowed. 'Well, enough. I am so done with this.' He stood up and put on his coat, slammed his body away from her, looking set to storm off.

'Don't go,' she said.

Kris swivelled on his heels and for a moment she thought he'd changed his mind. He reached over the table and snatched up his phone. He stared straight at her, his mouth set hard with anger. 'Your real mum's not magically alive just because some old gangster says she is, you know. She's probably still dead. And you go around listening to men like that, you'll be joining her soon enough.'

Sian watched him walk away. She felt sick and faint and very, very alone. Kris was right. She was doing exactly what she'd dreaded, staggering towards that crash she had always felt coming, hard coded into who she was. And yet she couldn't stop. She knew that Kris had a point, that it could be a trap but she also knew she was going to follow up and visit Angela anyway.

June 1971
Baby Jump

The Loggerheads pub

Pat held his gun straight and looked at Angela, bent double with pain and staring up at him with wide, frightened eyes. He didn't want to have to shoot her. But what was he supposed to do here?

'I need... the hospital...' Angela moaned out the words between angry breaths. Then she stood up straighter, her eyes slightly clearer. 'You won't stop me. You're not like that, are you? The kind of man who hurts women.' There was something steely in her now. 'You're not,' she said, very sure of herself.

Pat lowered the shaft of the gun. He took Angela by the arm and into the lounge bar, helping her to sit down at one of the tables. 'Problem is, you've seen too much,' he told her, sitting in the chair opposite. 'And your loyalty wouldn't be to me. Quite rightly, you'd be on the side of your feller down there.' He indicated with the barrel of the gun to the floor below them.

Angela shook her head, letting out a choked laugh. 'I've wanted to kill him a few times mesen,' she said. But she was crying, moans and sobs coming from her mouth out of her control. 'You'd be killing two of us,' she said.

Pat nodded. 'I am aware of this fact.'

'I'd never tell,' Angela said. 'I'd never breathe a word.'

Pat sighed and shook his head. 'You'd be amazed how many people say that when they're looking into the barrel of this.' He twisted the gun upwards slightly as he spoke.

'I don't speak to police,' Angela said. 'Just like you don't go round killing women and babies.' She looked at him then, her teeth gritted. 'Please. Please let my baby live.' Her eyes shone with defiance. 'If you don't, I swear, I will damn well find a way to haunt you.'

Pat smiled. 'Don't believe in ghosts,' he said.

Angela buckled with pain again and let out a yelp. Pat found himself reaching for her hand on instinct, and she grabbed his back. 'Fuck. You!' Her hand tightened on Pat's until her nails dug into him. 'Bastard!' Her hand tightened on Pat's even harder. He tried to pull away but, just in that moment, she was too strong. Then the pain seemed to ease off and her grip loosened.

'Hold up, gal. I wouldn't usually let anyone talk to me like that,' Pat told her, his voice gentle.

Angela's breath had gone deep and raspy. 'I need the hospital,' she said.

Pat shook his head. Maybe he'd deliver the baby himself.

'You got kids?' she asked him.

He let out a short, humourless laugh. 'Got some bitch who says it's mine,' he said.

'And you think she's lying?'

'Dunno.' He looked thoughtful and a little sad. 'It's not exactly the way I was planning my family,' he told her. He hadn't been able to get Kathy pregnant and knew a baby with another woman would break her heart in a terrifying way. 'I don't want to believe her,' he said.

'I'm having a little girl,' Angela told him. She sounded very sure.

'How the fuck can you know that?'

'Sometimes, you just know,' she said.

Pat stared at her. Something had changed in Angela and she didn't look afraid anymore. He had this weird feeling that she was right and that she'd be strong enough to protect that baby; wrestle the gun from him if she needed to. He knew that made no sense but there were lots of things in life that didn't. There was something in the air around Angela that made him think twice.

'My mam wants me to call her Sian.' She laughed, lightly. 'I don't like my mam very much, but I like the name.'

'Sian,' he said. 'That's a nice name.' He was shaking his head. 'And now you think I've heard the name so I won't do it now. Won't be able.'

'I don't think you ever were,' she said, 'That's not who you are.' Pat raised one eyebrow. She'd overestimated him; he'd done things many times worse than this. But, as he looked at her, the curve of her belly and the sweat across her brow, he realised that she was right. This time, at least, he couldn't do it. He sighed and put the gun into his inside pocket. 'Fine,' he said. 'Let's get you and Sian to hospital, sweetheart.'

'You can't take that with you,' she said, gesturing at his pocket with a nod. 'Into a hospital where there are mams and babies.' She shook her head. 'It's not right.'

Pat sat back and rolled his eyes. What was this woman doing to him? 'Fine,' he said. He stood up and walked over to the bar, stashing the gun up behind the whisky glasses. He'd come back for it later, before the pub opened that night. Come back for Angela too, perhaps, and whoever else he needed to, once the baby was here.

arrested the previous evening and was suddenly very weak with it. She put down the photo and sat on the sofa.

The little dog wandered over and gave Sian a detailed sniff, finding out everything she could about what kind of dog Elvis was and what that might tell her about this human. She seemed to decide that all was good and jumped up beside Sian on the sofa, eliciting an indulgent smile from Angela when she walked back in carrying a tray. 'She's not really allowed up there,' she said, but made no effort to make her get down. Sian smiled and thought that, yes, it looked like she really had found her mother.

Angela passed Sian a steaming mug of tea and put another one down on the coffee table for herself, as well as a plate of biscuits. 'OK, you deserve some answers. But I don't know where to start, so you're going to have to help me with what you already know,' she said.

Sian smiled. She liked getting to the point too and could tell she was related to this woman. She could feel her own genes, pulling to her. 'Pat told me he was there when I was born.'

'Oh.' A very different sound this time. Then a tiny laugh. 'No, duckie, he's got it all wrong.'

'Really? Because he seemed pretty sure.' She paused, wondering how best to phrase it. 'We found Harry's body, in my cellar.'

'I saw that on the news,' Angela said, 'about the bodies.' There was a weird distance in her eyes, like she was remembering a dream.

'Is he my dad?' Sian said.

Angela recovered herself and smiled at Sian. 'Maybe,' she said. 'But you're not my baby.' She put down her tea cup and got to her feet, walking over to a bookshelf and pulling down a small jewellery box. It had a lock on it, and she got her keys out to undo it, emptying its contents on to the coffee table next to the tea things.

There were a few tatty old photographs, a wedding ring and then something that made Sian take a sharp, deep breath. Another

Mizpah pendant. It felt like the room was revolving around her as she picked up the pendant and held it.

'My little Carrie-Ann.' Angela sighed and handed Sian the baby pictures. It showed a chubby little thing, with thin curls that barely covered her head and eyes that were a bright cornflower blue. 'She wasn't even two. Meningitis.'

Sian stared at the picture and wanted to cry. For the little baby who hadn't lived. And for herself, living and breathing and without a mother.

'The pendant,' Sian said. She reached into her pocket for her keys then pulled them out to show Angela. They placed the pendants together but they didn't match. They were the equivalent piece.

'Bobby's,' Angela said, with a whisper of a laugh. 'Harry bought them for all of us but Bobby didn't want to wear a necklace so I told him to put it on his keyring.'

'Both of the bodies had pendants like this. So, it was Marilyn down there with Harry? Your sister?' She didn't want it to be true, but she had to admit the police had a point that her uncle was the most likely person to have put them there. 'Do you know what happened?'

'Some of it, I guess. We were tight, back then, the four of us. But things went really sour. Bobby and Marilyn were at each other's throats and me and Harry only a little bit better.' She stopped, as if she'd said too much. 'When I saw the pictures in the paper, well, I just knew it was her. I think a part of me's known she was there all these years.' She gave Sian a very level stare. 'I ran off with my baby, as far as I could get. I only came back later when I felt safe. My Freddie.' She nodded towards the wedding picture with the shoulder pads. 'I knew he could look after me and Carrie-Ann, and so we came back.'

Sian swallowed. 'Were Harry and Marilyn having an affair? Is that why Bobby killed them?'

Angela let out a very strange, little laugh. 'Oh, no, it wasn't Bobby. Bobby didn't kill them!' She made the idea sound silly. 'Not Bobby!'

Sian took a big breath out, tension releasing from her body in a rush.

'There was nothing going on with Harry and Marilyn,' Angela said, her voice quiet and dreamy. 'I'm not exactly sure about Harry, anymore, who he really was and what he might have done. He was the kind of man who'd say whatever he thought you wanted to hear, you know what I mean?' She looked to Sian, who nodded an assurance that she did. 'He feels like a childhood memory, now – it all does. But I know about my sister. She would never have done that to me.'

'Who killed them?' Sian said.

'Oh, I know who killed Harry. I was there.' Her face was very serious. 'But it's not someone you talk about.'

'Pat Walsh?' Sian said.

Angela didn't move or speak; total silence. Enough to tell Sian that she was right about this, though.

'They were down there together, though,' she said. 'Marilyn and Harry.'

'I don't know about the rest. All I know is what happened to Harry.' Angela took the pendant from Sian. She ran the silver chain through her fingers. Then she looked up at Sian, fixed her right in the eyes, and Sian knew that she was telling the truth.

'Why did Pat kill Harry?' Sian said. She refused to be scared of talking about Walsh, would not be bullied into submission by his reputation. Her head was spinning. She felt like she might be sick.

'I never said he did and if you quote me on that, there'll be a problem.' There was a warning look on Angela's face, a deep frown; she came from a place where you don't talk to police, like Sian's uncle. That place where you stay so quiet, you don't even talk to yourself.

But then Angela looked at Sian again, properly, examining her face as if deciding something. 'I used to think that Harry had slept with Pat's wife,' she said. 'Kathy, her name was. Pretty little thing, she were, proper Irish colleen. And there was something he said that day Carrie-Ann was born that made me wonder.' She sighed. 'But there were other things he said, too. It's taken me a long time to put it all together but I think Harry had something on him. Knew something that the big man didn't want getting out. I don't know what.'

Sian nodded. 'You recognised me, though, when I came to the door.' She put down her mug and stood up too fast. 'You knew my name straightaway.' Her head swam and her stomach turned. 'Sorry.' She clung to the sofa back. 'Can I use the bathroom?'

'Are you OK, love?' Angela moved closer, her face full of concern.

'Yes,' Sian said, but it was a lie. She looked down and realised how tightly she was holding on to the sofa and that she didn't dare let go. 'I feel a bit lightheaded, that's all.' The words echoed and the room span. Angela's face warped larger then smaller. And then everything went black like shutters coming down. She could still hear Angela's voice, calling after her. *You OK, love? You OK? Love, love, love, love, love...*

JUMP

Angela's house

'Love.' The voice sounded far away. 'Love!' But very familiar. Someone was shaking her. Sian screwed up her eyes as she came to and pushed out her arms.

'Gettoff,' she said. She opened her eyes and tried to focus.

It was Kris. He looked very concerned. 'You OK, Sian?'

She tried to pull away but he held on to her tightly. 'Am fine,' she said. She giggled, lightly. She felt like she might be drunk and wondered if she'd had that whole bottle of amaretto, and then remembered what had happened to it. She sat up. Her skin was cold and clammy.

'You passed out,' Kris said. He took hold of her chin and examined her pupils.

Sian tried to remember what had happened. But as she saw the chintzy sofa and the shiny wooden coffee table, the baby pictures and the silver pendant, she remembered about Angela. She sat up straighter and sucked in a hard, deep breath. It felt like coming back from the dead.

Angela was sitting on the armchair across from her. Her mother. No, not her mother. That baby had died. Angela was smoking; something about the way she held her cigarette brought to mind Sian's childhood. 'I called him,' she told Sian. 'You passed out and I looked in your phone for your ICE contacts. I hope that's OK.'

'Yes,' Sian said. Then, remembering who else was on her ICE contacts. 'Did you call my mother too?'

'Yes.' Angela said. 'I think she's on her way.' There was a tiny catch to her breath. 'I haven't seen Ruth O'Quaid for about a million years.'

Kris cleared his throat. 'You feeling any better?' he asked Sian.

Sian nodded, remembering that they'd had a big row, that he'd said he'd had enough. 'I'm so sorry,' she said.

'I'll make more tea,' Angela said, getting up and picking up the mugs.

'It wasn't a trick, though,' Sian told Kris.

'Yeah, I got that,' he said. 'Turns out elderly gangsters sometimes tell the truth.'

'It was Angela's sister, Marilyn, that we found. She was married to my Uncle Bobby and I don't know who killed her, or why.' Her throat tightened. 'Angela says it wasn't Bobby but she doesn't know who it was.' She was no longer keeping things from Kris and found that she didn't feel that tightening of her throat and chest when she was around him now. Something had shifted between them. 'Pat Walsh killed Harry,' she told him. 'And then Angela had her baby, the same day.'

'You?' His voice was very quiet.

'No. It wasn't me. That baby died.' Sian was thinking and didn't speak for a few moments. 'She doesn't think Harry's my dad, but she must be wrong, because the DNA matched and otherwise...' her voice trailed off.

'Marilyn's your mum.' This was Ruth's voice, coming from the living room doorway, a clarification and not just a finishing of the thought. Sian turned to look at her. She had no idea how long her mother had been standing there listening.

'No,' Sian said. She had to swallow to be able to speak again. 'You're my mum,' she said, 'Marilyn was my biological mother.'

Sian's mum walked over and sat down beside her on the sofa.

'I'm sorry,' Ruth said. 'I know I told too many lies and, really, truly, I'm sorry. I was trying to protect you but I should have told you.'

Sian knew what it meant if her mother apologised; God knows she'd heard the rules about the word sorry enough, when she was a child. More often than jokes about noses and broken promises. She nodded. 'Why didn't you?' she said.

'Oh, I don't know.' Ruth glanced away then at Kris, as if he was the one owed an explanation. 'It's a total cliché but I just never found the right time and the longer it went on, the more it felt like I couldn't say anything about it without destroying everything.'

'What about when I realised that David wasn't my dad? Wasn't that a fairly decent opportunity to tell me everything?' Sian said.

'Well,' her mum said, 'maybe. But you were so angry. I thought that telling you I wasn't your mother either would finish us off'

Sian stared at her. 'You'd already given me enough trust issues; you might as well have gone for the set.'

Angela came back in with fresh mugs of tea. She busied herself, placing them down on the table.

'Will your husband be back soon?' Sian asked, wondering who he was, what he was like.

'Oh no, dear, he's gone,' she said. 'He passed away three years ago now.'

'I'm sorry to hear that,' Ruth said. 'I lost my David back in the 90s.' She didn't mention that she'd remarried.

'Was he good to you?' Sian asked Angela. Her voice was quiet, and she found that she really cared about the answer.

'The third time's the charm,' Angela said, with a wink. Sian noted that this wasn't really an answer but she guessed he had to have been an improvement on the previous two.

'Jack's dying,' Sian said. 'Dementia.'

'Good,' Angela said. She sounded completely matter of fact. 'Nothing like a bit of justice in the world.' She leaned her head right back against the armchair. 'Sorry, that probably sounds cruel. But he wasn't good to me.'

'I know,' Sian said. And she left it at that.

'Do you have any other questions?' Angela said. She looked around the room at all of them. 'Ask me anything now, and I'll answer if I can. Just don't record anything or ask me to write it down, and don't come back.' She put down her mug then looked at Sian full on. 'Please.'

Sian nodded. 'Do you know anything else at all about what happened in that pub cellar? Who killed Marilyn and why? Who would want to kill her?'

Angela shook her head, slowly, side to side. 'I can't help with that. I've really been wracking my brains about it, ever since I saw the news, but I just don't know.' She stared into her tea like she was reading a fortune. 'Maybe she killed herself,' she said. 'She was pretty messed up after the baby came.' She looked at Sian. 'After you came. Looking back, I guess she had post-natal depression. But we didn't know much about those things, not back then.'

Sian turned to her mother. She really didn't want to ask her, but she had to face the truth. 'Rob must've known they were down there. Did you know?'

'Sian.' Her mum's voice was quiet and gentle, soothing. Ruth took hold of both Sian's hands, then her wrists. There were still bruises there from the handcuffs that Jonny Breen had so brutishly applied and Ruth rubbed at them with her thumbs as if she might be able to rub them away. 'I knew he had secrets there at the pub. Course I did. But I had no idea it was anything like this.'

'But the police never looked? When everyone except Uncle Rob went missing? People must have talked about it.' Sian was confused. 'I know they talked about it. Les, and the rest on the street.'

'Big Pat's called that for a reason and it's not just about how tall he is,' Angela said. 'Bigger than the law. Always has been.'

'So, who was my father?' Sian said.

'I don't know,' Ruth said, simply. 'But Marilyn told Bobby that you were Harry's in the middle of a big row.'

'But that's not true.' If Harry had been her father, she'd have seen far more markers that matched hers on the mixed profile; it would have contained all of her DNA.

'I overheard that row,' Angela said.

Everyone turned to look at her.

She looked embarrassed, like she'd been caught looking at something she shouldn't. 'I didn't mean to listen in but we all lived close in that pub together. I heard a lot of what went off between them. And, as you can imagine, that one made an impression.' A short breath of a laugh. 'I can remember it word for word because I've mulled and mulled over it, and thought about those words for the rest of my life. She said "Ask Harry"; they were her exact words.'

Sian watched Angela's face as she spoke and realised that she still loved Harry, across all the years and despite the other marriage.

'Is there anything else you want to ask me?' Angela spoke quietly and it was obvious that she wanted to shake herself back to the 21st century, away from the past and all of the things she'd lost to the years.

Sian shook her head.

'Come on, Love, let's get you home.' Kris stood up and reached out a hand towards her.

Sian let him get her to her feet. 'Thank you, Angela McKenzie,' she said. The woman gave her the tightest of smiles. Then Sian walked away, leaning on Kris and letting him help.

GUN

Bank, Nottingham city centre

Ruth had handed Sian the key in the car on the way back from Angela's house. 'No more secrets,' she'd said. 'It's for a safety deposit box. I don't know what's in there but Bobby called it his insurance. He told me to take it to the police if anything ever happened to him.'

Sian sat in the waiting area, turning the key over in her hands. Did she want to find out what was in the box? She didn't, not really, but she couldn't help herself, either. She had to keep going until she found the truth. The clerk returned and opened the door towards her. 'This way, please, Ms Love,' he said. She got up and followed him,

The clerk took her to a private room where the box was sitting on the table. He discreetly left, locking the door behind him. Sian stared at the box. She slipped the key into the lock and opened it.

June 1971
Heaven Must Have Sent You

The Loggerheads pub: crime scene

Marilyn woke up to the all too familiar sound of the baby grizzling. It didn't even properly cry, just moaned and whimpered. She looked down at her belly, its swell and the angry-looking stretchmarks. She was struggling to guess whether she was awake or asleep, what was real and which parts of her life were just a bad, bad dream.

Bobby turned over in his sleep, muttering something to himself. He was wearing earplugs as usual, blissfully unaware of the baby and all of its constant needing of things. That was Marilyn's job, dealing with the baby. She had heard about women's liberation on the news, but that was in London like most things, and none of it bothered itself to get on the train and come here.

She supposed that she should get up and feed the baby but she didn't want to. Didn't want to feel its sucking, desperate grip on her. Bobby snuffled and muttered again and she decided to get up and get properly dressed, make herself feel better. She would leave him with the baby and see how long it took for him to realise it needed something. She slid from the bed and pulled on stockings, a nice dress. It rucked over her stomach but she tried to ignore that. She slipped her feet into her favourite red heels and tiptoed out of the bedroom.

The pub was quiet in a way that it only ever was early in the morning. As she walked she heard her heels clip against the stairs and had that weird sensation again, that she might be dreaming. She had dreamed that she'd woken up and walked around the house before and then had realised she wasn't actually awake, that the banisters were not really that colour, and woke up again, only to notice another little detail in the carpet on the stairs and realise she was still dreaming. She'd gone through several cycles of this waking into a dream before she'd woken up properly and had been scared, ever since, that everything might be a dream.

The further Marilyn got from the room, the quieter the baby's grizzling got and the better she felt. Maybe the baby wasn't real at all. Downstairs, she turned on the lights in the lounge bar. They were those modern fluorescent tubes, and they flashed and squeaked as they came on. The bar looked strange without any punters, haunted by the absence of them. There was a bottle of whisky out where Harry had left it most probably. Marilyn took a glass from the shelf above her to pour herself a drink. As she pulled it out she caught the edge of something else that was behind it and it almost fell on her. She grabbed it just in time.

It was a gun. Now she knew she was dreaming. She turned it over in her hands; the sight of it was raw and shocking and fully took her breath away. She felt the weight of it and it felt real, not like a dream at all. That was when she heard the noises coming from the cellar. It sounded a little like the baby grizzling but deeper. More like the growl of a wounded animal. Marilyn's eyes widened. What in the hell had happened here? She felt, for a moment, like she'd strayed on to the screen in the pictures, where she knew she'd always belonged.

Marilyn held tight to the gun and the banister as she walked down the stairs to the cellar. Halfway down the steps she could hear the voice better, its low moans and wails and the odd word. *Help me. Shiiiite. Fucking hell, help me.* She could hear the accent too and realised it was Harry. Her heels made the tiniest of sharp musical sounds against the steps.

She opened the cellar door and there was Harry, lying in a pool of dark liquid. The air was filled with the smell of beer, and the iron tang of blood and urine. Marilyn moved closer and inspected the scene, the gun heavy in her small hands.

Harry sat up slightly as he saw her and let out a loud groan. The barrel behind him had been burst open by gunshots too, and his blood made patterns and rainbows on the surface of the beer. 'Help me,' he said, his voice barely a squeak.

Marilyn stared at him. 'Why should I help you?' she said.

'We're pals, hen. Isnay that right?' He wheezed with the effort of talking. He was scrabbling for something; she could see it in his eyes. He thought he could talk his way out of anything. 'We're family,' he said. And, when he realised that this had not moved her, 'Yer wee sister loves me.'

Marilyn let out a weird shock of a laugh. 'My sister loves anybody who'll have her,' she said. It was the nasty side of true.

Harry's eyes softened. 'Please, hen,' he said, through another wet wheeze. 'I need hospital. I need ye to help.'

Marilyn nodded. 'Yeah, you do.' Then she smiled. She could feel something building inside her, a weird, manic energy that was not so much anger as excitement. 'But why should I help you? Have you helped me?' She was shaking her head. 'You bought and sold me like I was your bloody prize cow.'

'Naw,' Harry said. He coughed, and blood squeezed from his nose. 'It wasnay like that,' he said.

'It were exactly like that,' she told him. She looked at the gun in her hand as if she'd forgotten she was carrying it, then lifted and pointed it at him.

Harry held up one arm, cocked around his face. 'Please,' he said. But his voice had turned desperate now. 'Ye can be the singer.'

'But I'm not good enough,' Marilyn said. 'You told me that.'

Harry started to cry, grizzling like the baby upstairs then letting out a sob that made a bubble of blood form and burst in his left nostril. It didn't make her feel sorry for him at all. She kept the gun steady and pointed at him, then stepped closer, standing right over him so that there was no way she could miss.

Marilyn let out the tiniest whistle of a sigh as she looked down at Harry's frightened blue eyes. She wasn't sure if she was dreaming, or awake. She didn't know if she would shoot him in the head but she sure as hell wanted to.

November 2017

SUICIDE

Central Police Station, Nottingham

DS Meadows appeared at the door to the waiting room with a smile. She gestured towards Kris and Sian. 'Ms Love, DI Payne. Please follow me.'

The two of them walked behind her down the police station corridor, past offices and interview rooms, until Meadows stopped outside one and knocked on the door.

'Sian?' DI Jonny Breen emerged from the room with his professional face on. 'And DI Payne, a double pleasure.'

Sian turned towards Kris. He took hold of her hand and squeezed her fingers a little too hard. 'You're OK, Love,' he said.

'Shall we go in?' Breen asked them, gesturing at the door. Sian nodded, and Breen turned from the pair of them. They followed him into the interview room where DCI Swann was already sitting at a table, waiting with folders and labelled tapes, in case they decided to start recording.

'Take a seat,' Jonny said, gesturing. 'I can get us some tea or coffee, if you want.' He was reaching for the intercom as he sat down in the chair next to Swann.

Sian shook her head. 'I just want to get this over with,' she said.

'OK,' Swann said. She placed both hands on the table in a business-like gesture. 'What was it you wanted to tell us?'

'Well, first of all, I want you to know that I'm considering making a complaint to the IPCC, about my recent violent and wrongful arrest. I have photographs of all the bruises and have documented everything.' Sian's voice was flat as she spoke, devoid of emotion.

Breen was shaking his head. 'Okaaaay,' he said, his voice making it sound like she was acting crazy.

Sian cleared her throat. 'I don't care if it gets me nowhere. I will cause you a whole storm of headaches.'

The two police officers exchanged a look; they knew she meant business.

'Look, Ms Love, we just want to do our jobs and get to the bottom of this case,' Swann told her.

Sian could have laughed out loud. 'Really?' She rolled her eyes.

'Yes, of course, really.' Swann sounded genuine and perhaps she was, for all Sian knew, but she knew that Jonny Breen's real boss was not anyone on the force.

'You haven't even got the identities of the victims right,' Sian told her. 'The woman you found isn't Angela McKenzie. It's Marilyn O'Quaid.'

'Your Uncle Robert's wife?' Breen said. There was a strange smirk on his face, as if he thought he had something on her now. 'Did he kill her, then? Did you know about this all along?'

Sian shook her head. 'No, of course not. My uncle never would have done anything like that. It was Pat Walsh. It was all Pat Walsh and I don't know why he killed them, but he did, and I have proof that connects him to the murders.'

Swann frowned. 'You have evidence that you've held back from us?' Sian noticed that she didn't ask who Pat Walsh was.

'No.' Sian pulled out a pale blue folder from her bag. 'I have evidence that I've discovered since we last spoke.' She opened the folder and brought out a photograph, thinking how her uncle had gone to his grave without talking to the police, but here he was from beyond it with a lot to say. The photo was of a gun, wrapped in plastic, the one she'd found in his safety deposit box. She'd taken several pictures of it, including a very clear shot that showed the serial number. She had another document detailing the van-load of weapons that had been stolen back in the mid-sixties, the one crime that Pat Walsh had served time for. This gun had come from that robbery. 'The weapon is linked to Walsh, and it may well have prints, too,' she said. 'I'll give you access so you can find out. Once you've arrested him.'

DCI Swann held out a hand, and Sian bundled the folder back together and gave it to her. 'Thanks,' Swann said. 'We'll put it all on file.'

'Put it on file?' Sian's voice was incredulous. 'Please don't try to brush me off. I will not go away and I want justice for my aunt and for Harry.'

'You seem to forget that we're the detectives tasked to investigate this crime. And we'll keep investigating as we see fit,' Breen said. 'I have no solid evidence that points to Pat Walsh having had any involvement in these murders and a photograph of an old gun doesn't prove a thing. Now, if you don't mind.' He stood up and walked to the door, opening it for them. Sian and Kris got up and left the room; Meadows was still waiting for them outside, as if she'd known the meeting would be snappy.

Kris and Sian followed Meadows back through several corridors towards the waiting area and exit of the station. They were almost at the main entrance and Sian began to breathe a little easier.

'Sian!' A voice came up the corridor towards them, footsteps rushing behind it; Dominic Wilkinson.

Sian rolled her eyes at Kris then turned to face Dominic. 'What?' she said.

Dominic nodded at Meadows and Kris, as if dismissing them from duty. 'Sian, a word alone,' he said.

'You don't have to speak to him,' Kris said. 'If you don't want to.'

'It's alright,' she said. She stepped back and to the edge of the hallway with Dominic.

Dominic stood so that the rest of the corridor was blocked and no one else could see what he said. There was something different about his demeanour. Something she'd never seen before.

'What do you want?' she said.

'I just saw Breen on his way back to his office. Listen, Sian,' he said, 'please, be careful whose name you go throwing around.' He reached a hand to his forehead like it was all too much to take. 'You're putting yourself in danger, Sian.'

'OK, well, I'll take that under advisement.' Then she looked up sharply, suddenly putting things together. 'Oh my God, he's your boss now, instead of Gary.'

Dominic didn't dispute it. 'You don't understand the half of it, Sian.'

'I understand as much as I want to,' she said.

'Just be careful.' His eyes turned soft. 'Please.'

'Anyone would think you actually cared,' she said. She turned and walked away, back towards Kris and the way out.

BLONDE

Loggerheads

The Loggerheads sign was rattling in the wind as Sian pulled over the car. She'd taken Elvis to the park and watched as he ran around inside an enclosure. It wasn't exactly taking him for a walk, but it was a start and it would have to do until the cast came off. She got out of the car and opened the door for him; he was so well trained, trotting out and straight over to the front door where he sat and waited for her. 'Good boy,' she told him, digging into her pockets for the keys and limping to the door after him.

As soon as she walked in, Sian knew something wasn't right. She could feel it; whether it was a scent in the air or the tiniest of sounds coming from another room, her intuition was sparking. She thought about taking her dog and making a run for it but she knew she wouldn't get far with her foot in plaster. 'Bed!' she ordered Elvis, and 'stay!' He went into the living room and did as he was told. Sian hung up her jacket but kept her keys in her hand, pointing the longest, sharpest forward. She crept down the hallway and to the kitchen at the back.

From the kitchen doorway, she saw the large broad shape of an old man, wearing a smart suit, looking out of the window and smoking. He turned and grinned at her. 'Hello, Sian,' he said.

'Pat,' she said. Sian hoped that Elvis would be a good boy and stay put the way she'd told him because, above everything else, she didn't want her dog to get hurt. She would rather die.

Pat Walsh held out his packet of cigarettes to her. She took one; why not? There were worse dangers than nicotine, tar and a bit of arsenic right now.　She leaned forward so he could light it and sucked in a big drag.

'How did you get in?' Sian asked him.

Pat gave her a slow, lazy smile, and then held up a bunch of keys and jangled them. 'This was always my pub,' he said.

'Oh right,' she said. 'Because it appears to be my pub now.'

'Indeed, young lady. But I gave it to Bobby and to Harry before that. And, yes, legally speaking, Bobby did purchase the building.' He narrowed his eyes as he took one last suck of his cigarette then threw what was left on the floor. 'But it never stopped being my pub.'

Sian glanced at him, then down at the cigarette butt on her kitchen floor.

'H'excuse me,' he said, putting both hands up in surrender. He picked the fag butt up and put it in the bin. 'That was h'extremely rude.' He was putting on a weird, posh voice, the kind where someone drops their h's in the wrong places and adds them elsewhere.

Sian glanced behind her, praying that Elvis was still doing as he was told. He must be able to smell the unusual person in the house. But he could also hear that Sian was still and normal. She tried to stay calm. She knew that dogs could pick up on your mood and she was pretty sure that they could smell adrenaline on you, so she stayed mindful, controlled her breathing.

'I came for my gun,' he said.

Sian rolled her eyes. 'Word travels fast,' she said.

He nodded.

'You killed Harry. And you killed Marilyn too.' She stated it bluntly. Why not? If he was going to kill her as well, she might as well know the truth before he did it.

'No.' He was shaking his head. 'That's not true. And I definitely told you to stop digging, didn't I? When we last met. Are you not a woman of her word? You made me a promise.'

Sian half smiled. 'Promises are like noses—'

'Right, right.' Pat interrupted her, waving a hand across his face as if to wave away her words. 'Made to be broken. Yeah, I heard your old man say that a hundred times. We all did.'

'Bobby wasn't my dad,' she said.

'Who said anything about Bobby?'

Sian stared at him. Of course, why would he think that? He'd always assumed she was the baby that Angela had, the day he killed her husband. So Harry must have said that thing about promises and noses. Maybe Harry was where her uncle had got all of his sayings from. She didn't like that idea; it felt like losing a chunk of him all over again.

'So,' he said. 'That gun?'

Sian felt her mouth set hard in defiance. She knew that this wasn't her best chance of survival but she couldn't help it. She had never been able to do it, to accede in the way some men wanted her to. But that was their problem, not hers.

Pat Walsh came closer. 'It's OK, darling. I've got a spare.' He produced the weapon like it was a magic trick and tried to back her up towards the door, but Sian faced him off. She knew: it was easier to shoot someone in the back, always, no matter how used to killing people you were. Now, though, she was trapped. The locked side door of the house behind her led out into the yard, but not without the key that hung on the hook by the back door, and Pat was in between her and that hook.

Pat came closer still, pushing her into the corner of the kitchen, up against a worktop and the locked door. He came right up to her face. She could smell his breath. He stared into her eyes as if he was trying to work something out.

'What is it about the women from your family?' he said. 'Can't do what they're fucking told.'

Sian had an urge to spit in his face or to bite him on the nose but she held back. She knew that one false move and any chance she had of staying alive was over.

'Your mother was bad enough,' he said. His voice was low and menacing. 'But your fucking slapper of an auntie.' He grinned, showing two gaps and a gold tooth. 'You know, I fucked her any which way, your little Aunty Marilyn. A bunch of times. But I didn't fucking kill her.'

Sian stared into Pat Walsh's eyes. His brown eyes.

'She came running to me, whining. *I love you, Paddy.* She thought we had this special name but I wasn't Paddy, not to no one.' He spat out a disdainful laugh. 'Said she was pregnant but she never had no baby, did she?' His face was so close that their skin was almost touching.

Sian stared at him. She tried to process what he'd just said. She thought about telling him what she suddenly knew, and wondered if that might save her from a bullet in the head. Blood was blood. But, no, she stared into those dead brown eyes and guessed it wouldn't save her, the truth, even if he believed her. The truth was all she had now and she wasn't giving it to him.

'Now I'm going to kill you, just like I killed your fucking father.' He lifted the gun and she grabbed his arm, pushing it away so that the barrel was pointing at his chest. He pushed back, hard.

Sian leaned against the cabinet and couldn't help letting out a small yelp. It wasn't about the gun, or about dying. But her dog. Elvis had padded down the hall and was standing in the doorway, his head held to the side like he was trying to work out what was going on. Sian tried not to look at her dog, to say or do anything that might alert Pat to his presence there.

'He cried too,' Walsh told her, and he raised the gun upwards, towards her head.

June 1971
Devil's Answer

The Loggerheads pub: cellar door

Bobby had barely slept all night, haunted by bad dreams and the terrible thing he'd done to Harry, but he finally dropped off from sheer exhaustion in the early hours. When he woke up, the bed beside him was cold and empty. He sat up, looking over at the alarm clock as its digits flicked to 6:37. Whatever Pat had done to Harry, it was all over now. Bobby felt the sting of guilt in his stomach as he thought about Angela, sleeping upstairs with that baby in her belly, blissfully unaware that Harry was gone. He carefully took the cotton wool balls, one then the other from inside his ears. The baby was screaming. Where was Marilyn?

He stood up and walked over to the crib, looking down at his daughter. Her mouth was wide open and her face had turned red with the crying. He picked her up and held her to him. 'There, there, little one,' he said, patting her on the back, thinking how he didn't have a clue what he was doing. 'C'mon, baby girl.' They needed to stop arguing over what to name her soon, because you needed to know what a baby was called. He didn't like the name Marilyn was keen on though. *Sian* sounded too modern; he wanted something nice and traditional, like Jane or Catherine but, as usual, his wife wouldn't listen to him. He thought it was the worst kind of curse, to have a wife who wouldn't listen to you.

It was bloody neglectful of Marilyn disappearing off and leaving their daughter sobbing in her crib; cruel even, now he thought about it. Bobby patted the crying baby on her back and headed downstairs with her on his shoulder. 'Marilyn!' he called. 'Honey?' There was no response. The upstairs living room and kitchen were quiet and dark and, as he walked down the stairs to the bar, he couldn't hear anything there, either. He walked into the lounge, then the public bar. He could hear the vague sound of voices from the cellar.

'Marilyn?' he said again. He headed down the cellar stairs, the air around him getting cooler and drier with each step. He was about halfway down when he realised that Marilyn might have found something nasty down there, the leftovers of Pat's little job last night or, worse, Pat or one of his fellers cleaning them up. He held the baby at arm's length, considered putting her down on the stairs, but that felt more dangerous. He didn't have time to take her back upstairs; he needed to get into the cellar and make sure his wife was OK.

As he came to the bottom of the stairs, Bobby could hear crying but it wasn't his wife's voice. It was deeper and gruffer. Harry? How was that even possible? He turned and took in the scene. He held the baby close to his chest as if that could protect her. Marilyn had a gun and was standing over Harry, holding it right against his temple. Harry was bleeding out, slowly, from his stomach, presumably Pat's work. Bobby had no idea if something had gone wrong or if, worse, Pat had for some reason decided that he wanted Harry to die slow and painful and for Bobby or one of the women to find him like this.

'Marilyn, stop.'

His wife turned to look at him. She was dressed to the nines, as if she were out for a night on the town, not just up for breakfast. She kept the gun right next to Harry's head. 'You don't know the half of it, Bobby.' She turned then, the gun moving with her and, for a moment, pointing at Bobby and the baby.

Bobby held his daughter closer, coiled and ready to wrap himself around her and take the bullet if he had to. 'Marilyn,' he said. Her voice sounded like a tragedy.

'He said it was what was needed, Harry. That it was for the best.' Marilyn's voice was weird and sing-song, like she was telling him a story. 'He said it was just a bit of fun and no one needed to know about it. But it wasn't fun. Not for me.'

Bobby held the baby and stared at her. 'Stop it, Marilyn. I don't want to know.'

'But you have to know, Bobby. You have to know what he did to me. What he did to us. All of it's his fault. Him and Paddy.' She stared at Harry. 'You used me, didn't you. You and Paddy?'

Harry coughed up blood then tried to speak. No words were coming out, just a wet, garbled sound.

Bobby stared between one and the other of them, holding tight to his little girl. 'Don't do it, baby,' he said. 'We'll sort him out. We can sort everything out.'

His wife didn't move; there were tiny twitches playing on her face but she just stared into Harry's eyes, then at the gun.

'Please, Marilyn, stop.'

She moved the gun back so that it was touching the side of Harry's head again. 'I don't have to do what you tell me to,' she said. 'I don't have to do what no one tells me to.' She squeezed the trigger. There were no mistakes this time, a point blank shot to Harry's left temple. It made a sharp, wet sound and Harry slumped backwards.

'No!' Bobby screamed the word and closed his eyes; he didn't want to see what was left of Harry's brains decorating the wall or the side of one of the barrels. When he opened them again, he saw Marilyn put the gun into her mouth. 'No!' he screamed again. But it was too late. His wife squeezed the trigger and there was blood everywhere, the bullet and blood and bits of bone coming out the back of her head and hitting a barrel of beer, which exploded with a massive bang. The baby in his arms jolted in shock, and she stopped crying. Then Marilyn slid to the floor and the room felt colder and more silent than anywhere he'd ever been before.

November 2017
DEAD

The Loggerheads pub

Pat hesitated, the gun almost touching Sian's temple, and Elvis seemed to work everything out all at once. Two bounds and he was on top of the old man. He held him pinned to the floor, his jaw around the old man's throat. Pat made squeaks and squeals, flailing about. Sian knew there was a chance he'd start firing off random bullets if he managed to get a proper hold on his gun. She jumped on him too, pulling him into an arm lock and wrestling the gun from his hand.

Standing up, she pointed the gun at him. She took a step backwards and almost tripped on her cast, then righted herself. She held the gun tightly in both hands. 'I know how to use this thing. I'm actually a crack shot, better than you probably. So don't move,' she said. Her heart was slamming in her chest as she reached into her back pocket for her mobile phone. She carried on pointing the gun at Pat but the fight seemed to have gone right out of him. She considered dialling 999 but changed her mind and rang Kris.

The front door burst open before she'd even got through. Armed police officers came bolting down the hallway and into the kitchen. Sian dropped the gun and grabbed Elvis by his collar. She put up her free hand and raised the other as high as she could in a gesture of surrender. Elvis pulled against her, barking and trying to jump up at the men.

'Don't shoot, he won't hurt you!' she screamed, unsure this was really true after how he'd gone for Walsh. She stood in front of her dog so that they'd have to shoot through her. The men crowded into the small kitchen and stood waiting, guns poised. Then, from behind them, Dominic Wilkinson came piling into Sian's kitchen like he thought he was some kind of hero.

'What the fuck?' The words came out before she could stop them.

Dominic was all business. He directed one of his men into the room and held his hand out for his gun. He was wearing gloves. He took hold of the firearm and glanced at Sian and her dog then he raised it. She closed her eyes and screwed up her face.

Sian heard the gunshot but didn't feel the bullet hit. She heard Elvis let out a strange frightened whimper and felt him pull against her. Then she opened her eyes. A pool of blood was spreading across the kitchen floor. She stared, trying to take in what she was seeing. Pat Walsh was lying there, bleeding out on her kitchen floor. She let go of Elvis, who ran over to the old man and started licking his wound. She grabbed her dog again and yanked him back.

'What did you do that for?' Sian said, her voice a screech. Pat Walsh was a complete and utter bastard, and a dangerous one, but he was also an old man surrounded by people with guns and a dog who hated him. He hadn't been about to go anywhere. Despite everything, Sian was incensed with the unfairness, with the lack of due process. With the sight of Dominic Wilkinson-style policing in her own kitchen.

'I had no choice,' Dominic said. 'He raised his gun.'

FLOWERS

Loggerheads

Sian was curled up on her sofa, shaking. Elvis was sitting guard at her feet; one of the officers had brought in one of those silver-coloured blankets they use when people have run marathons and draped it over her shoulders. She was still processing what had happened and what she now knew about Pat Walsh. There were still traces of his blood on the floor, where it had pooled and spread, but she didn't need to take a sample to be sure. Because she knew it, as surely as their eyes were the same colour: *dark and exotic.*

Elvis sat up straighter, his ears pointed, and then Kris walked into the living room. He took one look at Sian and rushed over.

'Did he hurt you?' he said.

'No,' she said. 'I'm fine.' She gave him a weak smile and let him hold her, stopped talking.

Sian moved over so that there was room for Kris on the sofa. He sat down and put his arm around her, and Elvis licked Kris's left elbow.

Kris stiffened as Dominic Wilkinson walked into the room. Dominic frowned then closed the door carefully behind him. He sat down on the armchair. Sian noticed that he was still wearing his gloves and also had shoe covers on his feet. He had never been here.

'The forensics team are busy in there and will be for the rest of the day,' he said. 'Do you have somewhere you could go?'

Sian glared at him. 'What are you now, the fucking FLO?' Dominic let the corner of his lips curl slightly. Sian felt hysterical, like she might burst into completely inappropriate laughter or throw up or both. She breathed, and worked hard to hold it together.

'She'll stay with me,' Kris said. He held on to Sian, and she couldn't help but think he was talking about something deeper. She squeezed him back.

'Why did you do that?' Sian asked Dominic. 'And don't bother with all that *he raised his gun* rubbish. This is us, now. I was there.'

Dominic frowned. 'Sian, this mustn't go further than this room,' he said.

'OK,' she said, and Kris nodded, too.

'Patrick Walsh was a very dangerous man. Patrick Walsh in prison would have been as dangerous, possibly more so.' Dominic looked at the carpet, like there was something he didn't want to admit. 'You'd never have been safe,' he said, at last.

Sian could barely breathe with how angry that made her.

There was no way Dominic gave a shit about her safety.

'He's right,' Kris said. 'You know he is.'

'Yes,' Sian said. She gritted her teeth and turned to look at Dominic. 'So what, though? What's it to you?'

Dominic shrugged. His face had flushed slightly.

Sian let out a snort. 'Please don't try to pretend you care about me.' No, she was not having this.

Dominic looked at Kris then, and nodded, as if giving him permission for something,

Kris pressed a hand on to her arm and nodded, just perceptibly, in Dominic's direction. 'My source,' he said.

'What?'

'Remember, I needed help to get rid of Gary?' Kris said.

Sian remembered the login on the piece of paper he'd given her. *I can't reveal my sources.* She looked from one to the other of them. It took her a moment to be able to speak again. 'But you were horrible to me,' she said, her gaze fixed on Dominic and her voice very quiet. 'I was terrified of you.'

'Yeah,' he admitted. 'I was a shit to you. It seemed like the easiest way to keep everybody safe.'

For a moment, Sian actually thought he might apologise.

'What do you want me to say?' Dominic asked her. He stood up, and opened the living room door. 'I never claimed to be a good person,' he said, glancing back, 'but I care about my officers.' And he walked out.

The room felt very quiet. Elvis stood up and stretched, then trotted towards his bed.

'He's got a massive soft spot for you,' Kris said. 'Always did have. It was obvious to everyone.'

'Dominic?' Sian was completely flummoxed. She'd never got that impression from him at all. She thought about it for a moment. She pushed herself to standing using the sofa arm; her foot felt sore and itchy in the cast. 'No,' she said. 'I think he'd just had enough of Pat telling him what to do.'

Kris was shaking his head and smiling, one arm held out as if he thought he might need to help her walk.

'What?' she said.

'Only you would think that was a good motive to kill someone,' he said.

July 1971
Peace Train

Nottingham Midland Railway Station

They sat in the café with the carry cot on the table between them. Bobby looked at his sister. 'I can't cope with her,' he said. This was part of the truth; he couldn't cope with the baby any more than he could manage the pain of losing Marilyn. Trauma was like a virus, and you passed it along a chain to the people you loved. This little girl was better off without him.

Ruth had been trying for a baby since she'd got married over a year ago. As much as it hurt his heart, this felt like the right thing to do.

The guard blew his whistle on a platform nearby then there was the grinding sound of the modern diesel engine. The baby startled, and began to cry. Ruth cooed and picked her up. She held her close and bounced her. 'I don't know,' she said.

'Look at you. You're a natural,' Bobby said.
His sister flushed, but she smiled. She looked down at the baby; the little girl gurgled and flustered beside her. She looked back at Bobby.

'I want to see her, of course. But I'd be her uncle. I wouldn't want her to know owt else about it,' he said.

Ruth held the baby closer, kissed her forehead. Her eyes began to fill with tears.

'Oi, why you crying?'

Ruth tried to talk through the tears. 'I just can't believe it,' she said. 'That you'd do this.' She swallowed. 'For me.'

'She's supposed to be yourn, can't you tell?' Bobby said.

Now his sister was properly crying, her tears falling on to the baby, who had stopped and was looking up at the stranger holding her as if trying to work out what she was.

'OK?' Bobby said.

Ruth nodded through the tears.

'One thing.' Bobby's voice had turned serious, like this moment was the most important of the day. 'No one must know that she was Marilyn's. That must never get out. I don't even want David to know it, OK? Tell David, and any'un else who works out she's not yourn, you must tell 'em that this is Angie's baby. A'right?' He reached for his sister's arm, grabbed hold of it with some urgency. 'It's important.'

Ruth looked confused and slightly scared. She stared at his hand on her arm and he moved it off with a quiet 'sorry'. But she nodded yes and he was happy with that.

'Some folks. They think they can just take what they want, and that includes people. This is important. We need to keep her safe.'

Ruth looked puzzled. 'Me and David'll keep her safe,' she said.

'I know you will,' Bobby said with a sad smile. He shook his head. 'Thing is, Ruthie, Marilyn had been up to all sorts. I don't even know that the baby's mine.'

She let out a gasp of shock. 'No!'

'You don't even know the half of it,' he said. 'And if the father's who I think it is, I don't want him nowhere near her. Ever.'

'Oh, Bobby,' she said, her voice like a sigh.

'Listen,' he told her, reaching inside his pocket. 'This is important too.' He handed her the key. 'This is for a safety deposit box at Smith's Bank. You mustn't lose it so put it somewhere very safe.' He pushed the key hard into her hand, as if to seal it there like wax on a letter. 'If owt happens to me, give this to the police,' he said.

'The police?' she said, surprised.

'Yeah, the police.' He cleared his throat. 'It's to be a last resort. My insurance, so to speak.'

Ruth stared at him, opening her mouth to say something else, but an announcement cut in. She rocked the baby and they both sat quiet until it finished.

'Does she have a name?' Ruth asked him, then.

Bobby had thought long and hard about this, mulling over and reliving every conversation and argument he'd had with Marilyn on the subject. 'Yes,' he said. 'She's called Sian.'

'Sian.' Ruth said the name in a breathy voice as she looked down at the baby. 'That's beautiful.'

Bobby nodded. 'Her mother chose it,' he said. 'At least she could give her that.'

'Yes,' Ruth said. She smiled down and brushed the baby's cheek, then looked back up at Bobby. 'It suits her.' Ruth's face looked hazy like a drunk's and he could tell that his sister had already fallen for the baby, that she would love her like her own.

'Thank you,' Bobby said, simply, as if that were enough.

Ruth looked down at the baby again, then up at her brother. 'I don't know, Bob. I think she is yours.' She smiled at him, her eyes wet and happy. 'Look at her. There's some red in her hair when the light hits it. And she's got your eyes.'

'Well, she needs to bleddy give 'em back then,' he said, choking on a tiny laugh. Bobby brushed the baby's hair across her forehead. 'Maybe,' he said. He knew he could never know, not for sure. It was something he would have to live with, the same as not seeing her every day.

Job done, he stood up. He gave his sister a hug and his daughter a kiss on the head and then he walked away. It was the hardest thing he'd ever had to do but he knew, sure as each step, that he was doing the right thing.

December 2017
LEAVES

Loggerheads

Sian printed her resignation letter then signed it. She would decide tomorrow about whether to hand it in or not, but she was more than 90 per cent sure about it. She didn't like having a boss and being told what to do; she reckoned this was hard-coded in her DNA. She'd even considered reopening the Loggerheads but she wasn't convinced that running a pub was in her genes and, well, she wasn't about to start a crime syndicate, even if that was.

Clicking into her email, Sian filed the confirmation messages for the domains she'd registered, various combinations of her name, the words 'detective' and 'DNA'. None of them felt perfect yet for what she wanted to achieve, if she did go ahead and set up the agency. She wasn't sure she wanted to be involved in other people's messy lives. Her own had been hard enough to deal with.

There would always be people out there who wanted to know the truth about where they came from, though, and she knew she'd never be short of work. That was the thing about the truth; it didn't change. It was always there, immutable as Pat Walsh's dead brown eyes. It could only hurt you if you looked right into it and saw how little it cared for you. She wasn't sure she wanted to help people look into that kind of void.

Acknowledgements

Thanks first of all to Katherine and Clare and the team at Verve for their faith in this book and all their hard work bringing it to life. Also, to my tutors and fellow students on the MA Crime Writing Course at UEA, who have been there from the beginning of this project with ideas, feedback, imagination, waffles and occasionally too much wine! Thanks also to my colleagues and students at De Montfort University, as well as the incredible online writing community, who have provided encouragement, sanity and inspiration in countless ways. And, of course, to my friends and family, for everything.

About Nicola Monaghan

Nicola Monaghan was born in Nottingham in 1971, and grew up there on a number of different council estates. She studied Mathematics at the University of York, and went on to work as a teacher, and then in finance. She has lived in London, Paris and Chicago, but moved back to her home town in 2002 to study Creative Writing at Nottingham Trent. She has since written several novels and novellas, as well as scripts for short films. Her first book, *The Killing Jar*, won a Betty Trask Award, the Authors' Club Best First Novel Prize, the Waverton Good Read, and was selected for the New Blood Panel at Harrogate in 2007. She was the first fellow of the National Academy of Writing, based at Birmingham City University, and now teaches creative writing at De Montfort University. More recently, she studied crime writing at the University of East Anglia, where she wrote *Dead Flowers*, which was shortlisted for the UEA/Little Brown Prize. She lives in Nottingham with her husband, son, two dogs and – the real boss of the household – a cat called Dream Tiger.

To be the first to hear about new books and exclusive deals
from Verve Books, sign up to our newsletters:
vervebooks.co.uk/signup

VERVE
BOOKS